Black Camelot's

Assassins

Conspirators

By

Darius Myers

Book Six In The Black Camelot Series

FERO SCITUS

WEST NEW YORK, NEW JERSEY

Books by Darius Myers

Published by

Fero Scitus Books

The Publisher's Dilemma: A Big City Tale of Privilege, Power & Murder

Black Camelot's Dawn & The Return of Madame Hot Temper

Black Camelot's Days of War

Black Camelot's Dazed by Death

Black Camelot's Skeletons & Secrets

Black Camelot's Assassins & Conspirators

Author's requests:

1. I need your review. It helps a new author stand out in this highly competitive publishing world. Please take a moment to leave a review at Amazon, and

2. Please join my subscriber list at dariusmyers.com

Thank you. I appreciate these kind gestures.

Fero Scitus Publishing

6105 Boulevard East

West New York, NJ 07093

Visit our website at www.**dariusmyers.com**

First Edition: **November 15, 2024**

ISBN: 9798303554436

Black Camelot Series Cheat Sheet:

Reference page for first-time readers of the Black Camelot series

Names of Notable Characters

- **The Black Camelots,** the board members of the Oliver Harris Foundation: **Donald Alexander** (billionaire heir of the Harris Simmons fortune; **Kwame Mills** (heir to the Harris Simmons fortune; **Samantha Rivers** (nicknamed "Sammie"; Cornwall Harris's illegitimate socialite daughter)

- **Main Black Camelot Friends: David Banks** (husband of Margot Mosely); **Marsha Cherry** (Ron Cherry's wife); **Ron Cherry** (prominent banker, and respected elder statesman and consigliere to the Black Camelots); **Rev. Joseph Frank Hall** (Pastor of Freewill Baptist Church); **Danielle Jackson** (supermodel and Tom Wilson's wife); **Phaethon Malone** (basketball star who was tapped to become Mayor of New York City before being murdered by a white supremacist kill squad); **Marianne Michaels** (powerful management consultant, political connector, and friend of Donald Alexander's); **Margot Mosley** (award-winning poet, diplomat to South Africa, David Banks's wife, and college friend of Carrie, Susan, and Debbie's); **Michelle Nubani** (Economics professor and Kwame Mills's wife); **Carrie Sinclair** (photojournalist and Donald Alexander's wife); **Debbie Techelle** (Hollywood power lawyer, and college friend of Carrie, Margot, and Susan's); **Senator Susan Thomas** (former congresswoman from Maryland, and college friend of Carrie, Margot, and Debbie's); **Tom Wilson** (music industry executive and Kwame Mills' best friend); **Stevenson Strachan** (advertising agency CEO and Donald Alexander's neighbor in the Hamptons)

- **Celebrity Hack Patrol**, three top gossip reporters in Gotham who dubbed Donald Alexander, Kwame Mills, and Samantha Rivers the "Black Camelots" to create more content for their gossip columns: **Mike Desanctis** (*The Post*); **Jennifer Kung (nicknamed "TV"**; *The Ledger*); **Luke McFlemming** (*The News*)

- **The Harris Family: Cornwall Harris** (Oliver's older brother and Samantha Rivers's father); **Gill Harris** (murdered CEO of Harris Simmons); **Oliver Harris Jr.** (Gill's father and retired Harris Simmons CEO); **Samantha Rivers** (nicknamed "Sammie"; Cornwall Harris's illegitimate socialite daughter)

- **NYPD: Walt Bigelow** (NYPD Assistant Chief of Detectives); **Mac McClellan** (NYPD top detective); **Teddy Walker** (NYPD Chief of Detectives)

- **The Guiding Force ("GF")**, a secret society whose members wield power equivalent to that of world leaders: **The Black Camelots; Hardwick Bivens Jr. (nicknamed "Little Hardy"); Hardwick Bivens Sr. (nicknamed "Big Hardy"); Senator Janet Bivens; S.P. Curtin; Mauldin Daniels; Jack Zell Mulliken; Jacci O'Connor; Yancey Stuart Sr.** (real estate tycoon and retired GF member); **Kurt Wimer.**

- **Society of Protectors**, private army that serves The Guiding Force, to protect its members and carry out peace-keeping and mercenary missions across the world. Members include: **Carlos Alvarez** (Society of Protectors team leader at Donald Alexander's O&G Vineyard), **Paul Choice** and **Eric Leon** (Society of Protectors members sent to New York to protect Blaine Andrews, Tyrone Wheeler, and Constance "Flower" Yates); **Bones Jones** (Corrections Officer at Cell Block D, the prison facility used by the Society of Protectors)

- o **Project Maim:** Elite division of the Society of Protectors. Members include the brothers: **Doug and Darryl Duncan** (childhood friends of Michelle Nubani's); **Garry and Larry Miller; Keyur and Manish Patel**
- o **The Voice (given name Bernard Palmer):** Leader of the Society of Protectors

- **Before Emancipation ("BE"):** White supremacist organization leading efforts to kill the Black Camelots.
  - o **The Confederate (given name Max Briner):** The General's successor as leader of BE

- **The General (given name Jericho Station):** The deceased former leader of BE
  - o **Vail Boats:** The Confederate's defense attorney

- **The Artist Hitman (given name Jefferson Painter):** Highly paid contract assassin.

- **Whit Smart:** Retired contract assassin

- **Billy One-Shot (given name William Turner):** Highly paid contract assassin

- **Michigan Whites:** White supremacist organization and kill squad based in Michigan's Upper Peninsula.

- o **Wayne Johns:** Leader of the Michigan Whites

- **Pre-1860:** Powerful legacy secret society formed in the South after the abolition of slavery, that supports white business and political leaders' initiatives

- **Bivens Family & Friends:** Hardwick Bivens Jr. .(**nicknamed "Little Hardy";** former Governor of California and Guiding Force member; Janet Bivens's father); **Hardwick Bivens Sr. (nicknamed "Big Hardy";** former Governor of California and Guiding Force member; Janet Bivens's grandfather); **Janet Bivens** (Senator and Guiding Force member); **Elizabeth Charlotte Wall (nicknamed "Lizzy";** Hollywood actress, portrayer of the fictional character "Night Time Poison"; Lancaster Wall's wife); **Grayson Wall (nicknamed "Gray";** drug kingpin, Lancaster and Elizabeth Charlotte Wall's wayward son; Janet Bivens's godson); **Lancaster Wall (nicknamed "Cast";** Janet Bivens's childhood friend)

- **Damon Family**, owners of Southern Christian TV ("SCTV"), the powerful Christian, white nationalist television network based in Jeffersonville, North Carolina: **Detrick Damon Sr.; Detrick Damon Jr. (nicknamed "DD2");** **Detrick Damon 3rd (nicknamed "DD3 ")**

- **Delbert Tenny:** Mayor of New York City

- **Yates Family & Associates: Blaine Andrews** (Southern belle socialite, former beauty queen, Constance "Flower" Yates's younger sister; Skylar Andrews's wife); **Skylar Andrews** (nicknamed "**Hawk**" and known to his wife, Blaine, as "**Daddy**

Woo-Woo"; President of Yates Savings and Loan); **Dixie Bill Sessions** (Digby Yates's head of security); **Tommy Tubbs** (Digby Yates's chief of staff); brothers **Juju and Tyrone Wheeler** (residents of The Bottoms in Yates, Tennessee and employees of Digby and Flower Yates's); **Constance Yates** (nicknamed "Flower"; Southern belle socialite, former beauty queen, Blaine Andrews's older sister, Digby Yates's wife); **Digby Yates** (powerful and wealthy member of the Yates family in Yates, Tennessee; candidate for President of the United States; husband of Constance "Flower" Yates's)

Previous series incidents relevant to Assassins & Secrets

- **Harris Simmons shootings:** At the world's most powerful media company, the CEO, Gill Harris, is murdered; Donald Alexander is shot but survives. The murder becomes the most talked about story in a decade. In its aftermath, the Celebrity Hack Patrol names the Black Camelots.

- **Black Camelot weddings:** In one summer, three years after Donald Alexander sold the Harris Simmons media company, Donald married photojournalist Carrie Sinclair in June; their Black Camelot friend, music industry executive Tom Wilson, married supermodel Danielle Jackson in July; and Donald's protégé at Harris Simmons, Kwame Mills, married Economics professor Michelle Nubani, in August. The Black Camelots have captured the imagination of the world and cemented their reputations as the royals of Black Camelot.

- **Blaine Andrews murder/Digby Yates assassination attempt:** Blaine Andrews, the sister of Constance "Flower"

Yates and wife of Skylar Andrews, is killed by a Before Emancipation assassin in New York. Flower has left her husband, Digby Yates, and accompanied by Blaine, gone to New York to pursue her love for her one-time field hand, Tyrone Wheeler. Digby finds out and sends a kill squad to assassinate Tyrone, but Blaine becomes the casualty. Skylar is a banker by profession but in another life was a trained assassin. He vows revenge for his wife's murder, but only wounds Yates.

- **Murders of Friends of the Black Camelots':** BE kill squads murder the pro basketball Hall-of-Famer and Mayoral hopeful, Phaethon Malone, along with five other hoops stars during a basketball workout.

- **Police officer casualties: Bill Trombetta** and the **Harlowe twins (Holden Krist and Alec Reese)** are ambushed by Before Emancipation members who brought their fight against the Black Camelots to Gotham. Their murder of law enforcement officers protecting the Black Camelots ratchets up the war between BE and The Guiding Force, to which the Black Camelots belong, and police from all over the world come to New York in solidarity after the murders of their fellow law enforcement officers. Later, BE members kill **Captain Rosario.**

- **Bronx massacre:** Three Michigan Whites were engaged in a fist fight in the Bronx, a couple of blocks from the safe house where they were hiding out. They later took to a rooftop, and in a torrent of gunshots killed Captain Rosario, barely missed Walker, and tore into the crowd of police that had made its way to the Bronx from Kipp Meenan's bar, where cops from all over the world gathered as they came for funerals of Trombetta and the Harlowe twins. The cops, many of them inebriated, had rushed to the Bronx angrily after learning that BE members were involved the street fight. Walker spots The Artist Hitman in the midst of the chaos, and a chase and shootout ensue. The Artist escapes and flees to Rio, where he must make some hard decisions.

- **Freewill Baptist Church attacks:** On the day of Phaethon Malone's funeral, Before Emancipation members set out to kill the Black Camelots and their friends. Garry Miller, one of six members of the elite Project Maim team, is killed during the attacks.

Part One

12

Chapter One

Southern Hospitality

"Welcome to Yates Southern Hospitality, the finest hotel in all the South and the hometown of the future president of the United States, Digby Yates," the concierge crowed to the incoming guest. "Make sure you enjoy some Yates Meats while you're in town. You'll never experience better pork in your life."

Billy One-Shot registered under the alias Charles Williams. His blond wig covered his black hair, and the prosthetic in his upper lip and jaw made his face pudgier. His disguise and fake ID photo went unnoticed by the concierge and the front desk attendant who checked him in.

The concierge had met him at the hotel's outdoor entrance. Billy sized him up at five foot seven with a pudgy midsection, and found most noticeable his thick-heeled shoes. The assassin guessed the lifts were three inches thick. They clunked loudly on the marble floor of the hotel's entrance.

The concierge spoke with the energy of a carnival barker as he introduced the guest to the skinny blonde front desk attendant with a pearly-white, plastered-on smile.

"Meet Mr. Williams, Maudine," he said, his voice tinted with a distinct thick Southern drawl. "He's staying on the luxury suite level on Penthouse Row. I've already told him that Yates Meats is the best pork he'll ever eat in life."

"Sure is. None better."

Maudine's eyes and face brightened to match her smile.

"The best pork in the world is right here in Yates, Tennessee. Welcome to the hometown of the next American President, Sir."

The over-the-top greetings were mandatory protocol at Yates Hospitality. Any lesser greeting was a punishable offense. Hotel managers and lobby video cameras were always on the lookout to catch concierge desk or front desk staff not properly saluting guests. Four front desk attendants had been demoted or fired in the last two years for such violations. Just three weeks ago, Lucy Pearl, who had been in the role for four years and was the highest ranking front desk attendant, was sent home without pay and fined for two days because she had a toothache and couldn't smile. Lucy Pearl's suspension was on Maudine's mind as she smiled at "Charles Williams."

"Thank you," Billy said in a voice laden artificially with a heavy bass tone and an erudite air.

. The assassin was travel weary because of his early start and unamused by the high-energy hotel workers. He'd left his Hoboken home at 4 AM and was anxious to check in and remove his disguise.

Maudine, burdened by the fears of the hotel performance code was blind to the cloak, and the guests fatigue. She dutifully continued on in her greeting.

"You requested a room facing the Yates Corporate Towers. It, too, is owned by the next president of this great republic and is the biggest building in town."

Her voice had a lesser carnival barker's cadence and to Billy's relief wasn't as annoying as the concierge's.

Billy forced a weak smile and yawned as he looked Maudine in the eyes. He hoped she would note the cue.

She didn't. Instead, she focused on a video camera on the far wall recording her.

Her pearly whites glistened as she recited, "The Corporate Towers and the Water Tower are two of the four landmarks in this town. The third is Yates Meats, where you'll find the best pork you'll ever eat in life. The fourth is the Yates Southern Hospitality, where you are now, Mr. Williams. We are the only five star hotel within 100 miles of Nashville. And frankly," she whispered and leaned forward as if revealing a secret, "our hotel is a thousand times better than those big city hotels."

Billy One-Shot smiled weakly, this time in sympathy of Maudine's earnestness. The prostheses grated painfully against his gums.

"It's part of their job," he thought. "But this damn prosthetic, I need to get it out of my mouth."

Billy then slowly spun 360-degrees, ostensibly to admire the massive lobby. His real purpose was to case the lobby for the video cameras that he knew were capturing images of him in disguise .

"One, two, three, four," he counted.

He closed his eyes and memorized each location: one in front of him at the desk, another at the rear entrance, a third on the far-left wall, and a fourth at the main entrance near the concierge desk.

"That explains the show. These staffers know they are being watched. Now, so do I."

Maudine's high pitch rang out again.

"You will be staying on the seventh Floor as requested, and your room will face the Yates Corporate Towers, Mr. Williams. Senator Yates is running for President and we love it."

Nearly finished, she stared at a notecard and then at the Concierge Jack. He smiled smugly. She flashed him another contemptuous eyeroll.

"Mr. Williams," she said. "Senator Yates will make America what it used to be. Help make him the next President. Go Digby!"

She belted out the words with pep of a high school cheerleader.

Billy clenched his jaw tightly. If not for fear of his prosthetics flying out his mouth, he would have burst into laughter. His eyes watered. Holding back made his sides ache.

Jack giggled after the big finale, purposely to annoy his co-worker. Maudine's pretty face reddened, and she glared at him. He giggled all the more.

She leaned forward and handed Billy One-Shot a keycard.

"I have to say that corny line," she whispered. "Concierge Jack loves Senator Yates and enjoys that I have to say it. I'm a Democrat. He's a Republican. Yates is a scoundrel."

"Gotcha," Billy said, slow and low so as to not shift his prosthetics. He gave her a thumbs up and a wink.

She turned to her colleague, "Concierge Jack, seeing that you're not busy, can you please escort Mr. Williams to his room this morning?"

"Gladly," Jack said. He clunked forward, "I'm here to serve Mr. Williams at the hotel in the hometown of America's next president."

Both men remained in character as they rode to the seventh Floor. Jack attempted small talk and began to angle for a tip.

"Mr. Williams, you'll be here for two days. If you need anything at all, please don't hesitate to contact Concierge Jack. I'm here for anything you need: food, drink, sights, and entertainment. Especially entertainment."

Billy leaned against the rear wall. Jack stood in front.

"You should know, Mr. Williams, this is the Bible Belt, but there is also a, uh, red light district. If you have any needs, I can make some calls. As I said, Concierge Jack can provide you whatever entertainment choices you desire."

The concierge turned his head back and winked. Billy nodded. There would be no time for strippers or escorts. That kind of indulgence was a professional no-no, especially when casing out a job. Without a word, he pulled a pocket Bible out of his brown sports coat jacket and flashed it to Jack.

"Oh, I apologize. You, Mr. Williams, are a man of God."

Billy nodded slowly as the Jack's face paled.

The concierge turned forward and kicked the floor panel lightly.

It was a gleeful moment for Billy. Jack would now wonder if he would file a complaint to the general manager of the best hotel in the hometown of America's next president for soliciting sex workers. The miscue shut Jack up until they made their way to Billy's room.

Suite C was in the middle of the floor and faced the center of town. Jack rushed to open the curtains in the sitting room of the large, two-room chamber. The late morning sun was bright and the sky cloudless.

"You picked a great day for a visit, Mr. Williams."

The assassin remained silent. Jack, still humbled by the prostitute solicitation, said nothing more and hobbled across the sitting room to the exit.

Billy walked two steps behind, his hitman instincts on high alert. He was six one to Jack's five seven. They both weighed roughly 215 pounds, but the rotund concierge was particularly soft-looking in the middle. There was a fat bulge in his neck, and his clunking platform shoes didn't conceal the exaggerated lift to his right leg.

"Probably gout from too much good Southern eating," Billy guessed. "He'd be easy prey and not a problem to take down because he's out of shape and has that bum leg. I won't have to worry about him if I'm in a battle in this building. The girl Maudine, however, has a little fire to her. It's the South, so she's probably an expert in firearms and knows enough to defend herself against a horny customer. This sleazy moron in front of me has probably tried her a time or two."

Billy dug into his pocket and pulled out a wad of cash. Two $50 bills were on top. "Make sure the girl gets one of these. I'll be checking that she does."

The voice he'd created for Charles Williams came out perfectly. Deep, strong, sophisticated, learned. It was a far cry from his normal street tough, take no crap baritone.

"Will do," Concierge Jack said. His face lit up. A $50 tip was a good start of the day.

Billy stopped at the door and nodded to Jack as he exited. He pulled the Do Not Disturb sign off the inside handle and hung it on the outside, pushed the door shut, and turned the safety lock.

The room was well appointed. Instead of the usual wall to wall carpeting found in most hotels, it had Persian rugs laid out atop glistening, light brown, wide oak planks. The rugs were noticeably thick. Billy guessed they were padded enough to insulate the room and cushion sounds. His shoes clanged on the planks when he moved from the carpet to wood and approached a chair and table next to the window.

He read a card on the table titled, "Soundproof Rooms. We have twelve inches of custom foam insulation that makes noise from these wood floors undetectable to the level below. Walk in your shoes and dance on the sparkling hardwood floors. It's one of the extra steps we've taken to make Yates Southern Hospitality one of the best five star hotels you'll ever experience."

Billy imagined killing Concierge Jack and leaving him in a pool of blood. The insulated floors would conceal the sounds of a struggle and prevent blood from dripping to the level below.

He glanced across the view, taking in the Water Tower and the Yates Corporate Tower. From his due diligence he knew the penthouse level of Yates Corporate Tower doubled as the Presidential candidate's headquarters.

He pulled a burner phone out of his pocket. It held one number and one name, that of his client, Big H California, Hardwick Bivens, Sr. He looked at his watch. It was just after 9:30 AM on the East Coast, 6:30 AM out west.

"Too early still to call him. Let me check out the building for now."

In his luggage was a set of binoculars. He pulled it out and trained it on the building to see how closely it matched the layout from his Internet due diligence.

Billy didn't keep notes. They were taboo in his world. All of the specs were in his head.

"My room looks right into the top floor of Yates Corporate Center. The layout posted online was spot on."

The prosthetics rubbed against his gums. He walked to the bathroom and washed his hands, removed the prosthetics, and plopped them into a glass. At the same time he doffed the blond wig.

Billy returned to the large leather recliner at the window. Two bottles of water were on the table. He grabbed one and as he settled into the chair took three long swallows. He felt for a latch and leaned the chair back as he continued to canvass Yates Headquarters.

Fatigue overcame him, and he took another swig. The water flushed his abraded gums as the first gunshot rang out.

"Huh? What in the hell?!"

He tensed and froze. Then came a second gunshot, and a third, and several others. At five he stopped counting. Glass crashed loudly from the window of the building he'd just cased.

Billy lowered the recliner to full horizontal as his heart raced. An assassin or team of assassins could be surveilling the surroundings and training their guns searching for a witnesses. It's what he'd do. He lay petrified for thirty seconds.

"It's dangerous to wait any longer," he reasoned. "They'd risk getting caught."

Billy reached to the desk and grabbed his binoculars. He was certain where the shooter was. It's where he'd planned to scope out later in the day. The Water Tower was five blocks away but directly across from Yates Headquarters, with unobstructed views. A tall, lean man dressed in a black warmup suit with a long gun harnessed on his back, moved swiftly down circular metal stairs.

Billy focused the binoculars and assessed the assassin: "Six foot two or three, close-cropped hair, clean-shaven, handsome, athletic build. A face I've never seen. Don't know him."

He watched the man descend the stairs with cat-like steps and jump into a black SUV.

As the car motored off Billy's heartbeat lessened and he leaned back again in the chair.

"I wonder if the old man ordered another hitter? If he did, it won't matter. He'll still have to pay. You don't contract Billy-One Shot with a backup. If he tries to renege on our deal, I'll just remind him that I can always get his son and granddaughter."

He then ceded to his fatigue and laid back in the recliner. Billy One-Shot closed his eyes and took a nap.

Chapter Two

Pork for Lunch

Billy slept from 10:00 am until noon. He hadn't eaten all morning. The disguise had prevented him from eating on the plane. Famished, he grabbed the menu from the desk

"I am in the pork capital of the South. Or is it the USA?" he cracked. "This guy sure knows how to push his product. Let me see what they've got."

He massaged his aching gums with his tongue.

"The choices are a pork butt sandwich; pork-style sushi roll with avocado; a pork-infused sloppy joe; pork rib sliders; or a slab bacon, lettuce, and tomato sandwich. I'm sure, unless I come back here, I'll never have the chance again to enjoy a delicious pork-style sushi roll."

A woman's voice he was certain belonged to the front desk clerk was on the other end when he dialed Room Service. He made sure he adopted his Charles Williams voice.

"Hello, I'd like to order lunch delivered to Penthouse Suite C."

"Mr. Williams, Maudine here. I can take your order. How are you enjoying your accommodations?"

"Everything is perfect, Maudine. Thank you for asking. Let me order the sushi roll and slab BLT."

"Anything to drink? Sweet tea, maybe?"

"No thank you. Water will be fine, Maudine."

"Those are excellent choices, Mr. Williams. We'll have the kitchen deliver your lunch in fifteen minutes. It's part of our five star guarantee. At the…"

"Please Maudine," Billy interrupted, "You don't have to say, 'At the hometown of the next American President.' It'll be our little secret."

"Oh, thank you, Mr. Williams," she giggled. "We'll get your order up shortly."

"You're welcome, Maudine."

Billy felt sorry for the petite blonde as he put on his wig and prosthetics, and waited for his order. For a brief second, he considered not putting on the disguise, but his instincts were on overdrive. Fifteen minutes later, the voice that followed the door made him grateful he had.

"Room Service, Mr. Williams."

Concierge Jack's Southern twang was easy to recognize. Billy guessed he'd be pushing for another big tip.

"Jack's probably a bit of a scoundrel with the other hotel employees. Maudine's glares earlier told me all that I need to know."

Billy didn't respond. He just opened the door.

Concierge Jack burst through with unearned familiarity.

"It's a big day here, Mr. Williams," he said in high carnival barker mode. "Don't know if you heard the news, yet. Presidential candidate Digby Yates was shot. His chief of staff was assassinated. The shots came from the Water Tower."

Jack hobbled past Billy and set up the tray on the table near the window. His eyes and head cast about. Billy could tell he was casing the room. Jack's wandering eyes angered him.

"This guy doesn't know I can kill him and be on my way out of this hotel before anyone knows. I hate snoops, and if I knew Yates better, and had a hideout or escape plan, I'd kill Jack right now, take the lunch to go, and hit the road."

Jack moved slowly and continued his snooping. At the same time Billy's anger brewed and forced him to call on his inner controls. He didn't trust his voice to say anything more than a couple words.

After Jack set up the food, Billy pulled another $50 out of his pocket and said, "Thank you."

The nosy concierge's face brightened.

"Oh, thank you kindly. You are quite generous."

The assassin walked to the door, opened it and with lowered eyebrows stared at the concierge. Jack recognized his bothered expression but was too nosy to heed it. He deliberated, eyes still darting about. Billy's ire grew, and he reached for his waistband.

"If he doesn't leave in ten seconds, I will kill him. He's asking for it. Make that five seconds."

A six-inch blade was lodged in his waistband. At the count of three, Jack was still in the center of the suite's living room. Jack's awkward gait now worked against him. There was no way he would make it to the doorway. Billy's hand was perched on the knife handle. The blade would be open at the five count and his neck slit from ear to ear, with his last word a curdled shocked scream.

A beep then rang out on Jack's phone.

He grabbed it and said, "Hey Maudine, what can I do for you?"

Her wind-up toy voice rang out, "We have two guests down here who want some advice for a sightseeing trip. They want to see some of the old plantations that are now working farms. Please, can you come down here?"

With money to be made Jack ceased his suspicious scanning and hobbled to the door.

"Let me know if you need anything else, Mr. Williams. Happy to serve you. Enjoy your lunch."

Billy didn't say a word as Jack passed by him and into the hall. He shut the door as the fat man with the gimp's gait hobbled towards the elevator

"Still should have killed him just for being nosy. But I might need to come here again. You controlled your urge today, Billy. Good boy."

Chapter Three

Not a Casualty

"Mr. Hardwick. I have some important news," the butler yelled. "Digby Yates has been shot. It's all over the news. I've turned the television on to Channel 2 in the great room for you."

Conrad, Hardwick Bivens Sr.'s longtime butler, barked the news from the great room doorway in the left wing of the massive center hall colonial.

Big Hardy was in the backyard of the Beverly Hills compound. He had taken breakfast there and was preparing to read through a stack of political magazines. He still fancied magazines whose pages he could thumb through

The 91-year-old patriarch of the Bivens political dynasty jumped up from his seat with the ease of a 30-year-old. His mouth and eyes were agape. Bivens had been working out three times a week, doing light calisthenics and weights. He'd also been walking two miles a day. He'd begun the fitness regimen in anticipation of the rough grind of the campaign which would gear up in the next few months.

Conrad watched as Big Hardy hurried from the garden area, past the pool and guest house, to the doorway of the left wing. Sixty-five years earlier, while in law school, Hardwick was an amateur light heavyweight prizefighter known as the Fighting Counselor. He'd often brag about his boxing prowess to Conrad and anyone else who'd listen. He now had a small team of personal trainers that were working with him on his stamina and leg strength.

"I refuse to be one of these guys hobbling around the campaign trail with a walker. I'm determined to show that Hardwick Bivens Sr. is as strong as ever," he'd say.

All of his personal trainers commented about his endurance as they put him through fitness exercises.

His favorite was Livy Baltimore, a cute 25-year-old, who flirted with him regularly. The toned, hyper-energetic brunette said often after a good workout, "You have endurance uncommon for men half your age.

He'd respond, always with a wry smile, "You know my nickname, Livy?"

His granddaughter happened to be a visitor on one such occasion. She overheard him and knew that her grandfather was a walking lawsuit, especially in the modern world of political correctness.

Janet yelled out, "Don't you dare. Don't you dare say that, Grandpa."

The patriarch ignored her command.

"They call me Big Hardy." The long-ago amateur pugilist barked, puffed his chest out proudly.

He then winked at his snarling granddaughter and said, "The world must know that I was and still am a conqueror."

Janet hung her head in defeat.

Big Hardy strutted into the house with his head held high, posing as a victorious warrior.

Livy smiled and blushed. She told Janet afterwards, "He's harmless. Don't worry about him being politically correct, Senator. I'm happy his mind works that way. His body is following, and if that keeps him motivated, then good."

On this morning, both his trainer and granddaughter would have marveled at the energy he expended as he watched the news coverage.

His cell phone was laid on the table in front of him. It kept pinging with incoming texts and ringing with phone calls.

He ignored it and yelled at the television, "Is he dead? Will he die?"

"A sniper, yet to be identified, let off a barrage of bullets at the campaign headquarters of presidential candidate, Senator Digby Yates. There has been one casualty," reported Bartholomew Tony. The reporter then took a long pause.

The excitement of the moment left the journalist breathless, and for viewers, the pauses heightened the suspense.

"There is one known casualty," Tony said. He paused again as he flipped pages in his note pad. "Digby Yates is…"

Tony's eyes turned upwards to face his cameraman. At the same time, he pressed his earplug and cocked his head as he concentrated on the instructions coming from his newsroom.

Seconds later, he snapped over the open mic, "Stop yelling at me. I know what I'm doing."

The reporter then turned to the camera, "Digby Yates is wounded, but not fatally. I repeat, he's not dead. He is not a casualty. I repeat: He is not a casualty. The presidential candidate has not died, and our initial reports are saying that this is not a mortal gunshot wound. The casualty is his chief of staff, Thomas Tubbs. Tubbs was pronounced dead at the scene. This is a breaking news story."

Chapter Four

Yesterday Leads to Today

Billy One-Shot left the hotel shortly after his lunch was delivered. He didn't bother to check out of Yates Southern Hospitality.

"Police and paparazzi are likely everywhere looking for any clues. I'm an outsider, and they'd have every reason to stop and question me. I'll call and check from the airport."

There was a rear exit to the hotel parking lot. He had parked there intentionally and was glad now as he saw a batch of police and official vehicles logjammed at the hotel's front.

"Ten minutes later and I may have not gotten out of there without being questioned," he thought.

He called his client on his way to the airport. Anger laced his client's voice.

"You know Billy, I don't want to hear any excuses. I contracted your services for a million dollars. Fifty percent up front and the rest upon completion. What in the hell happened down there?"

Billy had carried his food out with him and chewed on a bite of the BLT as he drove. A chunk of meat lodged midway in his chest.

"Give me a second, Governor. I ate something too fast."

He muted the phone. As he did, the governor grumbled. Bivens was a man accustomed to a world of sycophants, and being put on hold even for a minute annoyed him.

The assassin opened the liter bottle of water in the center console and downed it in three gulps. It moved the big ball of meat, and his chest felt better. He returned to the call, his voice as angry as the governor's.

"Governor, are you serious? You're the one with explaining to do."

"What did you say?" Big Hardy snapped.

"I don't do clean-up work, Governor. The last person who asked me was Bronson Pagent. And if I see him again, I am going to kill him slowly and painfully. He cost me four good men doing clean-up work. I'm not doing any clean-up work on Yates. Do you understand me?"

"Clean-up work? What are you talking about? Who's Bronson Pagent? I have no idea whom you are talking about."

"Pagent hired me to kill the advertising CEO, Stevenson Strachan, then called me off the job while I had the guy in the crosshairs. He then hired me when Pagent was abducted, to rescue him, and I lost a four-man team. It was a job I should have refused."

"Billy, I didn't call you off the job. I want the guy dead."

"Then what happened? Did you hire two hitters?"

"No, I only hired you. And it appears that I hired the wrong man."

Billy chafed at the dig.

"What did you say? Did you forget who I am?"

Big Hardy couldn't see the hitman's tightened jaw or the dark emptiness in his eyes, but to the powerful former governor it wouldn't have mattered. Hardwick Bivens Sr. was afraid of no man, and no one talked to him as Billy was.

The assassin didn't scare, either. He bristled as his thoughts momentarily shifted to whether or not he would set out to kill the governor.

The governor responded to Billy's threat.

"Just whom do you think you're talking to, young man?"

"Let me remind you, Governor. I'm a paid assassin. One of the best in the world. Otherwise known as a ruthless dirty work man. And you hired me to kill someone, so I suggest you remember that. Otherwise I will f-…this will end badly."

Billy stopped himself from letting off the full F-word. His rage was at a full boil, but the governor was still a client.

He exhaled and began to explain, "Listen, Governor. Let me tell you more about my last client, Bronson Pagent. He double-booked me. Then, he calls off the hit. Then he calls me again when he is losing badly to his enemies, and rehires me to use my hit team to conduct a rescue mission, during which my team of four died. I'm a professional, not a street corner thug. In case you need to know: There's a huge difference. I can kill in a variety of ways: with a gun, a knife, a bomb, a rope, poison, my bare hands. Today, I saw the shooter escape the Yates shooting as he descended the stairs of the Yates Water Tower. He wasn't a novice or rent-a-thug, either. This guy had the look of a highly skilled professional."

Bivens snapped angrily, "How would you know?"

Billy's mind drifted back to the showdown where he'd lost his men to the legendary Society of Protectors' Project Maim team. Four months back, the foursome he'd sent to rescue the real estate baron, Bronson Pagent, was lured onto a two-lane road off a highway in New Jersey. When his team attacked the abductors, they responded with a missile from a rocket projector that blew up their vehicles. He had heard the entire exchange via cell phone. Bronson Pagent has not been heard from since.

"Trust me. I know a fellow professional when I see one. This is the second time in four months when my assignment crossed paths with guys who are just as talented as I. The abductors in New Jersey were mercenaries. They'd brought a rocket projector to a gunfight. The marksman today pulled off shots that only an elite mercenary or a world-class assassin could."

The explanation calmed the governor.

"Well, on my honor, Billy," Bivens said, his voice finally calm, "I had nothing to do with that guy. You are my last hope to get this done. I was asked to stand down by my granddaughter and son. But I was prepared to live with their anger as long as the guy was killed. Did you hear the news reports?"

"No. I was worn down from the travels this morning, and since I had nothing to do with the mysterious shooting, I took a nap after the commotion subsided and the sniper drove away."

"Well, Yates's chief of staff is dead. Yates is injured, but he will survive the bullet that went through his shoulder, unless the doctors missed something. This is the worst possible outcome."

"Give me one second, Governor," Billy said.

He plugged "Shooting in Yates" into his phone's browser. Each of the local news stations had breaking coverage. The first to pop up was Channel 5. He pressed a button, and the live feed began streaming. A banner appeared on the bottom of the screen that read, 'Senator and presidential candidate Yates wounded, but expected to survive. Chief of Staff Tubbs pronounced dead at the scene."

As Billy watched the live feed, the governor sat in a chair and looked at a sheet of paper Whit Smart had given him after he turned down the job. On it were the name and number of Billy One-Shot. The governor's conversation with Whit ran through his head.

"I'm retired. I'm fatter, slower, and probably lost my nerve," that assassin had said. "If you ask me, there are only two people who can do this job. One is down here, and word is he's too hot to come to the States for something this high-profile. The other goes by the name of Billy One-Shot. Both are world-class. Did The Voice tell you to call me?"

"Oh no, The Voice doesn't know about my needs, and he never can," The governor had answered. "And, I don't need you trying to put two and two together, either."

Twenty-five years ago, The Voice had had the governor interview Whit. The Voice wanted a hitman to kill GOP presidential candidate, Prescott Jefferson.

The governor asked The Voice to supply a shortlist of people that were not on the government's payroll who might be able to pull off a long gun assassination. Long gun assassins could hit targets from thousands of yards away and not get caught. The top four known assassins on the list were Billy One-Shot, Tim Moore, his brother Tom Moore, and Whit Smart. The Moore brothers hadn't been seen in ten years. They were believed to be living in the shadows in the Czech Republic under aliases, and married. That left Billy One-Shot and Whit Smart.

The governor, then as now, couldn't get permission from the Guiding Force to murder a presidential candidate. He paid Whit to give him a tutorial on how a long gun sniper worked. Smart, known as a raconteur amongst hitmen, gladly obliged.

"An expert long gun marksman could do it," Whit told him. "There are hundreds of marksmen trained for 1000-yard shots, but once we get to 2000 to 3000 yards, the group gets smaller and smaller. When you get to 5000 yards, only a select number of Americans, maybe fifty to seventy-five elite marksmen, have ever attained that status."

"They are called the 5's," Whit had continued, "because they can execute those shots. Nearly all of them are Army-trained and indexed in a military database because of their specific qualifications. Every 5 member is equipped with a custom-made sniper gun. The weapon is built with a specially designed scope, chamber, and hammer, and is calibrated for 5000-yard shots exclusively. The 5's are certified to navigate climate conditions, such as rain, wind, air thickness, humidity, cold, and heat, and to never miss beyond two inches."

Billy continued to watch the news and said to the governor, "I'm on my way out of town. Police searches will likely begin shortly. I pulled off the highway to make this call. Feds will be all over Yates and the hotel I was at because it has a front-row view of the crime scene. I'll be made because I checked in under an alias and there was a guy there, a nosy type, who'll likely expose me and my fake identity. I wanted to kill him."

The governor didn't hear Billy clearly. "Did you kill someone at the hotel? Is that what you said?"

"No, I said, there was a guy nosing around my suite. I wanted to kill him, and I know when the top investigators get into town, they'll find out I registered under an alias. I have another alias that will get me out of town. Before I hang up, you need to know the man who took that shot was a Level 4 or 5 marksman."

Billy rifled through his wallet. The blond-wigged guy might be made if the feds looked for Charles Williams. So from here, he would travel as James Smith with red hair and the same oral prosthetics. He had to get moving.

"The airport is an hour and forty-five minutes away, Governor. I need to get moving."

"Okay. But I paid for services. It was a lot of money, so we must reconvene about this."

Billy looked at his watch. With each passing minute, the risk of his being made at the airport increased. He knew that flying directly to New York would also be risky. A hideaway would be the safest place to retreat to.

A bag was in his back seat. He pulled it forward and unzipped the top compartment. In it were five passports, one each for Charles Williams, Mike Jones, Will Penn, Martin Rover, and James Smith. Relieved, he turned his attention to the call.

"Governor, you know what today means?"

"I'm afraid I do, Mr. Billy. It means we lost a great opportunity."

"Yeah, Yates is unapproachable now. His security will be impenetrable. I can't touch this job. I don't know anyone who would."

"I'm afraid you're right. I'll pay you the remaining fifty percent for your troubles."

"No, let's make that just $250k. It was a good plan. What we didn't factor in was that someone else hates this guy more than you. Good luck in the race."

"Thank you, Mr. One-Shot. It just pains me that we just made him the sympathetic candidate for the political Right. We're going to need a lot of luck now, for sure."

"I understand, Governor. If there are other ways to get this completed, short of a suicide mission, I am available for the task, but for now I've gotta get going."

As the phone clicked, Billy typed "Travelworld.com" into his browser. It was the site he used for last-minute flights.

"Better to be safe than sorry," he told himself. "It's been a few months. I need to visit my villa in Rio, anyhow."

Chapter Five

The Beltway News

"**12**:30. Dammit. There's no telling where they could be. My best hope is that they were nearby having burgers and a beer."

W.T. Hill texted his team. "If you are around the corner at Smiley's, put your beers down and get back here. Digby Yates's sister-in-law has been shot and killed in New York City. Yates has also been shot, but in his campaign headquarters in Tennessee. We've gotta get on this. Order some chicken wings or whatever garbage you eat from that place. It's going to be a long afternoon and night."

All of Hill's *Beltway News* reporters were either out for lunch or covering stories for their beats. The only sound in the 2000-square foot newsroom was the tick tock of a massive clock on the bullpen's far wall, 100 feet away. Each text to his top writers - Ron "R.L." Lawson, Geena John, and Marie Falcone - went unanswered.

Hill was lightheaded, and his heart raced. He took a deep breath and looked downward at this chest. It's what he did when he was agitated, as if he could see his heart pulsate. Of course, he couldn't.

He'd forgotten to take his meds this morning and looked at the pill bottles that sat on his desk. One was for high blood pressure, the other for high cholesterol.

Hill opened the first bottle, plopped a horse pill-sized 50 MG blood pressure tablet into his palm, placed it on his tongue, and swallowed. His face contorted, revealing how much, even as a fully grown man, he hated taking the medicine. On light news days he'd feel a degree of victory if he could take his blood pressure in the morning and his numbers would stay in the normal or slightly elevated range. Today's news made it all different.

As he dry-swallowed the cholesterol pill Jones Rivera, his assistant managing editor, burst through the bullpen entrance near the large clock. Hill smiled and choked lightly as he felt the pill navigating his body's middle passage. His trusted #2 was talented enough to run any newsroom in the country. She was also the newsroom's mother hen.

The Assistant ME went by the nickname Jones. It was short for Jonessa. Seeing Hill choking, she dashed into his office, a bag with takeout in her hand.

"You take your pills," she barked.

"Just did. I hate doing it, but I did."

"You're not smarter than science and the doctors."

"I know, Jones. I told you, I just took my pills," he snapped then coughed lightly.

"Drink some water. What's wrong with you?" she said. "This is just what I need on an afternoon like this. Me witnessing my boss choke to death."

Jones' voice was high-pitched, her Boricua-tinged accent now heightened to match her mean glare that was equal parts maternal and frustrated.

"Didn't I tell you to take those pills at 10:00 am? Isn't that the time the doctor said - right after you eat breakfast? You should've taken your medicine earlier. Don't cheat on what the doctors tell you to do, W.T. Hardhead."

Her office was right next to Hill's. And like his, had a floor-to-ceiling glass window front that faced the bullpen.

The newsroom often filled with hysterical laughter during the legendary yelling matches between the cantankerous managing editor and the mother hen. For the staffers it was must-see entertainment. Sometimes, they'd lay down bets on who'd win as the ME and his #2 argued and cussed at each other, and neither spared any histrionics.

Rivera had two grown daughters. One an actress, the other an accountant. Both lived in New York. Her husband, Gualterio, had died four years earlier from liver cancer. Work had since become her therapy.

When the headlines made the Internet, Hill knew Rivera would cut her lunch break short.

"I was going to call you," he told her. "I just left messages for our big three."

"They respond yet?"

Hill coughed again.

She glared at him.

"Drink some more water. Don't make me come over there, W.T. I'll pinch your nose and force that water down your throat. I swear I will. Besides, staying hydrated is good for you. What did the doctor say?"

"Drink more water and less scotch."

"Say that again louder, please?"

"D-r-i-i-i-n-k m-o-o-o-r-e s-c-o-o-o-tch." Hill enunciated each word really slowly with a devilish glint in his eyes.

"*Sabeltodo*," she said, calling him a smart-ass in Spanish. She'd often flip between English and Spanish when they'd argue.

"I've been called worse," he shot back.

Rivera remained stone-faced. She shifted her attention to the plan to cover the stories, "Let's get to work, here."

"What are you thinking, Jones?"

"Biggest story of the campaign season, so we can't give it short shrift, Boss. We have contacts everywhere, but I think we should send R.L. to Yates, Geena to New York, and Marie to work Congress. You will be on standby to help her with D.C. And I'll cover the newsroom," Jones said.

Hill spun his chair toward the wall behind him. A large map with markings for all red states, the state capitals, and the names of the governors, senators, and congresspeople was centered on the wall. To its left was a five-foot by five-foot sheet of paper with all 100 U.S. senators and 435 congresspeople, and their party affiliations.

Rivera wondered why he was looking at the map. Hill stared at it silently for ten seconds, then spun around.

"It's a good plan, except there's one more story I think we need to get."

"What's that, Hill?"

"Old Man Bivens."

Rivera knew her boss wanted this story for himself. He wanted to get the eldest Bivens talking.

"Man, that's a big risk. We talked about it. *No bueno*, I say. We need that door open. You want to close it quick, fast, and in a hurry with the senator? Go to Cali."

Hill nodded and sat back in his chair. It wasn't a secret that Hardwick Bivens Sr. was uncontrollable. The senator had politely requested that they give her some space when it came to her grandfather. Hill opened a bottom drawer and pulled out a bottle of single malt and two glasses.

"Nope, I'm not drinking."

"Come on, Jones. We might be here all night."

"Well, it's afternoon now, W.T."

He shrugged.

"It's five o'clock somewhere. This day already deserves a drink."

She cringed again. Hill knew the look. It was her bargaining face.

"Only if you drink a full bottle of water first. And, the booze can only be a small pour, just a shot size. We've got work to do."

*   *   *

Hill had been Rivera's mentor early in her career. Back then, she was a new mother with two small kids, and her husband, Gualterio, was a linebacker for the Capitals, Washington's pro football team. Rivera impressed Hill during a summer internship interview. Like a seasoned reporter, she had thoroughly researched his background and history as the favorite son of Waterside, the oppressed black community outside of Yates, Tennessee. She knew Hill's story as a high honors undergraduate from Sidrow and a Harlowe Graduate School of Journalism scholar. She also knew of the scandalous murder of his cousin, star football player, Bruiser Jackson, by the Yates Police Department. Rivera prepared the account as a feature article as if she were a local reporter in Waterside or Yates.

"Bruiser Jackson was the star running back of Sidrow College, the Harlowe of the South, and was murdered by the son of its legendary police chief, Johnny Tumult, and his deputy, Jinx Koop. News reports later substantiated witnesses' testimony that two police officers, Patrolman Jinx Koop and Assistant Chief of Police, Johnny Tumult Jr., the police chief's son, killed him in a jealous rage. Bruiser was a nationally recognized scholar-athlete, a college football star who had successfully made it out of Waterside with both academic and athletic honors. His life seemed to be set as a pro football player, then prized Sidrow alumnus.

Tumult had falsely stated that Jackson had been hyped up on drugs. Digby Yates, then a first-term senator and lawyer, had well-known affiliations with racial hate groups and was called on by the Tumults to cover up the scandal. The murder and cover-up were revealed when Harrison Newman came into town to investigate the story. At the time, Newman was the general counsel of Sidrow and in between his elected positions as State Attorney General and Governor. Newman was interested because he had personally recruited Jackson to Sidrow and had become a mentor to him. The death devastated Newman, and he vowed to uncover the truth and do his best to get the killers arrested and prosecuted."

Rivera didn't tell Hill that she'd learned that he had sworn revenge against Digby Yates. She also didn't reveal that she'd learned that Hill was banned, for his own protection, by his deceased grandfather, Chesterfield Hill, from ever returning to Waterside.

Despite its alluring name, Waterside was not an attractive community. The town was a swampy bedroom community below sea level and where blacks that serviced Yates resided. The other community was The Bottoms, another swampy outpost on the opposite side of Yates, from which Tyrone and Juju Wheeler hailed.

That interview was fifteen years ago, five years after Hill had started *The Beltway News*. Since then, it had become the most important political news source covering all of D.C. and national politics. Rivera's interview was scheduled for forty-five minutes but ran over an hour and fifteen minutes.

Both talked about their families. Hill told Rivera that he and his wife had had two sons. He'd been keen to give them common names, Mark and Michael, because of the disdain he'd endured for his uncommon given name.

"You take lemons and make lemonade, Jones. I make speeches all the time, and my first name, Word, is a great icebreaker at the beginning of my talks."

He then broke into the short speech he used.

Ladies and gentlemen: My parents have common names, Robertson and Millie. Those are good, strong Southern names. They said they'd named me Word so I would never forget my purpose. Even when I was a child, I hated that first name and wanted to change it to John or Robertson Jr.

Just so you know, my middle name is Thomas. And when my Mom would scream, "WORD THOMAS!" I knew my old friends, Consequences and Repercussions, were coming to visit.

He'd then rub his hindquarters and grimace.

I'd bring along their cousins, Ouch and Sorry.

Hill's icebreaker story always drew raucous laughter from his audiences. After the laughter, he'd continue as he did with Jones.

"As a child, I thought my name had predestined me to be a Southern man of God, someone who would bring HIS Word, as did many of the people from my small hometown of Waterside. But I've come to learn that I was actually predestined to do a different kind of public service work."

As always, Rivera smiled when he got to the end.

"I still hate the name Word. Who does that to a kid?"

Chapter Six

Memories Are for a Reason

Ronald Lawson, Hill's best friend since college and officially the number one reporter at *The Beltway News*, had gotten the message and rushed back to the office. He joined Hill and Rivera's conversation. Hill continued venting. They'd both heard it countless times and knew that while Hill would never say publicly that he wanted Yates dead, Yates's demise wouldn't sadden him.

"R.L., that guy is everything I despise. He's racist, privileged, and has made a mint from all of his diabolical practices. I hold him responsible first for the evilness of the town that bears his name and his part in hiring the police that killed my cousin, and second for the Tax Liberty con that fleeced America and made him richer."

Lawson, as Hill's loyal best friend, had come to despise Yates nearly as much as his buddy did.

"He deserved to go to jail for his part in both. How can he run for president? He's a criminal. In New York, the mobsters would give him two to the head," Lawson said.

Hill nodded, "Guys like that need God, R.L., but if I were God I wouldn't accept him." Hill lowered his voice to mimic God, "No, not you, Digby. Straight to Hell, you go."

"Good imitation," Lawson chuckled.

"I might be lucky, though. Yates is too proud to repent. He'll get his in the afterlife."

"You mean you're not going to pray for him, W.T.?"

"Why? He wouldn't accept it. Yates doesn't believe he's done anything wrong."

"I suppose you're right. You and your family are the servant class to him. It's illogical for him to see people of color as equals deserving of an apology."

Hills scanned the online report. Hope that the Tennessee scoundrel was dead or might die consumed him. He read the headline from the *World Media News* service out loud, "Tennessee Presidential Candidate Shot."

He continued, "Digby Yates, GOP presidential candidate, was shot in his campaign headquarters earlier today. The bullet pierced his shoulder. Initial reports indicate the bullet exited his body. His chief of staff, Thomas Tubbs, was killed. This is a breaking story."

* * *

Rivera was seated in one of the leather armchairs that faced Hill's desk. She had moved to its edge, her hands poised to grab the bottle. Lawson sat in the chair next to hers.

"I'm gonna grab that booze from you, Mr. Heavy Pour. *No bueno*," Rivera said. "We've got work to do."

"Not today, Jones. Give me a break. You know how I feel about that guy."

Rivera lifted her eyes to the map behind him. She gave up the fight for the bottle of single malt as Hill poured himself a double shot and another for Lawson.

As Hill popped the cork back into the bottle, Rivera spoke, her eyes still locked on the map, "Senator Bivens is wonderful lady, Hill. Her father, Hardwick Jr., is too. He is really a gracious man. But Hardwick Sr., on the other hand…he's a mess. You don't have to be a rocket scientist to see that he misses the limelight and wants it turned back on him."

"You got that right, Jones," Hill said.

He took a gulp from his shot glass and cringed as the scotch burn ran along his tongue and through his body.

"Well, Janet is far from stupid," Rivera said. "The insider betting says that she's gonna whoop Yates's ass."

"I wouldn't be so sure about that. That was before today's shooting," Lawson said. "There's a lot of sympathy out there for victims of assassination attempts. Yates has already won the religious right, and Southern Christian TV is building a huge platform for him."

"Damn. You're right, R.L.," Rivera said. "I'm sitting here thinking that common sense will prevail. But now that you mention it, it's looking as if it won't." She lowered her head. "Pour me a shot of that stuff, please."

Hill quickly complied. Rivera downed it in one gulp. She pursed her lips and inhaled to cool the scotch burns.

"Don't say that, Jones. I don't like that. That's giving up hope."

"I'm sorry, Boss," she responded. "We're both Americans with the same rights as everyone else. That's why our job here is so important."

"Common sense ain't so common, Jones. And it's exactly why Hardwick Bivens Sr. is the key here. Janet is too dignified. Her father, too. They ain't street fighters like the old man."

She looked to the ceiling and thought about her late husband.

"I get it. There's no goon in either of them. Gualterio would always say, 'Stick a knee in their back when they're down. Hurt 'em in the pileup when the refs ain't looking. Threaten them that if they come back his way again, more pain is waiting. And that changes your personality.' That's who Hardwick Sr. is. His son and granddaughter would help an opponent up off the ground and ask if they were okay."

"Yep. Your husband was right," Hill said. He then crossed his heart and kissed his hand up to God.

Rivera did the same.

Hill continued, "Fierce kung fu, dirty fighting is what's going to determine this campaign's winner. Yates is a racist with an agenda, and he will make promises to hate groups that will rile them up. He'll create expectations that the presidency is his destiny, and thereby their destiny. If enough people follow, we're looking at a landslide victory with both houses of Congress on his side. All Yates wants is power and money, but he's never been punched in the mouth until now. The reports say that he's gonna live, but I bet you he cried like a whiny bitch after he was shot."

Rivera nodded as she pushed her glass towards Hill. "Pour me another shot, please, and make it a double."

Hill pulled out the bottle. All the smiles were gone. When he passed the glass back, Rivera picked it up, stared into it, and swirled the brown contents around.

"I guess that's the end of us sticking to our credo of being a 'news source that reports news with no opinion and all facts.' We're putting that down for a while?"

"Jones, we're standing at the doorway of a historical event that will change our country forever. We need…" he paused as he downed his shot and grimaced through the scotch burn, "…we must be fearless. Bivens Sr. will call Yates's ass out. This race just turned into a street brawl. Bivens Sr. is the best in the business when it comes to giving it unfiltered, raw, and true."

"She's gonna hate you."

"I'll live with that, Jones. We'll explain to her what we did and why after she wins."

Part Two

Chapter Seven

Frustrations

Teddy Walker's phone vibrated. He recognized the D.C. area code and the exchange for a government official phone, and ignored the call. Right now, he had to calm the chaos in his town. He also was trying to end another phone call.

The Chief of Detectives was in his chauffeured car, headed north from the NYPD's Downtown headquarters. He listened as the young officer spoke on the line, anxiousness peppering his voice.

"Chief Walker, I'm Officer Roger Black, and I work out of the Midtown West precinct. We met a couple weeks back."

"I'm on my way to a crime scene in Midtown, Officer Black. Make it quick."

"I'll call you another time, then. You must be on your way to where the wife and sister-in-law of the former senator, now presidential candidate, from Tennessee were involved in the tragic shooting."

"It would be that one. Yes, Officer Black," Walker answered.

Black was a rookie Uni. Walker had met him just weeks earlier at a mentoring session. Black had asked if he could contact Walker in the future. The chief liked that he was a gung-ho, ambitious type and had given the rookie his number.

Teddy Walker knew multiple Roger Blacks in the force. He'd met thousands of them over his career. Many came out of the academy with good intentions to serve and protect. Some others had more brawn than brain; they liked the job because they could live out their Alpha male fantasies with pay and benefits. The smart ones had a plan. But for the vast majority, the plan was the same: Do five years and become a detective. If they didn't get a detective's gold shield by then, they'd spend ten to twelve years to become Precinct Commander, followed by another ten to fifteen years and then retirement. Those who were real stars and had a little luck could, in eight to ten years, become a member of a special division, and after a few more years could become a division head, and then they'd be plucked to be an assistant chief, then a chief, which automatically put them on the short list to Commissioner.

Walker didn't mind enthusiasm and ambition. It kept the best on the force behaving like boy scouts. They stayed true to the oath of protecting and serving, as opposed to the Alpha males who would soon become arrogant renegades with disdain for the work and for the creed to protect and serve. He wondered what Roger Black would be like in five years: a top cop, or a renegade.

"Call me next week at this time, Black. I promise we can talk. Today's incident is tragic and a headache. We'll spend some time then."

"Okay, Chief," the rookie said and hung up.

Walker also liked it that Black had his ear to the ground. Teddy had gotten all the details from The Voice about the Midtown shooting, and knew Roger Black was technically incorrect. He didn't mind the small error: No one died at the shooting. Blaine Andrews was pronounced dead a short time later, at the hospital. Miscommunication of that detail was a rookie mistake borne out of enthusiasm and ambition.

Most importantly for Walker, and what he learned from The Voice, was that if not for the Society of Protectors he'd be on his way to a mass murder scene. Blaine Andrews was dead, but her sister, Constance Yates, and Constance's companion, Tyrone Wheeler, had been saved by The Voice's team.

Riding along with Walker were his top aides, Bigelow and McClellan. They sat pensively in the SUV. Silence enveloped the vehicle as they motored north on the East River Drive to the 42nd Street exit. The driver continued west and began to navigate the bump and grind of Gotham's weekday traffic, whose normal congestion doubled as they approached the spectacular crime scene.

It was quiet inside the car now except for the outside noise. A thump over a pothole, the squeal of brakes, a blare from another vehicle's horn, and the roaring of the SUV's engine as it motored onward formed a dialogue unto itself to the men in the vehicle. Bigelow and McClellan were as tense and exhausted as Walker. Their faces, like his, were grim and tight-jawed. Finally, Bigelow broke the silence.

"When is it going to end, Teddy?"

"What do you mean, Bigelow?"

Walker knew what his #2 wanted to talk about. He didn't have an answer, but he had to let his deputy vent.

"The last six months, we can't catch a break. The deaths, the incompetence of Mayor Connor Tenny, and the inept uselessness of the Police Commissioner Chuck Safity have got you doing three jobs: yours as Chief of Detectives and theirs. Which means no sleep for me. All I want is a vacation, to get recharged. Our city sleeps through the night comfortably because of you and me and Mac working triple time."

Walker nodded and shrugged. McClellan, sitting up front, turned to look back at him and nodded his agreement.

"I hear you, Bigelow. What can I say? You're right."

Bigelow had made his point. He'd vented, and Walker had heard him. It had become their pattern on car rides. First there'd be silence. Then Bigelow would vent, Walker would acknowledge his complaint, and they'd continue the ride resigned to their reality. McClellan always remained silent. His nod in agreement was his way of participating.

They looked at their phones. Each busied himself reading the breaking news accounts. The stories released from SCTV News painted Digby Yates as a victim.

A ring on Walker's phone broke the silence.

"Who could this be? I know news travels fast, but come on, man!" Walker said when he again saw the incoming call's 202 area code and 505 exchange. "If the feds get involved, it's not gonna be good. But maybe that's what's needed? Maybe Tenny and Safity will finally do their jobs."

He ignored the call and surveyed the traffic in front of them. They were two blocks from the Park Avenue Five-Plex. Vehicular traffic had ground to a halt. The streets were flooded with people walking towards the hotel.

"Put the flashing strobe on the top of the car, and turn the siren on loud, really loud," he ordered the driver, Gordon. "Move that damned crowd out of the streets."

"I'll call Midtown West, Teddy. This crowd is crazy and dangerous. All we need is a driver hitting someone," McClellan said.

"Good idea, Mac."

McClellan put the call on speakerphone and dialed the Midtown West station house.

A man with a gruff, gravelly Long Island accent answered, "Midtown West, what's your pleasure?"

The desk sergeant on duty was a smart-ass and a prick way too often for McClellan's taste.

"Hey, it's Mac McClellan," the top detective barked. "I need every man in the area to get over here to the Park Avenue Five-Plex. There's been a shooting three blocks away. These streets are a mess. This might be Midtown Manhattan at lunchtime, but it looks like Bourbon Street during Mardi Gras. This is your area, your responsibility. This requires a disaster, big-event street team. What in the hell are you doing over there?"

"Sorry, Mac," Desk Sergeant Morrow responded.

He spoke with his mouth full and with a laissez faire tone. "Give me a second, will you? I've got to finish my sandwich. The corned beef is good today."

Walker's skin crawled as they listened to the man chew. Morrow's nonchalant indifference was intentional. McClellan didn't outrank him, and so Morrow didn't fear him. Morrow took another bite. Corned beef filled his mouth as he spoke.

Walker seethed. His phone vibrated. The caller from D.C. had already called four times. This time he picked up. On the other end was the familiar voice of a friend he hadn't talked to in years.

"Teddy, you got a second?"

"Not right now. I need thirty seconds. I'm on my way to a crime scene, and there's an idiot making this day worse. I've gotta pull rank and put this clown in his place. Just give me half a minute."

"Take a moment. Call me back when you finish, but call me back. It's important."

'I will, Sir. Promise. Can I call back at this same number?"

"Yep."

As he ended the call Walker turned and said to McClellan, "Give me that phone, Mac?"

Rumors ran rampant among the subgroup that resented Walker's success. Many were Long Island lifers, others second and third generation legacy patrolman and precinct desk sergeants who despised him because he'd blocked their promotions to detective. Walker put an emphasis on promotions to straitlaced by the book candidates. For decades before, the detective promotion was granted because of a system known for nepotism or cronyism. It included promotions to officers with checks on their records that should have had their rode to detective difficult.

As a result, they gave McClellan and Bigelow a hard time on basic administrative work such as transporting criminals, providing paperwork, fingerprints, and arrest records, and passing along phone messages. The plainclothes detectives that worked out of Midtown West were particularly mistreated because they were part of Walker's team.

The station house was run by Morrow, a twenty-five-year veteran. He was eligible for retirement but remained on the job for the paycheck, and the Midtown West daytime desk sergeant's paycheck often loaded with double and triple overtime was a good one.

Walker had turned down Morrow's son for a detective's promotion for two years running, and Morrow took it personally, even though his kid had a reputation for using his father's name to gain unearned privileges and for being sloppy with paperwork. He even had a couple of misuse of force complaints. The rejections put a stain on Morrow's son's record. They marked him and indicated that he wasn't headed to chief or assistant chief status.

At best, he'd become a desk sergeant, like his dad, and if he left to go to Nassau County or Suffolk County on Long Island, or to Northern New Jersey or Newark, the same would be true. Consequently, the desk sergeant despised Walker and blamed him for his son being marked.

Morrow, like all of the cops in New York, knew that Walker was running the department, and McClellan was one of his stars.

The desk sergeant took two minutes to get back to the call. McClellan and Bigelow decided not to wait. They jumped out of the SUV as its police siren blared.

"There is no telling how long -this clown will keep us on hold and get a team over here. I see a bottleneck of five cars and a box truck at the top of the logjam" Bigelow said to McClellan. "Let's do some old-fashioned traffic-moving and get this congestion cleared up."

Word of the shooting had traveled throughout the city, and pedestrians and drivers hoping to catch a peek at the crime scene filled the streets for blocks surrounding the hotel. Traffic in Midtown was at a standstill.

The situation required a massive police presence for crowd control. People had to be moved before the cars and trucks could. McClellan and Bigelow walked in front of Walker's SUV carrying bullhorns.

Mac spotted a couple of uniformed cops and yelled, "You in blue, get over here."

The young officers recognized Walker's vehicle, distinguished by a gold badge on the upper right windshield. They also knew Bigelow and Mac, as they were the two most high-profile detectives on the force. The young officers ran towards Mac and then stopped at attention, as they'd been taught in the academy.

"Pull out your batons. Make them visible. I'll be five yards behind you on the bullhorn. We are going to that box truck in the middle of the street half a block away. Let's get these morons out of the road before someone gets run over. Assistant Chief Bigelow will be right beside me. You guys take the front. Do you understand me? Are we clear?"

"Yes, sir. We've got to get these people on the sidewalks and out of the streets," the taller and more eager Uni answered.

"Good," Mac yelled. "Any of your buddies in the area? Call them. Tell them we need them here."

Too often, cops - like citizens - could become fans of the big moment. The uniformed police officers, even the detectives, sometimes became enamored and acted as fans during big events that blocked the streets such as parades, protest marches, and street concerts. This was one of those times. The shooting at a five star hotel in Midtown Manhattan with the presidential candidate's wife was sure to gather onlookers, for hours.

The street cops made the calls to their colleagues. In five minutes, six more uniformed officers ran toward Mac and Bigelow. These cops, like the first two, were rookie officers. Crowd control was a basic lesson in the academy.

"Y'all know what to do," McClellan commanded. "Just like you were taught. We need to move the crowd and get these streets open. Fall in line behind your buddies. We'll get reinforcements in to help. For now, keep Park Avenue clear from the 53rd to 54th Street stoplights so traffic can get moving."

Sergeant Morrow finally returned to the call and with an attitude.

"Mac, how dare you bother me on my lunch time? I don't give a hoot who you work for."

"That's good to know, Morrow. Just so you know, Mac is outside with my other top guy directing traffic. You know, doing the stuff you are supposed to have a team over here doing."

The line fell silent for the next twenty seconds. Walker waited for a response.

"Teddy, I mean Chief Walker, uh, ap-ap-apologies, Si-Sir. I was just getting to it. P-P-Promise I was," Morrow stammered.

Walker envisioned the heavy-jawed, potbellied desk sergeant's face reddening with fear. All the bravado from a second earlier had now turned into cowardice.

"Here are my instructions to you, Sergeant: Call your union rep and go home. You are suspended for two weeks without pay. Have as many of those corned beef sandwiches as you want during your time off."

"But wait, Teddy. I mean Chief Walker..."

"I don't want to hear it. Just pass the call on to Julius. Find him NOW," Walker yelled.

"Chief, can I protest?"

"Do you want three weeks? A month? Protest with your union rep."

As he realized his defeat, Morrow mumbled, "Sure, Teddy."

"Before you go, I need that done in fifteen seconds, otherwise the suspension will be for a month. We have an emergency. Someone has been shot dead, and people are out here walking in the middle of the streets. You're supposed to be leading a precinct and in times like this operating a command center. Instead, you are eating a sandwich."

"I apologize, Sir. Please accept my apology."

The desk sergeant knew he was in trouble. Gloating to McClellan about eating corned beef, refusing to respond to an emergency, and making the insubordinate comment heard by Walker were certain to be a problem for him, even with his union rep's help. If Walker wanted to really push it, a permanent mark or even a demotion could be forthcoming.

"Tell it to your rep. I want you out of the damned precinct in ten minutes."

Julius, a plainclothes detective, was patched into the call ten seconds later.

"Hey, Teddy. Morrow just called me. He said you suspended him. I'm at the front door and on my way to the crowd."

"I need you to hang back for a second. Do a quick call announcement. Get all the guys to meet at the precinct and march down here as a united force. I need everyone in that precinct here in ten minutes. Make it clear that anyone who doesn't respond will need to account for where they were and why. They'd better be doing something really important. I don't want to hear about some frigging lunch date or doctor's appointment. Anyone who is not saving a life or stopping a crime, and I don't mean giving out a traffic ticket, had better be with you on that line."

"Got you, Teddy."

"Julius, march them down here and get these streets clear. It's like a block party over here. I don't need anyone hit by a car or a truck, or engaging in pushing and shoving that leads to a street fight. Can you do that in ten minutes?"

"It'll be done, Teddy."

"Good, I'm counting on you. I've got to go. The attorney general just called me. I'm guessing he wants to talk about all that is going on. I have to call him back."

"Don't worry, Teddy. I'll get it done. Make your call."

Chapter Eight

He Can't Be Killed

"Teddy do you have a burner available?"

"Give me one minute, Mr. AG."

Attorney General Cameron Chase knew Digby Yates from their time together in the Senate. Chase was a three-term senator from Illinois and voted for Yates's devious Tax Liberty bill. Like many of the senators and Congress members, especially across blue states, Chase supported the bill believing that it would bring thousands of new hourly paying jobs to big cities in their states. He anxiously looked forward to the opening of new Chicago superstores and countless construction jobs across the state. But because the bill was a con job, all it turned out to be was a 10-year tease. After the seventh year, when it became apparent that the big box stores were not going to create the new megastores in Illinois, the senator suffered dearly. He barely won re-election and following his next term left Congress. Chase returned to private practice as the general counsel of a technology start-up that made him a multi-millionaire.

President Woodside Forest, a longtime friend, had pulled him back to D.C. as his attorney general. Tacked to a bulletin board on the far wall in his office were pictures of ten people. He called them his "Must Watch" list. These were people he would never take his eyes off of while he was the country's top cop. Digby Yates was at the top of the list.

"Mr. Attorney General, sorry I couldn't take your call. There's chaos in the streets here. You probably know that Yates's sister-in-law was murdered a couple of hours ago, and his wife was at the scene of the crime. We're still trying to get things squared away. Had to do some basic street cop stuff. You remember those days, don't you?"

The attorney general started out as a street cop on the Southside of Chicago, while attending Sheridan University at night and afterwards the Evanston University School of Law. After law school, he ran a private practice and eventually moved on to politics. Chase had the natural charisma required of a politician, the looks of a handsome boy scout, and a hard-scrabble Irish immigrant background.

His father, Posey, had changed the family name from O'Brian to Chase. Posey O'Brian never regretted the name change and, on his deathbed, reminded his family of their purpose.

"We came to the United States to chase the American dream and a better way of life, so that will be our family name, forevermore. What better reminder than to have your name match your mission? I will be looking at you from the heavens. Never give up the chase."

Now, Cameron Chase had called to tell Teddy Walker, top cop-to-top cop, to say that he was all in on the pursuit of Digby Yates.

"I just want you to know that whatever you need from me, you got it. I have never shared with you how corrupt I think Digby Yates is. The news reports make the attempt on his life look like an assassination attempt. I have to play it down the middle as the attorney general, and because he's a presidential candidate we have to find his shooter. The Department of Justice will be levying an investigation and trying to find out what went on in Tennessee, so I may not be able to speak to you directly again. I have to keep up appearances on this one, Teddy. Just wanted to let you know."

"I understand, Mr. Attorney General."

"Geez man, call me Cam, Teddy. We've known each other twenty-five years, too long for the official stuff."

"Sorry Cam, I just want to show the proper respect."

"I understand. Anyhow, that's the official reason for my call."

"What's the unofficial reason Mr. AG

"As much as I despise Yates for luring me into his Tax Liberty con, he's a threat to the state for even worse reasons. He's not directly affiliated with Before Emancipation, but he is a known supporter of white supremacy. That makes him an enemy of the state, in my opinion. At least someone we need to keep an eye on."

"We know that, but the rest of the world should know it too, Cam."

"I agree. Anyhow, we suspect the reason for the shooting today in New York is that he couldn't stand the idea of his wife's being with a black man, and the embarrassment it would bring to him and his campaign."

"If that is true, can I go after him? That is a conspiracy to commit murder and a crime."

"He's a presidential candidate. This ain't easy stuff. But nobody is …"

Walker cut him off, "Nobody is above the law."

"Yes. He's not a good guy, Teddy. Yates is as corrupt as they come. Worst yet, he is a budding political strongman, an authoritarian, and if he gets in office, we may never be able to get him out. He'll wreck our country."

"Then do something, Mr. Attorney General. Take him down."

"I am working on it. If he ordered the shooting, Teddy, we'll find out and end his campaign."

The attorney general let out a loud sigh. Walker guessed there was more to the call and waited for him to say more, but instead there was dead silence for five, then ten seconds. Walker looked at the phone.

"Is there anything else, Cam?"

"Yes, your friend Bernard Palmer. I don't have direct access to him. I need you to deliver a message."

Walker didn't deny he knew Palmer aka The Voice. It was a secret, and only a select few knew they were friends. He knew why the AG brought him up. As powerful as the Society of Protectors and its ruling body, the Guiding Force, were, the United States government was infinitely more powerful.

"What do you need, Sir?"

"Let him know that Yates can't be killed. There is really nothing we can do. I get it. Believe it or not, Yates is too powerful. Even I can't threaten him at this point, especially with the growing relationship he has with Southern Christian TV. If The Voice kills him, there will be anarchy."

"Mr. AG, we understand that there are things you can't do, but people look the other way all the time. You know that as well as I."

"Teddy, this situation falls under the category of 'I wish I could.' Truly, I'd love for The Voice to have a run at him, but Yates is not The General. Yes, we know what Palmer did to The General. He can't shackle him to a chair and shoot him in the head or ship him to an abandoned island like he did the General. Yates is a presidential candidate and a former three-term senator, so we're going to give him a protective detail after he leaves the hospital. Just tell Palmer that he's untouchable, please."

"Duly noted," Walker said.

"Okay, Teddy. Good luck. Call me if I can help with what's going on in New York, but I trust you have it under control. Remember, Yates can't be killed. That's a non-starter."

'I'll pass it on."

"Okay, now be sure to throw the burner away. I'll speak with you soon."

Chapter Nine

He Doesn't Know

"Can I ride in the ambulance with you guys?" Dixie Bill Sessions asked. "I'm not certain he knows quite yet that he's been shot. The senator is, uh, not aware that his chief, uh, I'm sorry."

Sessions, Yates's head of security, couldn't finish the sentence. He'd just watched Tommy Tubbs's brains explode and the words, "He's dead," couldn't come out of his mouth. He covered his eyes with his massive right paw.

"I hate my boss," is what he wanted to say.

Two other rants ran through his head, "I should have shot him when the assassin missed. If the shooter had aimed a half inch to the left, he'd be in a body bag, too."

The gray-haired paramedic interrupted his thoughts.

"Dixie, what is it that you were saying about the senator?"

He and the younger paramedic knew Dixie. They were father and son, separated by twenty years.

Everybody knew the former football star. Dixie was the town hero, the fullback and linebacker who took Yates to the regional championships fifteen years ago. They lost the game by a missed field goal in the waning seconds. An attempted field goal chip shot that the kicker, Bo Nix, missed wide and to the right. It was Nix's only miss of the season. Nix and Sessions both made the all-state team. Dixie didn't pan out at the college level and returned home. Nix ended up at Sidrow and became an all-American field goal kicker. He never missed a kick wide right again.

"I'm sorry. What I meant to say, Big Wick," Dixie said. He nodded to the older man, "is the senator doesn't know that Tommy Tubbs is dead. He also doesn't know that his gunshot is a through and through. He's not in any danger of dying, but the pain will make him think he is."

"How do you know it's a through and through?" Big Wick asked.

"Because I saw the exit wound. I saw all the blood and watched him pass out. Afterwards, I checked to see if any other gunshots wounds or vital organs were at issue. I turned him over."

Sessions grimaced as he recalled the moment.

The Wick's looked at Yates. They imagined the yeoman task and strength required for such a deed. Sessions was still very strapping and certainly strong to turn the oversized, 250-pound senator.

Big Wick's eyes fluttered anxiously. Any information could be helpful as Yates laid unconscious. They needed to make as complete a report as possible. The time they spent transporting him to the hospital would be critical before delivering him to the Emergency Room team.

"How did you know what to do? Where'd you learn how to check him out without jeopardizing him in any way?"

"Got that from my training for the Yates National Guard. They taught us how to stop the bleeding, pull out a bullet, patch a wound. This was a through and through. Besides, I also saw the bullet. It's in the wall behind his desk. About four feet high and to the left."

Sessions' mind drifted again. He could see the bullet lodged into the wall just left of center where Yates positioned his desk and chair.

"It's right there for the police to see. It won't be a problem to find once they begin the investigation."

Dixie thought about how Digby, once the bullet was recovered, would memorialize the spot where he nearly died and create a trophy case for the projectile. He gritted his teeth as he thought about all the ways it would be publicized and monetized in the weeks, months, and years to come.

He thought to himself again, this time with more venom, "I'm a damned coward. I should have shot him, dammit."

Yates's eyes suddenly opened, accompanied by a loud acknowledgement of his pain and predicament. Sessions closed his eyes again as the voice of his boss, now high-pitched and nervous, grated on his nerves.

"I'm not dead. Thank God. Oh, Lawd, I'm not dead."

"No, you're not dead, Sir," Big Wick said. "You are going to be okay. We just need to get you to the hospital."

"Oh, Lawd. Thank you, Jesus. I can't die. It's not my turn. I have so much to do yet."

He moved slightly. The shift caused a bolt of pain.

"Ooh, my shoulder hurts. What happened? Did I get shot? Can you tell Tommy to get me an aspirin? I need pain killers, dammit, and a shot of scotch."

"Sir, we are in an ambulance. You are on the way to the hospital. You can't have any aspirin or scotch."

Yates's eyes then locked on Sessions.

"Dixie Bill, what in the hell happened? You've got one job. Keep me safe. You're fired. You hear me? You're fired. But first, get me Tubbs, dammit, and some aspirin."

"Senator," Big Wick said.

He covered Yates's mouth and nose with a gas mask.

Yates continued to bark orders through the mask. His voice began to slur and twenty seconds later, he was out.

"What did you do?" Sessions nervously asked.

"He's in shock," Big Wick said. "You're right, Dixie, the bullet hole I checked for is a through and through. I remember seeing it in the wall when we went upstairs, and even though he's a large man, I turned him just enough to see the exit wound. He won't bleed out or have any internal ricochet wounds as a result of the gunshot, but he is at risk of a stress-induced heart attack. The gas is a light sedative. It will slow down his heart rate and calm him until we get to the hospital."

Chapter 10

Darkness in Gotham

Blaine was in the cold room now. It was actually the morgue, but they called it the "cold room" at City Hospital. The room was kept between 35 and 40 degrees Fahrenheit, and the space was large enough to hold fifty bodies. Blaine's was one of only five in there at this time.

She'd remain there until an official identification was made and plans were made to move her for her burial. Dulany assumed it would likely be made by the distraught woman sitting in the ER waiting area with the handsome, muscular black man.

"That lady has gotta be the deceased's sister," Dulany said to Johnson. "Even with her teary face, she's just as pretty as the dead woman. I need her to claim the body."

"Okay," Johnson said. He was the paramedic supervisor whose ambulance had delivered Blaine to the City Hospital.

"The dead woman is wearing a wedding ring," Dulany told Johnson.

He nodded as did his partner, Lucas. The ring typically meant she was married, but as this was Gotham, a wedding ring could also be a disguise. Dulany knew that game and told the paramedics.

"A woman that beautiful, fellas, might have used a wedding band to hold off the hounds."

The men nodded their understanding. Dulany was curvaceous and buxom, and guys flocked to her. The more fearless men never hesitated to shoot their shots. Dulany kept a wedding ring on her, in her bag, or in her locker just for that purpose. She wore it when she joined the members of the team for a cocktail, and especially when they would go to Kipp Meenan's bar on 23rd Street. Meenan's was the cop hangout and always filled with a bunch of Uni's. The rookie Uni's that hadn't yet been to City Hospital would jaw drop at the site of the fiery, freckle-faced redhead. They'd run to her like dogs at dinner time, panting and slobbering. She'd brandish the wedding ring, and for most men it was a force field that stopped them in their tracks.

In the Emergency Room, two men wearing blood-splattered clothes had just finished talking to the Celebrity Hacks. Dulany yelled for them, a strong New York-accented attitude filled her voice.

"Hey, you! You two with blood all over you. Get ova here!" she snapped and gestured with a swing of her head, which - like a magnet - pulled the men to her.

Eric Leon and his partner, Paul Choice, were the men.

Dulany's summons unnerved the Society of Protectors partners. They'd hung around just long enough to find out for sure what was going on but needed to get going. Flower Yates, their assignment, had covertly slipped out of the Emergency Room. She and her black boyfriend had jumped into a private car. A backup

Society of Protectors team was following them, and Eric and Paul needed to join the pursuit.

"Ma'am we've gotta go," Eric said.

"Don't ma'am me. Get your asses ova here, now."

Eric was African-American, Paul was White Anglo-Saxon Protestant. Both heard their angry mothers, or big sisters, in Dulany's command. It turned them into little boys as they trotted to her.

"Sorry," Eric said.

"Apologies, Ma'am. I mean Miss," Paul uttered

"Look, here's the deal. That woman who just left is the sister of the woman who was killed. Judging by the blood on your shirts, you know what went down. Are you witnesses? The shooters? Who the hell are you?"

"Witnesses, Ma'...I mean Miss," Eric said. Dulany eyeballed him. She sensed him angling for a suitable lie. The head nurse tilted her head, and Eric gave up the attempted fabrication.

"We are her bodyguards, and we are devastated. The older sister was here, and now she's gone. There may be other people chasing her and the black guy, her boyfriend. We need to go."

They turned towards the exit. Four hospital security guards stood protectively at the doors. The guards stood ready to put up a fight but would not have stood a chance against the Society of Protectors mercenaries.

Eric and Paul looked over their shoulders at the four guards locked in arms.

"Please ask them to stand down, Nurse," Eric said. "I beg you. We have to follow that woman. If you don't want her to come back here dead, let us do our job."

Dulany sensed the men were different. She'd seen in her years on the job all kinds of killers. The boldest would come into the hospital on the losing side of a battle.

"I need to know that you were not here to finish the job, gentlemen."

"That's why we're here," Eric responded. "Had she lived, we would have needed to keep her safe. Now that she has passed, we have to make sure the bad guys don't get to her sister. You have to let us go and do our jobs. Otherwise, she and her boyfriend will be joining her sister in the morgue."

"Then go and find her, please. Beg her to come back. We need her to officially identify the body. She knows her sister is dead. I told her to take a moment to get herself together. When I came back, she was gone."

"We'll get her and bring her back," Paul said.

"Thank you very much. Get going and be safe."

She waved her right hand in a magic wand circle, and the four security guards unlocked their arms and removed their blockade of the exit.

Eric and Paul exited without a word to the security team. Outside, they were greeted by the dusky cool of the fall evening that had replaced the warm, sunny day.

"The head nurse is right. We've gotta find her, Paul," Eric said.

"Yeah, Eric. You should call The Voice and tell him. It's gonna be dark soon in Gotham. Anything could happen now. We need help."

Chapter 11

Yates High School

"Can I ride with you to the hospital?" Dixie Bill asked again.

"If you were Bo Nix, we could squeeze you in," Little Wick wisecracked.

"Come on, Man. This ain't the time for that. Besides, I caused the fumble, if you remember, to get us the ball. Bo Nix missed the damned field goal. That missed kick messed up my life."

"Mine, too," Little Wick said. "I suppose you're right, though. Damned Rubber Arm Nix."

Neither of them laughed. Both had moved on with their lives from the football game of fifteen years ago. But the memory was still clear, and its loss still hurt.

Larry Wick Jr. was the starting wide receiver. A pass play was called on third and seven, with fifteen seconds left against Memorial in the mid-state regional championships. Nix wasn't a confident passer, so much not that his teammates nicknamed him "Rubber Arm." He could make short throws accurately, but beyond fifteen yards, his accuracy was unreliable. Fifty percent of the time, Nix might airmail a pass or short hop it to a wide open receiver, the other fifty percent, he'd make the completion. The play against Memorial called for an easy across the middle down and in. Little Wick, the receiver, ran ten yards downfield, cut, and darted five yards to the middle of the field hashmark.

On the snap, Nix deftly moved into the passing pocket and looked downfield. As the play formed, Wick Jr. ran downfield swiftly, his defender backpedaling. In the backfield, Dixie Bill pulverized the rushing opposing Memorial linebacker and created an open passing lane that should have made the pass attempt easy.

"Let it go! Let it go!"

Dixie Bill yelled to Nix as Little Wick cut and moved to the spot where the ball was to be. Nix stepped and whipped the throw with confidence. The ball cleared the battling offensive lineman and continued to ascend, however, missing Little Wick's high jump by three feet. It fell into the defensive backfield ten yards away from any offense or defense player, as an incomplete pass.

The crowd of Yates fans let out a collective groan. Nix hung his head.

The Memorial defenders knew he had choked and as they trotted back to their huddle began yelling barbs at him. Trash talk chants rang incessantly.

"He's yella."

"Bo Nix is choking."

"The Rubber Arm nickname is true."

"Game over."

"I knew it then," Dixie told his father after the game. "There's no way he makes that field goal. Bo makes that chip shot every day in practice, never missed anything under thirty-five yards all season. This one, a twenty-five yarder, he shanks wide right."

For Dixie, the shanked field goal was an even bigger miss. The Yates team's star linebacker was also recruited at Sidrow, at Sheridan in Chicago, at Grande Point in New York, and at Big Cal in Los Angeles. No one promised him a starting spot except for Middle Tennessee State, "MTS," as it was referred to in The Big Bend State. That promise to start was rescinded two weeks into summer training camp when it was revealed that he just wasn't better than the guys he competed against. After two seasons, Dixie had lost his passion for the game. It led to his being relegated to a special teams player and third string linebacker. Angry about the demotion, he packed it in.

Fifteen years back, Larry Wick had a hot post-season. The team won four games in the state playoff rounds. The team's run was largely due to Larry's emergence as an offensive threat and the primary receiver of Bo Nix's completed passes. Little Wick suddenly found himself being recruited by smaller schools than Sessions and Nix. Larry Jr. was fine with that. He just wanted to continue playing football and have an opportunity to get out of the small town owned and controlled by the sausage king of the South. His fallback option was his father's business.

Larry Wick Sr. was an Army veteran, and his military occupational specialty was as a paramedic. He successfully transferred that skill out of the Army when he won a contract to become the primary paramedic for Yates General Hospital. When the college football recruiters never came through with scholarships, Larry Jr. followed his dad into the family business. He did go away to school for a little while. It was for one year at the Nashville Paramedic Academy.

After returning home, he and Dixie Bill often talked about the big game. Today as they stood in front of the unconscious Yates the missed moment of the big game was recalled one more time.

"I knew he was going to miss that kick," Little Wick said. "Especially as the Memorial guys started to trash talk and call him a choker. Maybe Coach should have just run you two times up the gut."

"No, it was the right play, Little Wick. Nix was a good kicker. Some people just don't have the stones for the big moment. They have the talent, but not the stones."

"You both had 'em. Big balls," Big Wick chimed in. There was regret in his voice as his gaze shifted between Dixie and his son. Dixie felt their pain and knew why Big Wick's eyes were grim. The old man had vicarious regret in him that he had yet to reconcile. For Big Wick, the pain was as strong and intense as if the miss fifteen years ago had happened yesterday.

Dixie understood it. Big Wick wasn't the only Yates resident to not get past the loss. Many of the folks in Yates had lived through his success as their local football star. Big Wick was proud of his son's play on the team, especially his late season emergence. The sting became even more pronounced after Memorial won the state championship.

"It's a shame it had to end that way," Big Wick said.

"Yes, Sir," Dixie replied.

Big Wick finally responded to Dixie's earlier request to ride in the paramedic unit to the hospital.

"What Junior meant to say is, you've still got a linebacker's body. You can't fit in here. You should follow us. We'll keep you patched in via phone. We're only a mile away."

Little Wick had remained one of Dixie's best friends. Bo Nix, they heard, became citified while he was at Sidrow. He was a starting place kicker and punter there. Because of his rubber arm, he never played quarterback again. As a kicker, Bo wasn't quite good enough to make the pros, but because he had a great career at Sidrow, his professional career was off to a better start than his high school teammates'.

"We gotta get going, Dixie. Follow us," Big Wick said. He reached for the ambulance's left rear door. Dixie grabbed the door on the right and swung it towards Big Wick.

"I'll be right behind you, Mr. Wick."

"See you in a second, Dixie," Big Wick said.

As the doors closed, Big Wick yelled to the unit's driver, "Let's go, Scooter."

"Roger that, Dad."

Scooter, Big Wick's second son, shifted the idling ambulance into Drive. He pressed a button that turned on the siren and revolving red roof beacon. Onlookers had surrounded their unit and craned their necks hoping to see something through small windows on each side and rear of the unit. Many clasped their hands in prayer. The sight angered Big Wick as he looked out the back windows while Little Wick held the mask over the unconscious senator.

"This man is a damned fool. What in the hell is Dixie doing working for him? I always thought he was a good kid."

"Yates owns the town, Dad. The only thing that doesn't have his name on it is this sick-person taxi that you own. He's a god to these people. It's not a coincidence they are praying for him."

The father and son stared out the back window. Word had gotten out about the shooting. It forced Scooter to exit slowly. For the first quarter of a mile, it appeared that all of Yates had come to the Yates Corporate Complex. The town wanted to see what happened to the favorite son, their very own presidential candidate.

"He's delusional," Big Wick said. "We're just a sleepy town in the center of a middle-of-the-road state. It can't be that the best thing we got going for us right now is this guy. Really? He is a con artist and will embarrass us all."

"You'll get no argument from me, Pop. You see the gunshot wound. Just two more inches to the left, and he'd be like Tubbs."

"That's right," Big Wick said. "So close, but so far."

He then turned his attention to his other son.

"Scooter, has the traffic cleared? Pick it up, Son. You're moving at a snail's pace. We've gotta get back here and pick up Tubbs. It's a crime scene, and I'm sure the Medical Examiner is on his way."

"Yep, Dad. We're just about through the crowd. The people came out for Yates. They love him."

Yates, roused and heard Scooter's statement.

He mumbled, "They love me. I know they love me. My shoulder is on fire. Where's Tubbs?"

"Yes, they do," Big Wick said. "They certainly do love you, Senator."

Big Wick nodded and signaled to Little Wick, who turned the knob to increase the flow of sedative gas. Yates began snoring again.

"He's gonna be a real mess when he comes to and finds out that Tubbs is gone. That was a sight, Son. His face splattered by the gun shot was bad as anything is I've seen in war. Whoever was doing the shooting is good. Really good. Yates is really lucky. Tubbs, RIP, was not."

Chapter 12

Call Me Flower White

Flower walked to the late model American luxury car for hire in City Hospital parking lot. The driver had the bearings of a professional chauffeur. He was reading on a tablet and, with one look at Flower, put his device down. He straightened upright in his seat and peered into the rearview mirror as he adjusted his tie. She was lucky. He was on duty.

"Sir, are you available?"

"Yes, I am. Where are you going, Ma'am?"

His voice Boricua, and to Flower and Tyrone just another dimension of what made New York unique.

"The Five Park Place Hotel. Can you get me there?"

"You mean the Park Avenue Five-Plex?"

"Yes, that's it. That's the hotel."

Flower's voice hid the pain of her loss. Her Southern belle training was to not let people see her stress and frustrations. She'd wiped her tears from moments ago. The driver had no idea of her drama.

It helped that she was outside. Inside the Emergency Room, she had felt hemmed in and claustrophobic. Outside, she breathed a little easier. The early evening brisk air calmed her.

Tyrone was two steps behind her. He heard her talk to the driver and didn't like the destination she'd given him.

"We can't go there, Flower. There are likely killers waiting to ambush us both there."

She turned and faced him.

Her voice lowered, and her head dropped as she whispered, "Where do we go baby? I don't know New York City that well."

Tyrone took a deep breath. He looked hard at his woman as she stood at the passenger side of the large car. Protecting her was his job now. His mind scrambled with ideas of places to go and hide out. None were safe. He couldn't take her his mother's place. That would endanger his mom and her. He had been to the Freewill Baptist Church a couple of times. This past Sunday, he saw the machine gun-tattered outside of the building. It was under repair after the attacks by Before Emancipation attackers following the Phaethon Malone funeral a couple months back. The Church had become a construction zone during the week, which eliminated it as a hiding place. For now, their only destination was the hotel. Tyrone's face lit up. There was a second entrance to the hotel that he'd found just days ago.

"I know a private entrance to the hotel. We'll see if we can sneak in there. We'll get a few things and get you to a safer place."

"You won't leave me? Right, Baby?"

"I'm never leaving you, Flower. Don't worry."

Getting to the hotel and getting her belonging would buy them time to find a safe place.

Tyrone found his strength in the moment. It came from his anger knowing that Digby was behind all of this. Vengeance was on his mind as he and Flower sat in the sedan's lush back seat. He took her into his arms, kissed her passionately, and whispered in her ear, "I'm not a killer, but I will do everything in my power to protect you."

The driver, Paco Torres, saw the kiss from the rearview mirror. His heartbeat quickened as he recognized them from the tablet. He looked down and saw the pics from the front page of *The Post*. That woman and man were in the back of his car. The pic was from when they'd kissed like crazed lovebirds hours earlier, at the same hotel she asked him to take them.

He turned to the backseat and said loudly.

"Sir, Miss, you do realize that you are all over the Internet? You two are famous."

Paco spoke hurriedly. His thick Boricua accent now nearly unintelligible to the Southerners in his back seat.

"Huh, what did you say?" Flower asked.

"Sorry, *Mami.* I mean, Ms. My accent gets in the way sometimes. *Mira.* I mean, look. See here," he said excitedly.

The driver reached backwards and handed them the tablet. The couple stared at the pictures of themselves kissing in the cover story in *The Post*. Paco. He turned further and faced them.

"Permit me for interrupting, but you can't go to that hotel. The police will be everywhere and now, right now, you are the most free you will be in New York. I'm surprised, honestly, you don't have all the press following you."

Flower and Tyrone knew the driver was right. But because neither had a suggestion they looked away from Paco at each other and said nothing.

"Here's a thought," Paco continued. "We'll drive by the Park Avenue Five-Plex, and if you don't like what it looks like I have a safe place to go."

"Can we trust you?" Tyrone asked.

Paco Torres grabbed with his left hand the rosary beads that he kept on the doorframe. He raised the beads for both to see.

"Trust? I put all my trust in God each day to protect me on these mean streets. He hasn't failed me yet. And there's no reason for him to fail me now. My name is Paco Torres. I will be your driver for as long as you need me tonight. It's a pleasure to meet you, Mrs. Yates."

"Call me Flower White. White is my maiden name and what I'd prefer. And no "Mrs.," just Flower. This is my man, Tyrone Wheeler, Paco Torres. Today is our official coming out to New York and the world."

Chapter 13

I Could Have Finished the Job

"**W**here are you? Are you safe?" AnneMarie Casanova asked.

Dixie Bill sighed and took a deep breath.

"I could have killed him, but The Voice called and ordered me not too. The fat man suffered a through and through. He's safe. Tubbs, on the other hand… Goodness, gracious, AnneMarie."

Tubbs's face exploding flashed in his mind.

"I never want to see anything like that again. Poor guy, never saw it coming. If there's any consolation, he didn't feel any pain. How could he?"

"Oh, I'm sorry for him and you too, Baby, to have witnessed that. You are safe, right? Did the gunman shoot at you?"

"No, he wanted Yates and to a lesser degree, Tubbs, I guess. I wasn't a target."

"How do you know? How can you be so sure?"

"Because he called and threatened Yates. The shooter is Blaine's husband, Skylar Andrews, the banker. Blaine is dead, too. Killed by a damned BE team in New York, on Yates's orders. He'll deny it, but the bastard deserves to die. Tubbs tried to talk him out of it, but Digby wouldn't listen."

"Jesus," AnneMarie said. She was alone in the nurse's break room by herself and paced nervously in front of a large, worn sofa. "I have to sit down. This is too much."

Dixie Bill continued lamenting his cowardice.

"That woman is dead, Tubbs is dead, and now this man will use the moment to try and start a race war. He'll do it because he's humiliated about her leaving him for a black man. I could have finished the job and then lobbied with The Voice to spare my life. I should have taken the risk."

"No, Honey. You made the right decision. You don't know The Voice that well. It would have been a huge risk to hope he wouldn't kill you for not following his order."

"Some things are worth the risk, Baby. I'm behind the ambulance and pulling up to the hospital, now. I'll see you inside in a minute. Don't tell anyone what we just talked about."

"Whom would I tell, Dixie? No one would believe me." "It's a small town, AnneMarie. People will believe anything. Right now, this fool has them all believing he can be President."

Chapter 14

A Safe Place for Now

"Are you aware that your husband has been shot, Mrs. Yates?" Paco asked.

Flower saw the headlines on the tablet. She gritted her teeth but showed no other emotion. The pain she'd felt over losing Blaine and her rage at Digby had emptied her emotional tank.

"Yes, thanks to you. But he hasn't been my husband romantically, ever. The man killed my sister, tried to have Tyrone killed, maybe even me, too. Knowing how his devious mind works, he'd make it look like a murder-suicide and use it to catapult his ratings and get sympathy votes. Instead, my sister is dead, so I don't have much grief for him. All my feelings of love are with Blaine and Tyrone right now."

"I understand," Paco said.

The ride took forty minutes. Both the hospital and the hotel were on 53rd Street. The cross-town drive from 10th Avenue to Park Avenue, on any other day at 5:30 pm, would have taken ten to fifteen minutes, but as they made it to Fifth Avenue, just two blocks from the hotel, their car didn't move at all for fifteen minutes.

"What's the deal with this traffic?" Flower lamented. "Welcome to Gotham," Paco said. "Every cop on duty is probably sitting there having coffee with a spike of Irish cream. I hear it's their late-afternoon pick-me-up. You should know that all this is for you. They are all waiting for you guys to show up."

"Jesus," Flower cried.

Paco's confirmation caused her heart to leap. His tinted windows hid them from the tragedy stalkers who rushed past his car.

"Look. See, there are hundreds, maybe even thousands, of New Yorkers rushing to the Park Avenue Five-Plex just to get a glimpse of you guys," Paco said. He then pointed to the train of television camera trucks parked on both sides of the street that had narrowed the drivable area to a sliver. "All these trucks on both sides of the road are news trucks."

Paco then identified newscasters and notable New Yorkers as they passed by. "That's Shawn Cooper from Channel 2, and there's Mo Daniels from Channel 4, and Teri Pretty from Channel 7. Ooh, you see that tall, gangly blond dude who looks like his panties are bunched too tight, and the pretty Asian? They're two members of the Celebrity Hack Patrol. There's the third, Desanctis, the handsome dark-haired guy. He's my favorite. Writes for *The Post*. I read him every day."

Paco picked up his copy of *The Post* and proudly waved it at them.

"They were at the hospital," Tyrone said.

"Well, you're lucky they didn't bear in on you. Especially Luke. He's a *bona fide* pain in the butt. At least, his reputation says he is."

"Are they all waiting for us?"

"Yes, Ma'am," Paco said. "It's what I feared."

"We can't go in there. What shall we do, Paco?"

"*Sí, Mami.* That place is *no Bueno,*" Paco said mixing languages again. He flipped back to full English.

"I told you I had a couple of ideas. My suggested destination is away from the action, and it may be just late enough in the day for you to get there and stay undercover until you can figure this out. Plus, my friend has way more connections than I do."

"Okay, Paco. We trust you," Flower said.

She squeezed Tyrone's hand and looked to him for reassurance. He nodded his agreement with the decision.

Finally, Tyrone said, "I'm all in now, Flower. I will protect you."

Paco clicked on his speakerphone, and the phone dialed loudly. A man picked up after one ring.

He barked happily, "Paco Torres! You owe me five dollars."

"*Papi,* not now. Save it for later, Juan," Paco said. "This is serious."

Paco's friend didn't pick up on the seriousness of the moment.

"You coming down here tonight? Are you hungry? We're having dinner in an hour. Bring a bottle of wine."

"I'm coming, Juan. But it's work. You follow today's big news story? The shooting at the Park Avenue Five-Plex?"

"*Sí, Papi, sí.* It's the worst. The woman died, poor thing. It's all over the news. So sad."

"*Sí, Papi, muy triste.* Well, the woman's sister and the guy she was with, who was also at the scene, are in my car."

"*No, mi amigo. Que quieres decir?*" Juan barked. "How'd they avoid Teddy Walker and his people?"

Paco turned to Flower and Tyrone. "Walker is the Chief of Detectives. The top cop that gets everything done."

Flower and Tyrone nodded.

He returned to the phone call.

"I don't know. I just know they are in my car. We've been stuck in a bottleneck in Midtown for a half hour trying to get them back to their hotel."

"No, Paco. Don't take them there. They'll get assaulted by the press. Maybe the killers are still chasing them. *No, Papi, no.* Bring them down here. I'll make a few calls, and we'll make this is a safe place for them for now."

Chapter 15

Keep Them Safe

"They are in a black car. We followed them from the hospital. She is with the black man, the boyfriend. We are one car behind them. Traffic wasn't moving at all. It looked like they wanted to go the hotel. They sat in a bottleneck for a nearly thirty minutes, and I guess the sight of the press and all the police scared them away. Now, we are headed downtown," the Society of Protectors member said.

"We're heading to join you. I've got Paul with me. Keep close to them. I'm going to call The Voice and find out what he wants us to do.."

"Roger that, Eric," the driver said.

Eric Leon was the lead on the Society of Protectors detail. His assignment: Guard Flower Yates and Tyrone Wheeler. Eric guessed the police would be looking for Flower. Normally, a uniformed team would have followed the ambulance to the hospital, but this was another purposeful miscue by Sergeant Morrow at the Midtown West precinct.

He whispered contemptuously, "Let Walker and his guys figure it out on their own. It's just another shooting."

There was glee in Morrow's whisper. Vindictiveness was why he didn't send anyone to the hospital and didn't alert the detectives at Midtown West. Hours after he was suspended, he hoped that the Chief of Detectives wouldn't do a post-mortem to uncover his purposeful sabotage. Follow ups of this sort were normal, particularly when someone died.

Morrow regretted his pettiness as he drove along the Long Island Expressway. His mind raced as he began to weave a tale to tell his police union rep. Then caution took over.

"Trying to make Walker look bad is now costing me money. I could get fired with loss of pension if Walker digs deeper and learns of the intentionally missed steps. I probably should just take the loss. I hate Walker for what he's done to my son, but I brought this one on myself," he thought.

Now that he was exposed, Morrow knew a suspension would be worse if Flower and Tyrone were assassinated. Walker would see to it. The desk sergeant hadn't been thinking that far ahead. Now, he was trying to protect himself.

A once devout Catholic, he called in a prayer, "I'm sorry God. Please forgive me. I'll spend some time in mass over this suspension, promise. I've worked too hard. Cover me through my errors. Amen"

In the city, keeping Flower and Tyrone safe was now Eric Leon and Paul Choice's problem; they and their team were doing the NYPD's job. Eric called his boss to give him an update.

"Voice, Ron and Tom are following the sister and her boyfriend." Eric paused to corrected himself, "I mean Mrs. Yates and Tyrone Wheeler."

"Are they being followed?"

"No, and strangely, no one was at the hospital. No police at all, detectives or uniforms."

"Are you following them?"

"The backups are. We are catching up to them. We got delayed at the hospital, too."

"What do you mean, delayed? They, well she, is your assignment. Nothing is to happen to her. Do you understand?"

Eric decided not to tell The Voice about the standoff with Dulany and security that prevented them from leaving. He could tell from his boss's tense voice that he might take it as an excuse. For The Voice, excuses were not tolerated when lives were on the line.

"Roger that, Sir," Eric said. "Do you want her on the streets? She can't go back to the hotel, and the hospital needs her to identify the body and advise where to send it for burial. She's married; maybe we should get her husband involved."

"We can't, Eric."

"Why not?"

"He's the guy who shot Senator Yates. He's underground now and could be anywhere. More than likely, he's keeping his ears to the ground in Yates and waiting to get a prognosis on Digby. He wants him dead and won't miss a second time."

"Yates will probably get a detail from the Government Protection Agency now. He'll be untouchable."

"I suppose you're right," The Voice said. "But he is a master killer. My sense is, right now, the Hawkeye Andrews I know is prepared to die. The Governmental Protection Agency detail guys are good but no match for him. It just depends on how dark he decides to go. He's a friend. I don't want him dead."

"Have you told Walker?"

"No. Everything is happening too fast, and I'm not certain I will tell him. Teddy has enough on his plate in New York."

"What do we do, Voice?"

"Don't let those people die, Eric. Get them, wherever they are, and bring them to the Millennium Club. We'll keep them safe there."

"Roger that, Voice. We're on our way to get them."

Chapter 16

Back Home, They'll Say⋯

The phone buzzed in the pocket of Flower's tan designer slacks. Dried blood speckles ruined the $1000 pants. As the phone vibrated she saw that blood also spotted her royal blue blouse. The splattering across her breast and midsection was thickest. Flower knew then that she'd never like either of those colors again.

This was the first time she'd taken notice of her phone. There were already fifty messages. Most were from the nosy members of the Yates Women's Club. She wasn't surprised. This would be the story of the decade for them, especially with Tyrone being her paramour. She and Blaine laughed about it on their plane ride this morning.

"Oh, you are about to be the lead player in the most scandalous tale the South has ever seen, Big Sister. It will be must-read gossip and scandal-ous," Blaine teased.

Blaine emphasized that last syllable for a laugh.

Flower grinned.

It was just hours ago when they laughed and joked in the most mischievous way. Flower closed her eyes and remembered the jokester, prankster, and teasing temptress her little sister could be. She smiled as she recalled the laughter on the plane.

Blaine mimicked the voice of a gossip reporter breaking a story. She stuck her phone in Flower's face.

"Hey, Big Sister. Do you know they gonna hate on you something terrible? All those women with their potbellied, tobacco chewing, fart trail husbands," Blaine had said. "Do you care to comment on the big story? Everyone wants to know about you and the handsome Tyrone Wheeler."

Flower stifled a laugh as she tried to make sense of her sister's description of the men of Yates. Blaine was known for her one-of-a-kind phrases that often defied definition. Now was one of those moments.

"Fart trail? What in the heck are you talking about, Blaine?"

"You know exactly what I'm talking about, Big Sister. Those men who walk and pass gas at the same time. Think for a second, Flower. You know a fart trail walker when you see one. Imagine a dance or an aerobics class, and the instructor leading it being a big, fat, redder-cheeked version of Digby. Step one. Fart. Step two. Step three. Fart. Step four. Don't be downwind from them, outside, oh Lawdy, Lawd. Birds fly off, squirrels run for trees, ants roll over dead, bees fly around in circles, confused, and drop dead. Fart trail walkers are one-man biohazards."

Flower's smile was so big that her teeth stuck to her lips.

"How? What? Girl? Where do these crazy thoughts come from? You clearly have too much free time on your hands. Fart trails. I never."

The siblings were drinking tea when a man broke through the curtain separating the main cabin from First Class. They sat in the last row of First Class. He hurried to the bathroom with a purpose that was clear to Blaine: an unstoppable bowel movement was imminent. The lead flight attendant looked at him and considered preventing him from using the First Class restroom. She was a handsome, middle-aged woman with a warden's disposition. The man sideswiped her without an apology as she shoved a luggage item in an overhead bin. She stood next to the sisters and shot a dagger's glare at the coach passenger. For that violation, she'd not let the large man use her restroom. Her eyes locked in on him as she slammed the overhead compartment. Blaine called out and stopped her.

"Excuse me, Ma'am?"

The flight attendant turned, her face bearing a determined scowl. Blaine flashed a charming smile as the attendant asked, "How can I help you, Ms.?"

"That man," Blaine pointed.

A thud reverberated as the bathroom door closed.

In seconds, a series of determined grunts echoed throughout the 10-row, First Class cabin.

"I just made a mercy intercession. That man, he needed to go. We're from Yates, Tennessee, the sausage capital of the South. We know the look of a constipated man. Don't we Flower?"

Playing along with the gag, Flower nodded with raised eyebrows and deceitful pursed lips.

The flight attendant's eyes lit up. She covered them and then her mouth, to cover the wide grin that replaced her scowl as Flower said, "Yeah, that man, he had the look."

Blaine waved her hand. She bore the same trickster face as Flower, and beckoned the flight attendant to come closer.

"If you made him hold it," Blaine whispered, "We were about to have a fart trail of epic proportions. Might have cleared out First Class."

The flight attendant's face turned pink, then red. She burst into laughter.

"That is hilarious. Oh, my gosh. That is so funny."

A few seconds later, the man walked out of the bathroom. He rubbed his hands together. Blaine grabbed Flower's arm and squeezed it.

"He's a handwasher, thank God."

The flight attendant choked back her laughter.

The large man's jeans rubbed together, and his cowboy boots banged on the floor heavily as he passed them on his way back to his seat.

Now Flower grabbed her sister's right arm and the flight attendants to her left. They stared at each other through water-filled eyes.

The man opened the curtain and clunked along to his seat. The three women waited five seconds and then, like teenaged schoolgirls, erupted in laughter.

The flight attendant's name badge read, "Mildred."

"I'll be right back," she said. "I'm opening a bottle of champagne for you two. I needed that laugh so badly. You want it straight or mimosa-style?"

"Mimosa," Flower said. "We've got a big day ahead."

As the sisters enjoyed the mimosas - they had two each over the three-hour flight - they realized that their lives would be different from now on.

They didn't know, though, how far Digby would go or that their laughter would, hours later, be replaced by death, tears, and pain.

Chapter 17

Skylar's Request

"Skylar, do you know?" Flower asked.

Her sister's newly-widowed husband answered, "Yes, I do. Do you know what I did?"

"Huh? What are you talking about?"

She hadn't talked to anyone except Tyrone and Paco, the driver.

"I called your husband when I first learned of the shooting in New York. I told him that I'd kill him if Blaine died."

"Did you kill that bastard? I hope you did it with your bare hands and made him beg for his life before killing him."

Her no-holds-barred, "vengeance is mine," streak bared itself.

She closed her eyes and imagined Skylar pinning Digby to the ground as he choked the life out of him. It would be most gratifying if Digby died slowly while he flapped his legs about and begged. His death would be merciless and end with the cracking sound of his neck. It was the only method she might approve of; anything less would be unsatisfying.

"I shot him, and I missed. I made the mistake of shooting Tubbs first. I got too emotional."

"What do you mean you missed, dammit?!" Flower yelled. She had crossed the Rubicon. A genteel, sophisticated lady of the South she was no longer. Her brother-in-law had made the same shift and reminded her of it.

"I tried to take him out from the water tower. I should have just walked into his office and shot him with a sidearm. Anyhow, I shot Tubbs and splattered his brains. I got Digby in the shoulder, but that wound was not a kill shot. Maybe subconsciously, I wanted to make him suffer before I killed him. One to the left shoulder, another to the right shoulder. The third one to the brain. That was my plan, but he ducked and hid. And I had to get away to recalibrate. I'm going underground now. You may not hear from me for a while. Do me a favor, please?"

"Yes, Skylar. What do you need?"

"Claim your sister's body. The house is paid for. There's a nice shady tree right next to the guest house in the back. Bury her there. If I am killed, bury me right next to her. Can you do that?"

"Killed? You can't die. Don't talk like that, Skylar."

"I have nothing to live for, Flower. Blaine was my heart and soul. She's gone. I can't bear living without her."

Flower felt her heart break even more. She, too, was mourning her sister. But she knew that Skylar was right. Digby deserved to die. She took a deep breath and tried to process all that her brother-in-law had just shared.

Finally, to change the conversation, she muttered, "What about your bank?"

"That's all taken care of. Nashville Federal will take it over. They have the same ethical practices, and will protect the bank and people of the community. That part of my life is over. I'm never going back. After you bury my wife, your sister, you leave that one-horse town, too, Flower."

"Oh, I am, Skylar. I'm never going back. But, where will you be? How can I reach you?"

"Don't change your number. I'll reach you. If I survive this, it will be my way to reach you. Goodbye, and good luck."

He closed his eyes and hung up the phone. A smiling Blaine and Flower staring at him during his wedding flashed in his mind.

The phone went dead, and Flower said, her voice cracking, "Goodbye, Skylar."

She turned to Tyrone.

"I guess you heard some of that. Skylar killed Tubbs and tried to kill Digby. He's on the run. He wants me to go back to the hospital to identify the body and then bury my sister. I don't know if I can do all that alone. You can't come back to Yates with me. Going back would not be safe for you. How am I going to get all of this done by myself?"

Chapter 18

Juan's Place

"We're two blocks away," Paco said. "Traffic has been crazy, but we're almost there."

"Good, I'm waiting outside," Juan said, anxiousness rippling his voice. "I'll be ready for you guys."

Paco told Flower and Tyrone a little bit about his friend.

"We are going to the store of my friend, Juan Mendoza. It used to be a bodega. Juan renamed it The Neighborhood Eatery. One side is still a grocery store, with fancy items that cater to the snooty types that infiltrated our East Village neighborhood.

"Juan is a man of the people. Everybody loves him. He's also a friend of the Black Camelots. Are you familiar with them?"

Tyrone could not recall and shook his head.

"The Black Camelots are the New York's equivalent of black royals. They are the talk of the town, and the country for that matter."

Flower said, "Yes, I have heard of them. They are a big deal with high society types and were married in a series of glamorous weddings last summer. My sister and I even hosted a couple of garden parties during the summer weddings."

The mention of summer weddings jogged Tyrone's memory. He and his brother, Juju, had worked both parties, one each at Blaine's and Flower's estates.

A nostalgic rush coursed through Flower as she thought about the summer festivities in Yates.

The events Flower and Blaine hosted were must-attend parties for Yates society, and invitations were highly coveted. Women purchased dresses that costs thousands of dollars and spent months starving themselves look their best. Women aspiring to be the most fabulous and prettiest belle at the balls made the summer's functions competitive, and at the same time, the most regal in Yates, ever. The lead-up and the balls themselves gave attendees, especially the members of the Yates Women's Club enough fodder for small-minded, cutthroat gossip to last them for decades to come.

Skylar and Blaine hosted the first event at their home. It coincided with Donald Alexander's and Carrie Sinclair's wedding.

The second event was hosted by the real estate magnate Piker Shoehorn and his wife, Sarah. It doubled as a way to formally introduce the Shoehorns to Yates society and as an excuse to invite Sarah's friends from New York, Los Angeles, and Miami to Tennessee for a weekend of adult fun. The Shoehorns hosted their event the weekend of Tom Wilson's wedding to supermodel Danielle Jackson.

Digby had had great reluctance about hosting the third event. Tubbs had to push him to do it.

Flower had decided she was going to host the third event whether Digby wanted to participate or not.

Tubbs then advised, "Your wife is right on this one. These garden parties are the rage of the South. Invite donors, and you get a chance to present as a high society leader, look presidential, and, importantly, make your wife happy. When you want to run for President, she's going to have to stand by your side. You can't say no."

After Tubbs's urging and the demands of his wife, who also threatened another sex lockout, Digby agreed.

"I remember the Black Camelots well," Flower said. "My sister's and my parties commemorated the excitement of their weddings. Tyrone, you remember, don't you?"

Flower's face turned grim as she remembered how she and the other women had objectified Tyrone, the man she was now madly in love with, and she suddenly felt shame.

"I'm sorry, my love," she lamented.

"No apologies necessary," he said. "Those were different times. We'll put that and all this behind us, and move forward."

Paco heard the conversation between the two lovers even though it had turned to whispers. He interjected when they were just seconds from their destination.

"Juan still opens up the store himself at 5 am, meets with all the vendors, and does all of the thankless work of a small storeowner and operator. The success of his memoir, *A Friend of the Black Camelots',* told his story of how he met Tom Wilson, and shortly thereafter, Tom's friend, Kwame Mills. The book follows his life from projects kid to his inclusion in the Black Camelot family."

"Sounds like a wonderful story," Flower said.

Paco continued, "That best-seller book and a negotiation for film rights made Juan a millionaire in just months. He used some of the proceeds to buy a vacant dry cleaning establishment next door. That's now his private events room. He calls it the Black Camelot Quarters. We're here."

Juan paced outside. His face turned grim when he recognized his friend Paco's sedan. He traded his dour visage with a nervous smile as he opened the passenger door.

"Welcome, folks. Come on in. This is a safe place."

Juan led Flower and Tyrone through the bodega. The handful of people in the store stared, not because of the headlines but rather because of Flower's bloodstained outfit.

Juan said, "Don't worry about the stares. Just follow me to the private room."

In seconds, they made their way through the store and into a large, dark, quiet space. He turned on the lights and pointed to several large sofas, end chairs, and coffee tables that made up the luxuriously furnished sitting area at one end. A large dance floor took up the middle, and separated the sitting area from the bar and dee jay booth on the other end.

"Welcome to the Black Camelot Quarters," Juan said. "Grab a seat over there."

He pointed towards the sofas in the lounge area.

A large man with an AR-15 followed them in the room. He surveilled the space, then walked to the right of its entry door. His face bore an intensity that was unnerving.

"Lady and gentlemen. The bad guys have found you. They are outside the store, across the street. We guess they are considering how to breach this establishment. Do you have a weapon?"

Tyrone and Flower shook their heads. Paco nodded. He reached down and pulled a small revolver from an ankle holster. The man with the AR-15 pulled two more powerful handguns from his waistband.

"You need more firepower. One for you, Sir."

He handed a firearm to Paco.

Flower walked to Paco and extended her hand. The driver gave her the gun.

She stared at it carefully and said, "Glock 20 Gen4 10mm Semi-Auto Pistol, 15 rounds. I have one at home. I can use this, if needed. I can hit a fly's wing. I'm a gun expert."

Flower then pulled the chamber out, looked into it to make sure it was clear, reassembled the gun, and pointed it. She stood in a crouched stance with her right leg in front, left leg a half step back. She held the shooting position as she panned the gun at the wall, circled the room, and trained her eye on a series of targets.

"Lady, you look like you can handle a weapon as deftly as the protectors on our team. If those assassins come in here, mow them down. It means they got past us, and you are on your own. Juan, I need you to come with me and get Lillian before the shooting starts. She's petrified. But don't worry, our team is filled with bad asses. We never lose."

"*Oh, mi esposa.* Don't let her get hurt."

"She'll be fine. She's just hiding behind the counter, calling for you."

The man then turned to Paco. "Sir, are you as good with a firearm as the lady?"

"No, sir. I keep this weapon but never shot one at a human or animal in my life. Just in target practice."

"Well use it today."

He then turned to Tyrone, "Sir, how about you?"

"I can handle weapons."

He handed the second Glock to Tyrone. Tyrone ran a check on the weapon faster than Flower had.

"We kept four of these at home in the event of a late-night attack by BE members," he whispered to Flower. "Two were hidden in the front of the house, two in the back. Growing up in the Bottoms, Juju and I were trained since we were kids to be ready to defend ourselves and our home from Before Emancipation and other white terrorists."

Tyrone turned and told the man with the AR-15, "Firearms are a way of life for us down in Tennessee, where me and the lady-" he corrected himself, "my lady are from."

Flower looked at Tyrone and rubbed his massive bicep. The strength in his arm and his mastery of the firearm were additional assurances that he was worth the chase.

"Okay, you guys know what you're doing?" the protector asked.

"Yes. So, who is coming for us?" Flower said.

"Probably more of the guys who came for him this morning. They are here to finish the job."

Flower looked at the man more closely. Her eyes widened with recognition.

"You were at the hotel and then at the hospital. You saved us. You and some other guys."

"Yes, I was there. I'm Ron. My teammate, Tom, is outside with Eric and Paul. I'm sorry your sister did not make it. That won't happen again. We are here to protect you. Now, stand against the wall and remove the safeties from your firearms. Juan and Lillian will announce themselves when they arrive. If anyone else on our team tries to enter, they will say that they are part of Society of Protectors. Let them in. Anyone else dies. Do you understand?"

"Yes, Ron," Flower and Tyrone said in unison.

"*Sí, Papi*," Paco said.

"Don't worry, we're good at what we do. Come with me, Juan. We need to get you to your wife and you guys back in here. Everyone else, we'll see in a second."

Chapter 19

Gunshots

"Lord Jesus!" Flower screamed as gunshots rang out. She hugged and squeezed Tyrone. With each shot, she cringed, and squeezed him tighter. He stood with a steely-eyed glare focused on the door. If the attackers breached the door, he was prepared to die.

The gunshots ended abruptly. They could hear no words during the gunfire. Now the only sound coming from the main store area was that of local Spanish-language radio station, NYPR, New York Puerto Rico.

Juan kept the station playing on the store's sound system to create a native atmosphere for customers. It was background noise and never loud.

"I don't hear anything," Paco said. He stood next to Flower with his small handgun in one hand, and his rosary beads in the other. He looked up to the ceiling and whispered another prayer.

She could only make out the final words as he said them in English, "In the name of the Father, the Son and the Holy Ghost."

He crossed his heart as the sounds of his rosary beads echoed in the otherwise silent back room.

Paco turned and said, "Ms. Flower and Mr. Tyrone, please do after me. Cross your heart three times. We need God's protection for all three of us. Let's not shortchange God as we ask for a hedge of protection. Y'all are believers, right?"

They both nodded. Neither was either Catholic nor as devout as Paco. But in the moment, they agreed it made sense to make God a priority.

They followed his lead, touched their heads and chests, and then completed the sign of the cross with a touch to their left and right breasts.

The driver then said, "God's got us. We need to trust our faith now."

Tyrone, his eyes still steely, whispered to Flower, "I counted ten shots. If they get through here, lay down on the ground. I'll take them out."

Paco heard him and agreed on the shot count, "I heard ten also, but now..."

The radio's volume in the store suddenly lowered. Tyrone reached for Flower's weapon.

"Give me your gun, Flower, and lay on the ground, please."

She shook her head vehemently, "Not a chance. This is all my fault. I brought all this drama to New York. I'm a good shot, Baby. We'll do this together."

"Please make a decision," Paco said. "Someone is at the door. If they are the bad guys, it's kill or be killed, and I ain't ready to die."

"Okay, Flower," Tyrone said. "Get ready."

"*Papi*, Paco. It's us, Lillian and Juan. We're coming in. Don't shoot us. We know you guys have guns. The good guys won. It's over."

"Keep your gun on the door. Paco, they could be forced to say that," Flower yelled.

"*Sí, Mami.* Yes, Ma'am. You're right, Ms. Flower."

They stared at the door as the locks released and the door handle moved.

"Get low and be ready," Tyrone said. "Use the sofa as a barrier, if the bad guys are with her."

Lillian walked into the room, and Juan followed. They closed the door behind them. Both froze in their tracks when they saw the guns trained on them.

"Jesus, Joseph, and Mary," Lillian yelled. "Put those guns down. I told you the good guys won. My heart can't stand this."

Lillian was a petite brunette. She stood five foot two, and — even without makeup - had the face of a Hollywood icon. Her hair was pulled back, and her white teeth glistened as she glared at Paco, Flower, and Tyrone.

"Oh, my goodness" she cried. "What a day! Juan, you owe me big-time for this. I need a vacation."

"They told us you guys were coming in here before the gunshots. We didn't know," Flower said. She then led an introduction

"Lillian, my name is Flower and this is my man, Tyrone. You guys saved our lives. Thank you."

"My husband told me everything. I was behind the counter when the bad guys jumped out of their truck across the street. I couldn't move I was so scared. We were stuck in a crawl space underneath the counter. Thank God I'm a teeny weeny. We were stuffed back there like a pretzel. Now I need a drink."

Flower was leaning on Tyrone and rubbing his arms as Lillian spoke.

"You two are in love. That is so special. I can see it. I saw the headlines in the papers, but my eyes don't lie. Y'all have made quite a story. I'm sorry to hear about your sister. That is sad, really sad."

"I need a drink," Juan yowled

"*Sí*, Papi," Lillian said.

Juan walked to the bar and gave them a rundown on the activities outside.

"The Society of Protector guys are amazing. I could see it all through a big mirror we have behind the counter. They took out the bad guys and they fell like bowling pins: four guys in the store, and two outside. Pop, pop, pop. Those guys didn't stand a chance."

"Yes, now they are out there cleaning things up. It's all pretty professional. A van pulled up. Eric told us to come back here and sit tight, and the store will be clean in twenty minutes."

Juan grabbed a bottle of champagne and popped the cork. The sound startled Flower, Tyone, and Paco and they quick turned and pointed their guns at him. Hs face froze, and he raised his hands with the bottle.

"*Lo siento, lo siento*," he barked. "I'm sorry."

"Oh my," Lillian said. "Be careful, *Papi*"

Eric Leone then burst through the door, his partner Paul behind him. They panned the room with their AR-15s.

"Everything okay in here."

"We are okay," Juan said. "My mistake. I opened a champagne bottle."

He acknowledged everyone with a nod. Eric stood six four, and his glare was no-nonsense.

"Okay, everyone. We are just about done. You two," he pointed at Flower and Tyrone, "we are going to get you out of here in five minutes. Say your goodbyes. We have a safe house, and our orders are to take you there."

He continued, "Mr. Paco, Juan and Lillian, thank you for your assistance. You helped us, otherwise the bad guys may have won today. We are grateful."

Chapter 20

Mr. Mayor, You Handle It

Nurse Dulany called Chief Walker. She was the only person at City Hospital who had his mobile number. He picked up right away. Dulany never called to chit chat.

"The woman, she just left," Dulany said. "It's been the weirdest day ever. Usually, survivors are too stunned to leave on their own after shootings. Plus, a uniform team is almost always at the hospital. You know how your uniformed guys work. They are always bucking for a promotion, and solving a crime like this could be that golden ticket, so they wouldn't let an eyewitness leave. But she and the man with her left before any of the uniforms arrived, and no one – not even security - stopped her, even though that woman had blood all over her clothing. I expected to see McClellan or one of your other detectives. Teddy, no one from the police department talked to her."

"I'm sorry, Dulany," Walker said. "But I know why that happened. Thanks for the heads up."

Walker's mind flashed back to Morrow. He inhaled deeply and let out a long exhale as he began to seethe, knowing the desk sergeant was responsible for not having a team covering the hospital.

"I know for sure that she's scared, Teddy. Get that girl and that guy. Make sure they get back here safely. And somebody has to officially identify the body. I don't want them to be brought back here in Johnson and Lucas's ambulance, and end up in my cold room."

Bigelow was in the first floor conference room at the hotel, with Walker. Mac McClellan was there, too. Walker had all the talking points for the press conference, and - like Bigelow and McClellan - he wore sad, exhausted eyes.

A knock on the door surprised them all. It was Mitch Williams, the head of the Mayor's security team. Williams didn't exchange pleasantries. Walker didn't expect any. It wasn't Williams's style.

Williams said in a deep baritone, "He's in the alley and wants to know if it's clear to come in."

His eyes turned downward. Walker knew he was embarrassed. Mitch had large black eyes and a massive barrel gut. He was six foot seven and long ago had been a pro basketball prospect. Mitch was a bit undersized for the center and power forward positions, but had a proclivity for rugged elbow throwing, spine tingling pick setting, and punishing blocks. Had he been two inches taller, he would have been a journeyman American pro and would have played for a dozen years. Nonetheless, he'd managed to cobble together a nice international career, for exactly that: twelve years. But there is a huge difference between international earnings and American League earnings. Mitch needed a job after his hoops career ended. Delbert Tenny liked the idea of having a massive black male protector and had Mitch transferred from the first role he'd held after his retirement: Police Youth Patrol leader. It was a cushy PR job for which he visited schools and made speeches warning kids about how a life of crime wouldn't pay.

Like Walker, Mitch despised the mayor, but he couldn't tell anyone.

All his years playing basketball had given Mitch, at 35, the knees of an arthritic 65-year-old. He walked moving his feet one in front of the other in an unsteady gait that expended way too much energy. Knee replacement surgery was required to steady his strut. He also needed surgery to address his cardio and respiratory conditions that would otherwise culminate in congestive heart failure. The doctors had him on a diet to lose ten more pounds. He'd ballooned to 300 pounds after his playing days, and they wanted him down to his playing weight of 250 for the surgery. He'd been stuck at 260 for the last eight months. Losing those final ten pounds was a frustration for him and his family.

Walker was a star to him. The community where Mitch still lived, the now gentrified Bedford Stuyvesant, reminded him daily that he was working for the wrong man. He heard it every visit to the barbershop, grocery store, church. They were recriminations that stung.

"Tenny is a sucker, Mitch. Safity, too. You better get with Walker, Brother," said a street hustler named Slick Slack.

"We taking away your rights to the cookout home slice," Barry, a resident loudmouth, would berate.

"He taking the shine off your star, my Brother-in-Christ. Tenny is a fool," Deacon Charles would whisper every time he'd see him at Bed Stuy Baptist, the local church.

The worst degradation from the neighborhood was a variation of a hip hop line. It came from a bunch of kids shooting hoops in the park at the end of his block. It was led by 12-year-old Marky Banks. Mitch knew his mom and dad. Mark Sr. and Lori were lifelong friends. Mitch had even taught Marky how to shoot a jump shot. The wisecracking kid didn't mean to hurt the old basketball pro's feelings. It smarted, nonetheless, to hear, "Uncle Mitch. You know your boss is a sucker. Safity, I mean. The mayor ain't much better."

The old basketball pro chose to respond thinking that his shooting student would appreciate his point-of-view.

"The mayor is my boss, Marky. I'm his head of security." "Oh, heck no, Uncle Mitch. You might catch fire for that fool. Nah, Man. Drop that zero. Time for you to find a new hero. Get with Walker."

That moment was two years ago. Mitch never forgot Marky's words, and today at the scene of the crime, the mayor was there to steal some headlines. Mitch was sent ahead to make sure it was okay. The task was embarrassing.

"Is Safity with him?" Walker asked.

Mitch didn't say a word. He just nodded.

"What do you think they want to do?"

"They have to be here. It makes them look good. A presidential candidate's wife is involved. Tenny is a Democrat; Yates is a Republican. It's all about party politics," Mitch said.

"Yeah, I get it," Walker said.

"I know you hate Safity and Tenny, Teddy, but the mayor thinks he's solid, aces with you."

"Why does he think I only hate Safity? And not him?"

Mitch looked down at the floor and rubbed his thick black mustache.

"Safity is an easy mark, that's all. The mayor is just a narcissistic nerd bustin' the chops of another nerd," Mitch said. He lifted his head and looked at the three men. "Please don't tell them I said that. I've got ten pounds to lose to get this knee surgery. Probably would have lost that weight already if I wasn't sitting my fat ass in the car all day, and being tempted by sweets and bad carbs at all those fancy breakfasts and lunches."

He then whispered under his breath, but loudly enough for them to hear, "I hate this job."

"I hear you, Mitch. Go get your, I mean our, boss. Tell him we're excited that he's here, both him and Safity," Walker said.

Ten minutes later, Mitch's labored steps, followed by three other sets of footsteps, echoed in the hallway as they approached. Mitch opened the door. Behind him were a somber-faced Tenny, Safity, and Peggy Smith, Tenny's newly hired PR maven.

They did their best to enter dramatically. Tenny's every move was calculated. The mayor and Safity were in campaign mode. No one had announced as a Democratic opponent for either man's job, but when word got out that Donald Alexander was not interested in politics at this time, Tenny hired Peggy Smith.

Smith's presence irritated Walker, and angered Bigelow and McClellan. She was known as both a crisis manager and as a dynamic campaign front person.

Walker flashed a smile and greeted them all, "Mr. Mayor. Commissioner. Peggy, I've heard only wonderful things about you. I'm glad to finally meet. Thank you for joining us today. Your reputation as a crisis manager is unparalleled. And let me tell you, today we have a doozy."

"Thank you, Teddy, I mean Chief Walker."

She knew her place and didn't want to act too familiar and exercising first names calling.

"Yes, this is something else. What a d-d-day," she said.

Smith spoke in a shrill, nasal voice as if she had cotton balls stuck in her nose. Walker and his team were distracted by her voice and her stutter. Finally, she got her words out, the stutter giving way to an upper crust New England accent.

Bigelow took a deep breath. He was already aggravated by the PR maven.

Teddy shot him a look. His #2 was seconds away from exploding. The only two people on the force who may have had more reason to be upset with Tenny and Safity were McClellan and Bigelow. Walker had done a great job of keeping them away from the mayor, but now that they were in the same room during another crisis, anything could happen.

McClellan was rubbing his hands together, and then he anxiously scratched his neck. Walker stared at him until McClellan felt his glare and looked back.

Walker needed his top two aides to calm down. The room remained uncomfortably quiet for the next thirty seconds. It stayed that way until Walker was sure he'd reined them in.

The three new entrants were too narcissistic to detect the contempt for them, but even if they did, it wouldn't have mattered. The Chief of Detectives and his aides were subordinates. Tenny and Safity had forced Walker to do all of their work for their entire terms. Tenny had failed miserably during the massacre in the Bronx, and Walker, as usual, saved him. Now, the mayor had an overpriced PR flack to guide him along. She was hired by his mother, Jane Tenny, who had tired of managing him and serving as the de facto Mayor. The press had viciously attacked both him and Jane, the former daytime television host, but with due cause. They saw her guide him during that last crisis in the Bronx Massacre when he was at a loss for words. Today, Walker was one step ahead of them.

"Mayor, it's good that you and Commissioner Safity are here. We just got a call alerting us to the whereabouts of the senator's wife," Walker said. It was a lie.

Walker didn't know Flower Yates' whereabouts, but he strongly believed The Voice and his Society of Protectors team would.

The lie was to push the mayor and Police Commissioner to do their jobs, for a change.

"Would it be okay to ask you and the commissioner to handle this?"

"Can't someone else secure the senator's wife for you?" Tenny asked.

The color drained from the mayor's face. He hadn't considered that his front man Walker would not be at his side. He'd never done a big press event without him. Peggy Smith tiptoed to him and leaned over to whisper in his ear. Walker and his aides read her lips.

"This i-i-s good f-f-for y-y-ou," she stuttered.

The mayor's nervous face did not change.

Smith was a pretty, petite redhead. Although polished, she was known for being exploitative and a know-it-all. That reputation fed into Walker's contempt for her. He had a particular disdain for such personality types.

"Chief, are you sure you can't do this for the mayor?" she asked. Smith tried to get Walker to relent with a pleading look.

"Sorry, we can't," Walker said, and looked at his watch. "We have a confidential informant. They won't speak to anyone else, and we need to get going. As it is, we have an underground route that will cost us ten minutes before we can drive to our informant. And it's still rush hour."

Finally, the mayor's contorted nervous face returned to normal.

"Go ahead," Tenny said. "Get to them. Do your job, Teddy."

"That's assertive. Mayoral. Gubernatorial, even," Smith said. She pumped her fist for emphasis.

Walker gritted his teeth reflexively. Smith had begun to eyeball him. She was sizing him up as a mayoral rival.

He didn't look at Smith as he responded, "Good luck Mr. Mayor."

Walker stood up, as did his team. Mitch Williams patted them all on the back as they walked past him and out the door. In a couple of minutes, they were at the alley entrance of their secret passage to the hotel. It was the same one that Tyrone Wheeler had just learned about and had hoped to sneak Flower and him into the Park Avenue Five-Plex. They needed to get two blocks away to 53rd Street and 5th Avenue. It took them down a flight of stairs and along a well-lit underground path that ran along 5th Avenue, where Walker's driver was waiting. They walked silently until Walker spoke.

"That guy wouldn't have shown up if he were not running for office," he said.

"Did she say, 'Governor'?" Bigelow barked.

"They looked right through us," McClellan snapped.

"And those looks mark the moment I made a decision. I am now considering a run for Mayor of New York City."

Part Three

Chapter 21

What's Going On?

Dawn Davis Stuart's eyes were red and her face tear-streaked. She wiped her tears and reached for the remote control. A shocking newsflash banner on the TV screen distracted her from the tear-filled conversation.

"Political wife and society figure involved in murder at Gotham hotel."

She turned up the volume.

"This is Shawn Cooper from Channel 2 News. We are here at Park Avenue Five-Plex, the scene of a dramatic shooting earlier today. Our reports are that there was a casualty: a former beauty pageant queen from Yates, Tennessee. The victim, identified as Blaine Andrews, had arrived in New York hours earlier with her sister, Constance Yates, the wife of the long-time former senator and current Presidential candidate Digby Yates. Initial reports suggest that the senator's wife is having an illicit romantic relationship with an employee of the Park Avenue Five-Plex. The police have not given us any details about what led to the shooting. This is breaking news. We will report details as they become available. This is Shawn Cooper from Channel 2 News."

Stuart turned the volume down and her attention away from the television. Steven Strachan sat across from her.

She threw her head back and took a deep breath.

For Dawn, the distraction provided by the news allowed her to get her emotions in check. Her facial features were now taut as she focused her teary, reddened eyes on him.

"Need I remind you who I am?"

"No, you don't, Dawn."

His gaze was calm and measured.

"I understand very clearly who you are," he continued. "But, do I have to tell you once again that I am madly in love with you? And Dawn, my dear, I know my love is reciprocated. Have I ever told you that you make my heart burst each time I lay eyes on you?"

The answer did not melt the beautiful heiress. She reminded him again of her reputation.

"You don't get it, Stevenson. I'm the infamous Madame Hot Temper. I shot and killed my husband for cheating on me."

She paused and covered her mouth. The symmetry of the breaking news report and Strachan's love overture was too much. Her tears resumed.

"Oh, my God. Oh, my God. That news report brought back so many thoughts of the person I once was."

They were seated in the living room of her Upper West Side penthouse. The sun shone through the large floor-to-ceiling windows and highlighted her face and body. She was dressed simply in her signature color, purple. Her yoga pants and matching top clung to her body and highlighted her curvy breast and flat stomach. Her brownish red hair was pulled back in a ponytail.

"I understand, Dawn. Killing your husband was a very tragic event," Strachan said. "But it was a long time ago. You are a different woman, now. As for me, I would never play with your emotions. You're way too important to me and my heart."

"You'd better not," she snapped.

He smiled. Strachan had a Hollywood-perfect smile that gave his dark skin and broad nose and large oval eyes a leading man's attractiveness. There was also a charm and coolness to the top advertising agency executive that comforted her and helped her fall head over heels in love with him. Those traits were on display now and stopped her tears.

"Thank you for those lovely words. They matter. You're a good, sweet man, Stevenson Strachan."

Dawn was making an important move with the new love in her life. Strachan was the leader of The Best Practices Advertising Agency, the world's largest advertising and media company. He had won her heart after besting two other world-class suitors: the investment banker Kurtis Van Weston and technology executive, Wills David.

The couple had tried to keep their romance clandestine. Strachan had met Stuart at Donald Alexander's wedding, the first of the fabled Black Camelot weddings. She had attended as the guest of her father-in-law, Yancey Stuart Sr., a retired real estate mogul and inactive Guiding Force member.

"I never thought I'd fall in love again, but watching this news report and the other Black Camelot stories on the Internet, I know that, like theirs, ours is a true love story. Passion and love are what I feel for you, Stevenson. I've got it bad. Look at me here, pleading, almost begging you to be my man. Don't break my heart."

"You're not begging, and if you think that's begging, then I am a lucky man to have you beg me."

Dawn's proclamation was new for Strachan. It was the first time she'd shared her heart with him this way. And it was a huge relief. Just days ago, he'd told Donald Alexander how he felt about her. Both were in the Hamptons during the evacuation period of Gotham for the Black Camelots and their friends. They stole some time away in what had become a custom for the two men during their weekends on Long Island's east end. They'd take an afternoon walk across their abutting properties. Alexander brought up the relationship.

"Aren't you dating the notorious Madame Hot Temper? I've been reading that in the press."

Strachan snickered, then stopped and turned to his friend.

"Well, you of all people should know not to believe everything you read. I never made you out as a follower of gossip, Alexander."

Alexander responded with a lie.

"Oh, I'm not. My wife, Carrie, told me. She likes Dawn and asked me why she has never been out here with you. Frankly, I didn't know you two were an item."

Strachan stood a couple steps behind and hadn't resumed walking yet.

"Uh, huh, Alexander. That's a terrible fib, brother."

Alexander decided not to admit to the falsehood. He was having fun at his new friend's expense.

'Let's keep walking, Strachan. We've got a lot of land to traverse. Won't get across these 100 acres stopping."

Strachan stared as Alexander started whistling. He then averted Strachan's stare-down with a sheepish grin. Alexander was right they had a lot of walking to do. They were making their way across the adjoining grounds, each a fifty-acre compound.

Alexander then fessed up. Strachan was anxious to talk about his new love and didn't have many people to confide in. This was a moment for confidential discussions between friends. Their friendship had progressed to where they trusted each other as confidants. When Alexander brought up Dawn Davis Stuart, he was glad. He needed advice.

"I like where this is going. She's a serious woman, and far more than a society dame. Very smart and low-key. She likes to stay in, read, watch good movies. She's got chef level skills and loves to cook for me. It's why we rarely go out publicly. I would have brought her here, but the house is packed, and it would have been a bit unfair to have her out here during this time with all of your friends around. She's the marrying type, for sure. My lifestyle as an international business leader is far from stay-at-home, but if I were to marry someone it would be her."

That conversation of just a few days ago ran through Strachan's head as he gazed adoringly at the beautiful woman who'd just declared her love for him. Dawn's story as the killer of her playboy husband and the reconciliation with his father, Yancey Sr., was legendary. Her face didn't reveal the pain of her past as a murderer and convict, of her second broken marriage, or her desire to become a mother. Instead, it was the face of a once-in-a-lifetime beauty in her late 30s, with a flawless complexion that did not hint, until you looked deep into her face, that she was mixed-race. And once you called it out to her, it was a background she was proud of and had never denied.

"I will not make you beg, Dawn. If anything, I should be begging you."

He got up from his sofa and crossed the room to her. He kneeled before her. "We have complicated lives you, and I. But you make it simple for me. I want us to enjoy years of simple love together. Will you marry me?"

Her tears began again.

"Yes. You know I will. Come here and kiss me, Honey."

Chapter 22

What Did You Say?

"How'd you do it, Man? Running Harris Simmons with all those brand presidents running their little fiefdoms. I'm generally pretty good at this, but all you need is one that goes off the rails. Now I have a runaway."

It had been a few years, five exactly, since Donald Alexander had sold Harris Simmons and stepped away from the cutthroat antics that take place inside large, complex organizations. But he had battle scars and memories that he'd never forget. They flashed in his mind as he responded.

"Trust me, I know that. Gill Harris was a great man, but if you crossed him, he was mean as a snake. If he thought you were throwing him a line of bull, he'd take your head off, and he didn't care who was watching. That set the tone for what would be tolerated and what would not. If someone went off the rails, most of the time I just sat back and watched. I didn't have to chop off too many heads. He wanted me to look like the darling prince of the business world and high society and spared me that. I'm glad he did. Saved me from a lot of sleepless nights. What happened that's got you so worked up?"

On this Saturday Stevenson Strachan was antsy to do their afternoon walk. He had a big business problem and needed Alexander's advice.

"I caught the CEO and COO for our Dallas agency stealing. We bought their nice, high-performing boutique agency two years back. Since the sale, they've been siphoning off money into their own production agency. When we bought them, they were bringing in $50 million a quarter and had been for the previous five years. Our auditors are rock solid, so we trusted their due diligence. The performance numbers continued that way for the first year after the sale. We purchased them for $200 million and made them wealthy. They'd wanted $300 million. We'd wanted to pay them $125."

Donald nodded. "So, they decided to steal the rest?"

"Looks like it. As far as we can trace. Revenues are down 50% over the last four quarters. A quick calculation shows that they pocketed $100 million."

Donald shook his head.

"They really wanted that $300 million, I guess."

"I get it," Strachan said. "The owners are two 55-year-old guys. They've been at it thirty years. It's their life's work, but now I have to decide how to proceed."

"What you gonna do?"

"Oh, they tried to punk me, Alexander. I got pimp tendencies for people who think I am soft."

"Now, you are reminding me of Gill," Alexander said. It was a clear day. He stopped and looked up to the sky and began to reminisce. He shook his head as memories of Gill's viciousness flooded his memory. "I can be a tough guy when I need to be, too, but Gill, that guy…"

"Gangsta, huh?" Strachan said.

A half smile crossed his face.

"Nuclear, buddy. Got it from his old man. Everyone thinks the Harrises are just a bunch of wealthy guys living a good life. Oliver tortured Gill. And remember, Gill's Uncle Cornwall was the one who tried to kill me and did kill Gill. That's as notorious as it gets."

"How'd you avert their rage?"

"I was making money for them. Lots of it and giving them a good face in public. Turns out - and I didn't know this until the crazy uncle shot us - I was keeping up appearances while their family was imploding. They had me on a need-to-know basis. I had no sense of the rivalry in the family or who Cornwall really was. The dude impregnated his best friend's wife and kept it a secret from his family. He also sired Sammie with a black lounge singer and then abandoned them. The man was pure evil; Hell on two legs. As selfish and as bitter a human being as they come. He forced his entitled, sexual predator of a son, Wynne, on the company but kept that bastard's background their secret. That showdown was bound to happen."

"Jesus. I guess these guys' stealing a million dollars from me is nothing compared to the Harris Simmons drama."

"I'd say. I'm not soft, but I can't be like them. I have crazy cousins in Cleveland who were bona fide gangsters. Cornwall and Oliver would get along well with them. They were tough street types, one who did hard jail time. The kind of guys who would look at you hard, and you'd empty your own pockets."

"I need guys like them right now."

"No, you don't. My cousin, Mario? Dead. They say it was a revenge killing. Took a shot to the back of the head. Colorful guy. Protected everyone. Even played a few years of professional football, but the word on the street is that his death was revenge for guys that he beat up and embarrassed. You don't want that following you."

"I'm not joking. I need a Mario now," Strachan said.

He turned to Strachan as a scowl crossed his face. Strachan furrowed his bushy eyebrows and tightened his jaw.

Alexander stared at him. Of every top executive he knew, male and female, the best had a trigger and dark side. He was suddenly curious about Strachan's and what he would do to get his money back.

Strachan continued, "You know how my business works, Donald. Advertising clients don't want their brands associated with controversy. Ad agencies are plentiful nowadays; there's one around every corner. I guess these guys thought they'd take what they felt they were due and back us into a corner because if we went public, the clients would walk away and everyone would lose. So, these dudes knew we'd catch on. They played a hand believing once we found out, we'd avoid controversy, and the worst we'd give them would be a tongue-lashing, or we'd fire them quietly."

"Did they guess right?"

"I told you: I'm a pimp when it comes to my money, and I'm getting it back," Strachan snapped. He suddenly had even more fire in his voice. The sophisticated, world-class CEO's composure had been replaced as his roots and a distinctive Bahamian accent took over.

"Me Donovan, Baby Boy. I fear no man, no challenge. They see me as a chump boy, Alexander. Can't have that. Let one get away, tomorrow another boy try me. Nah, Man. Me no chump boy."

Alexander looked at his friend. Strachan's scowl was now even darker.

"I agree. You have to put the hammer down. That means you only have one course of action." He continued, "But, 'Me no chump boy?' I need a second to process if that's gangster enough. Do they really say that in the Bahamas?"

Strachan's body language shifted. A smile replaced his scowl. "I don't know. I just made it up. These guys had me so angry. And I think you are trying to clown me, my friend. Are you hinting that I am taking myself and these guys way too seriously?"

"Well, that clowning part is true," Alexander said with a hearty nod.

Strachan's smile brightened.

"Okay, I get it. Point made: Bully and goon stuff is what lawyers do. For the record, I already let them loose on those guys."

"Now, you're talking. What did the lawyers say?"

"We should fire them."

Strachan took a long deep breath and stopped as he spotted a rock. He picked it up and hurled it like a baseball player as far as he could. A smile crossed his face as he watched the rock soar and disappear. As the rock landed so did his smile. He turned back to Alexander and rubbed his shoulder.

"Good arm, Strachan."

"Was an outfielder in my early life."

"I could tell from that toss."

"Anyhow, to continue: For now, it means a lot of work for me. I have to go down there and visit clients myself for the next couple of weeks. Salvage as much of the business and client relationships as I can."

"Are the lawyers filing any charges?"

"We decided to give them forty-eight hours to show how we can get every cent back. The lawyers already discovered that the guys' homes are attached to the production company. We can't trace the cash yet. It might be in foreign accounts, but we'll have them jailed on Monday, so they can feel some pain, and proceed with next steps while they are posting bond. It's going to be ugly."

"Good moves. The law's on your side."

"Yes, there is a ton of case law protecting us and exposing them to long jail sentences. But we have to go after them hard. One hundred million dollars is a lot of money, and we have fifty boutique shops around the world. We have to send a strong message. If we don't, everyone will start to cheat, and we'll be in trouble. I'm not going to allow that."

"I know you won't. You're too good for that. Keep me posted, please. Is that all you wanted to talk about?"

Chapter 23

Chump Boy

"It's Dawn, Donald. I got it bad for that woman. She's got me spinning in circles."

You're not going to be a chump boy about her, are you?" Alexander teased.

Strachan didn't mind the razzing or his new friend having fun at his expense. Alexander was five years older and a big brother he never had. The teasing was all good fun.

Before, their conversations had never been more than pleasantries, and he was excited and pleased that they had become more. He lowered his head in mock shame.

"I shouldn't have come up with that Chump Boy line. My damned temper. I say silly things when it comes out."

"Oh, you do for sure," Alexander said. "Don't worry. I'll keep that between us."

"I'd appreciate it."

Their walk had moved from Strachan's wooded trail to Alexander's vineyard. Aside from getting a little exercise, they used these walks to inspect their grounds which they'd leave for weeks, sometimes months, at a time.

Strachan had another issue to share, a far more personal one than the thefts by the boutique agency CEO and COO in Dallas.

"I want to talk about Dawn, Donald."

"Let's hear it, Buddy. I don't know a lot about her. How is that going between the two of you?"

"Dating her is like dating a movie star or A-list celebrity. I've never had to deal with someone like this. Do you know she has a press following led by the Celebrity Hack Patrol?"

Alexander stopped and nodded.

"Oh, they are the worst. Particularly the tall goofy one, McFlemming. He thinks he's a star. I don't mind the other two, Kung and Desanctis. They act like they have home training."

"Yeah, Home Training Rule #1: If you embarrass the family name, there'll be hell to pay when you get home. That guy definitely never learned that lesson."

"Ooh yes." Donald's eyes widened as a memory from his childhood kicked in. "My father was always on the road, but Mom had her four gigantic cousins, the Morgan brothers. The gangsters in my family I talked about. She'd threaten to call one, in particular, to straighten Rick and me out when we'd get out of hand."

Strachan's eyes lit up with his own recollection.

"I didn't dare try my father, Donovan. We're talking about a real man's man. With him, things never got out of hand. He was a construction worker. Worked as a stone mason on all the casinos and hotels that dot the landscape across Nassau and Freeport, and then on the weekends ran a fishing boat for tourists. The man rose at 5 am daily, had breakfast, said his prayers, and returned at dark each day with fresh flowers in his hand for my momma. First thing he'd say was, 'I love you, Ella.' Second was, 'Dat son of mine give you any headaches today? Do I need to give him the strap?'"

Strachan smiled as he recalled his youth.

"Did you ever get the strap?"

"No, never did. I thought I might the day I took some of Momma's flowers. I gave them to a girl I had a crush on, Tildy Moore. Momma told daddy. She thought it was cute. My dad then confronted me and told me that Momma was his woman, and if I wanted flowers for my woman, I needed to get a job and buy them with my own money."

Strachan smiled and continued, "I was 8, and I thought I had done something really bad. But my dad then winked at me and said, 'I'll bring some flowers for your girlfriend tomorrow. Okay?' I'd come to learn later that a wink was his sign of approval. He later told me that when I took my momma's flowers that day to impress a girl, he knew he was raising a gentleman."

"Giving flowers to girls at eight. That's style. You still do it?"

"Every time I see Dawn, I bring fresh flowers. She loves it and tells me that I've re-awakened the romance in her. I see it, too. It's in her eyes. She doesn't take them for granted and is surprised each time. It doesn't matter what type of flowers I bring - roses, tulips, carnations, daisies, mixed flowers - she gets giddy."

"Good home training does have its benefits, Buddy."

A big smile framed Donald's face as he realized they'd both had similar strong male influences in their lives.

"My dad wasn't a disciplinarian. He wasn't around enough, but if there was anyone built for that job it was my cousin Mario. My mother's first cousin. He spoke with a lisp. When he yelled at Rick and me, his lisp worsened. Mario also had a country accent. Between the accent and the lisp, Rick and I couldn't understand much of what he said. The truth is, when he came over to discipline us, he just gave us a crazy look. Then he'd leave. Mom had told us he went to jail for killing a man with his bare hands. That was enough for us."

"Killing a man, really?" Strachan said.

"Yeah, that part is true. But the whole talking crazy part was an act. He killed a man in a bare-knuckle prizefight. The fight was illegal, so Mario went to jail. He told us after we got older that he would never have put a hand on us. The crazy look was my Mom's idea.

"He said then, 'Y'all family, but you were boys and needed a little threat now and again to keep you in line. That was my job, seeing that your father was always on the road.' "

"Can you call him and tell him to come visit Luke? He's cramping my style. The guy's everywhere. We go out to dinner in the city. He and his hack friends are there. We come out here and take a walk on the grounds. They're here. Dawn comes to my place in the city. They're there. Luke's the loudest and most obnoxious. The other two, like I said, are respectful."

"Well, this is what you need to know. There's competition between them. Kung, in my opinion, is the smartest and most talented. She beats out Desanctis by a hair. But he's the most well-mannered, the kind of guy you'd want at a dinner party. He'd be almost invisible. Luke, on the other hand, he'd take over the hosting role at your own dinner party. He's got to be the center of attention."

"He's wrecking my game, Donald. I know she's seeing other guys, and I like this woman, a lot. I've got to do something a bit different."

"Okay, then. I have a tough question, and I need an honest answer."

"Sure, what is it?"

"Is she into you as much as you like her? Her nickname is Madame Hot Temper. You don't want to break her heart if you are not serious. Is this for real?"

"Dawn told me that she's looking for love and that other men are chasing her, but she makes time for me when I ask her to. I think I am in first place."

Donald nodded.

"Well, the rules of dating are pretty simple, Buddy. If a woman tells you that you are the one, take her at her word. Sounds like Dawn Davis Stuart issued a marching order. You'd better step your game up, or she's on to the next guy. She's being honest. You couldn't ask for more."

Alexander stopped. Their walk had taken them to the middle of his vineyard. He plucked a handful of grapes off a vine and wiped them on his shirt. Then, he held up a grape and kissed it, as if asking God to clean it, and popped it into his mouth. As a child, they called that kissing it up to God. Strachan grabbed a handful of grapes and did the same.

"Is she worth it?" Alexander asked between chomps of grapes. "Do you want what comes with being a partner with the infamous Madame Hot Temper? That's a lot of baggage."

"Oh, she's a sweet lady. The most beautiful woman I've ever dated, and she's warm, affectionate, witty, smart, and kind-hearted."

"How do you know all that? I mean you only met her at my wedding."

"I can feel it, Man. And Yancey Stuart called me to vouch for her. She told him that I have the inside track. He wants her to be okay. Yancey sounds like a character, too, but he cares deeply about Dawn. She'd probably be really pissed off at him for calling me."

"I'd say," Donald said. "What did he say?"

"The man let me know he's an original, a true throwback gentlemen's gentleman. Rich as hell, and don't give a damn."

Strachan continued, "I can imagine him in his heyday. The guy told me, 'I'm a bit too involved in her affairs, but so what? I'm a fabulously wealthy old man, and I do want I want.' "

Both men laughed loudly. Alexander knew Yancey Stuart Sr.'s legend. He was a retired Guiding Force member, but he had yet to spend any time with him. Strachan learned of Yancey's legend as a real estate tycoon when he started dating Dawn and had been unnerved when the old man phoned him.

He shared more of the phone call with Alexander.

"The old man was calculating. First, he texted, 'This is Yancey Stuart Sr. I'm calling you in one minute. Make sure you pick up.'

"The phone rang, and I answered, 'Hello.' "

The voice on the other end was strong, lots of bass, no nonsense, "Stevenson Strachan, this is Yancey Stuart Sr. I saw you across the room at Alexander's wedding. The first Black Camelot wedding this summer. We didn't meet, but I saw you when you were dancing with Dawn. She is my daughter-in-law, you know, and we live together."

"I didn't know how to respond. I thought it might be a prank. All I could say was, 'Excuse me?' "

"This is unorthodox I know, Strachan," he continued. "Here's what you need to know. You've got the inside track. I've heard good things about you. I already had you checked out. No criminal records, no kids on the side. You don't drink excessively or do drugs. Some womanizing in the past, but that also appears to be behind you. Every man has to get it out of his system. My assessment is you're a fine fellow. So, don't deliberate with Dawn. She's ready to date and wants only serious suitors. If you're not serious, step aside."

"I still didn't trust that it was Yancey. Hell, it could've been one of the Celebrity Hacks fishing for a story. I hadn't had a conversation with him so I couldn't even tell if it was his voice. I thought to hang up on the caller. Instead, I decided to play along.

"I said, 'I am serious.' "

"Good, then step up your game, Son. Pull out all the stops. And don't ever tell Dawn we had this conversation. She'd hate me for meddling."

"He hung up, and I've been pulling out all the stops since."

"Well not all the stops, Strachan. Do you have your own plane?" Donald asked.

"I'm not that wealthy, Alexander. Far from it."

"But your neighbor has his own plane," he said. "I have a pilot and a flight attendant on call. You can use them any time you want."

"I couldn't do that."

"I insist. Look behind us."

They both turned around. There were four men twenty yards behind them. Alexander waved his hand at them. They all nodded and waved back.

"You may as well. I'm pretty much on house arrest until this Black Camelot tension breaks. I'm not going anywhere."

"But Donald, that's a bit much."

"No, it's not. You'd actually be doing me a favor. The first place I want you to go is a private island we own in the Caribbean. It's called Oliver's Oasis. It's beautiful with white, sandy beaches and a 10,000-square-foot mansion. We'll have a kitchen staff sent there to give you five-star service."

Strachan shook his head. The offer was too excessive.

"No. It's too much."

"Why are you arguing with me, Donovan's son? No one has been at the island house since this thing started. Someone needs to air it out, and the plane is collecting dust. I can't travel; it's too dangerous for me. Please accept this mutually beneficial offer. Don't be a chump boy."

Strachan scratched his head and searched for another rock. He picked it up, wound up, and threw it twice as far as the first toss. They both admired the rock's soaring arc and descent.

"Stevenson, come on, Man. This is what wealth is really like. Remember those expense budgets and the old expression? Use it or lose it. I'm losing days, if not months, of my life because of this Black Camelot war. You have some fun, my friend. Okay?"

"Okay, my friend." Strachan smiled wryly. "You got me. I won't be a chump boy."

154

Part Four

Chapter 24

The Hideout

Jefferson Painter knew how lucky he was to make it out of Gotham after his showdown with Teddy Walker, but now he wondered if the pied-à-terre he kept in Rio was the hideaway he needed. Too many wayward characters were in Brazil for his comfort. Just two nights ago, Whit Smart had spotted him as he picked up produce at a farmstand a mile away from his place.

Whit was a retired hitman, thirty years older than the 35-year-old Jefferson Painter aka The Artist Hitman. Whit was celebrated in the business for making over fifty contracted hits and never getting arrested or wounded. In retirement he drank too much. Painter didn't know if Whit was a drunk, but he could sometimes be a loudmouth..

"Here between jobs, Artist?"

Whit was leaving on his motor scooter. Two bags of groceries rested in his scooter's rear basket.

"Yeah. Do me a favor. You didn't see me. I don't want to have to leave while I'm on my break. You understand?" Painter said, his voice ice-cold.

Smart got the point.

"Sure, I never saw you. That's the business. I've been out for ten years now, but I still understand the code. This place has been good to me, and I don't need people snooping around. If they come after you, I might be recognized and then folks will be coming here looking for me. Do you think you may have some visitors?"

"I don't know, Whit. I just know that I don't want anyone to say they saw me around Rio."

"Well, just so happens, I'm leaving for a place I have in Costa Rica. I spend three months there, three months here, two months in Vancouver, and sneak down to the States for a minute to see people. Breaks up the monotony, you know. I'm outta here in a week. So, if you're hot, I won't be around to talk to anyone that might be snooping. Good luck to you."

"Thank you, Whit. Safe travels."

"See you when I see you, Painter. You stay safe, too."

As Whit sped off on his motor scooter, Painter assessed him. Whit used to be six feet tall, but Painter's hawk-eye vision measured a man that had shrunk at least an inch since his last sighting, twelve years back. Painter also knew Whit's full life story. It was the cautionary tale of a lonely hitman. Whit confided to him when the younger man just started in the business.

"I never married. I had a couple of kids from short-time girlfriends. The women understood my life as an assassin and were attracted to me because of it. They liked bad boys, but once they become mothers, they think that your past is going to go away. They don't know that we will always have a price on our heads from both the law and the dark world we are a part of. It's why I never married or got too serious. It just isn't safe; not for me, not for the women, not for my offspring. I sent money annually, $100,000 to each of my baby mamas, with the understanding that the money continues until the kids turned 18. After 18, I sent money for college, and after that my girls are on their own."

Being responsible alleviated some of the grief for being an absentee parent, but not all. The hitman had deep regrets, especially as he saw his daughters grow into beautiful women.

"I've got two daughters. One from an Irish lass and the other from an Italian temptress that I bedded," he'd told Painter. "They are beautiful girls, yes indeed, I tell you. If you like pretty girls, you'd fall hard for them. They're just a couple years apart in age and don't know each other. That's a shame, man. One lives in Seattle and the other in Los Angeles, college grads both. As I said, my agreement with their moms was that I'd see them through college. I'm proud of that. I retired from the work after they graduated ten years back. I got another $50K set aside for each when they get married. I fantasize about going to their weddings and walking them down the aisle, but that will never happen. The girls don't know me. Besides, I couldn't bring that drama to their wedding days. But yeah, Painter, they are easy on the eyes. The Irish girl has a thick crop of red hair, green eyes, and ivory white skin. She's my height, a full six feet tall.

Her sister is five four, with dark hair and a breathtaking face. I cry inside each time I get a picture of them."

"You are a proud papa," Painter had said.

"I am, but I am tortured. That's the hell I pay on Earth for the life I've chosen. It's what you'll have to contend with in this game, too, if you live long enough and evade capture. And trust me, if you have a child, you'll know what I mean. You're a pup in this game and getting a little reputation. What's your nickname again?"

"The Artist Hitman."

"How'd you come up with that?"

"I guess it's a play on our line of work and my true passion. I'm also a sketch and oil paints artist. It's a gift that I've had since I was a little boy, and I use it to relax now. I'm more of an introvert than you, Sir. I spend a lot of time by myself with my paints and easels in between jobs."

"You called me, Sir. You sassing me young man?"

Whit looked at Painter with a crooked smile.

Painter answered with a controlled grin, "Not at all."

He smiled at the memory of that conversation over a decade ago. It helped him remember why Whit was so outgoing. He was a man who missed his family and was tortured by it. Whit couldn't sit in his homes in Rio, Costa Rica, or Vancouver and spend time with his daughters. When they were young and asked about him, he told their mothers to tell them that he'd run off with another woman who was a jealous bitch. The other woman wouldn't allow him to have a relationship with his daughters, and their father was a coward.

"Tell them that until they're old enough to really know the truth. When I die, tell them to write a book on my life story. I'm keeping a diary, and they can access it and make a lot of money. It'll be a great screenplay. That'll be their inheritance."

He kept the diaries in a safety deposit box at the Bank of Vancouver. Each year, he'd add cash to the safety deposit boxes. Since his retirement, he'd added more diaries. Smart knew they would be worth a lot when he was dead. He'd hired a Vancouver law firm to contact the daughters upon his passing and disclose the diaries.

Jefferson Painter was young enough to be Whit Smart's son. Each year that Painter stayed in the game, his legend as The Artist Hitman grew. Having crossed into his mid-30s, in a deadly business that forced one to live each day as if it were their last, he now understood Whit's master class on what awaited him in the future. Whit told him there would not be a normal family life for him.

"All the simple joys, you can forget. Dropping your kids off to school, coaching Little League, or watching them in a school play, being involved in a church, or going on a family vacation. Forget about it."

Painter kept a large loft in the countryside on the outskirts of Rio. The canvas paintings that he'd created there were stacked in three rows, each row twenty deep, would never grace the walls of any gallery. Not while he was alive, anyway. The joys of that kind of life would never be his.

His hideout, twenty-five miles away from the busy center of town, was perfect for Painter as it was just rural enough to ward off the tourists. They mostly stayed in the central district for the restaurants, late night bar action, and local beaches. Besides Whit, one of the few people who knew that Painter lived there was a favorite call girl he'd nicknamed Jasmine Bronze. The name had clicked in his head because of her scent. She did smell like jasmine and had brown skin that glistened. The call girl was 23 now, and while in Rio he'd see her for weeks at a time. Their relationship had become so normalized that she would fantasize about being more than his concubine; she thought of herself as his pied-à-terre wife.

Jasmine's flawless face still had a glow of innocence. Her body was lean like that of a track athlete. She had a round bottom that moved in a hypnotic cadence, and even five years into their relationship, Painter never tired of it. Her bosom wasn't large or pronounced in any way. Her firm breasts stood at attention without a bra. Painter guessed they would expand in width and weight as she got older, and as they became feeding tubes for her future babies.

Her real name was Gisele Costa. Painter learned it when they met five years ago. He had sneaked into her wallet while she was in the bathroom. She'd left her bag on a table near the door.

"Why are you looking in my bag? This is not a good way to start."

Painter was a world-class sniper, but a terrible spy and thief. He was caught red-handed with the bag in his hand.

"There are things I must know," he said. "There are also things about me that I must protect at all costs. The people around me can neither know nor share these things."

"Oh, you sound way too serious."

Gisele waved her hand dismissively. Her flippancy set off alarm bells for Painter.

"I think you should leave," he said.

"Why, did I offend you?" she shot back. Her manner and answer was saucy and off-putting to the high alert code he operated by. "I'm sorry, then. You're handsome, and I can see that you are dark and mysterious. I like that in a man."

Five years ago, she was a college student. Her father, Humberto, had died when she was just 3 years old. Her mother was an accountant at a local firm. Gisele didn't have to be a working girl but liked the adventure. She'd become that way in reaction to her overprotective Mother, Marisol, who'd kept her under a watchful glare after Humberto's sudden and tragic death. Humberto, was a victim of a hit-and-run car accident in the center of town. The driver was a Rio drug lord who had control of the local police department. He had people visit Marisol to promise retaliation if she made a big deal out of the accident and pursued an investigation.

A week after his death, Marisol was visited by a short, spectacled man with a backpack. She opened the door and glared at the man. He was dressed like a banker in a dark blue suit, white shirt, and blue tie. When he extended his hand to shake hers, the gleam from his gold cuff links, initialed NW, was so intense that Marisol averted her eyes.

Marisol knew what the initials stood for. Friends had told her they would be coming and warned her to not be difficult. She had a 3-year-old daughter to raise and protect. Still, she refused his handshake, which he acknowledged with a nod as she crossed her arms and glared at him.

"People are talking. They are saying the hit-and-run driver was one of our couriers, but they don't know what they are talking about. People are known to make stuff up. You shouldn't listen to talk from such people in the street, as it is just talk. But we are saddened by your loss."

Marisol's glare cut through him. Even with a small child to care for, she did not hide her contempt. Her husband, the love of her life and father of her kid, was gone, and nothing would be done about it.

"We are gifting you $50,000 as a token of our condolences. Nothing you can say or do will bring Humberto back. My advice is to use the money and take care of your little girl. And please do not push this with the police. The Night Workers would not take kindly to that. Have I been clear, *Mami*?"

Marisol, lowered her head. Her raw anger was all-consuming. She had stopped listening to the messenger. Instead, she imagined spitting in his face and scratching his eyes out. But a sweet call from her baby girl broke through her thoughts, *"Mami, Mami, see? I finished!"*

Behind her in the living room was Gisele. The toddler proudly held up the large baby bottle whose milk she had just finished drinking. Her calls melted Marisol's rage and grabbed her attention. They did the same for the messenger.

"She's a beautiful baby. Here, take the money."

The man pushed the backpack through the doorway where they both stood and towards Marisol. She pushed it back.

"You may think I am a terrible person, but right now I am doing a job. Please know that my heart is broken, even more so now seeing your beautiful, innocent, happy little girl. Use this money and give her a good life."

"Leave us alone, please, Sir. Just go away."

Marisol attempted to close the door. The man tossed the backpack through a small opening. Marisol didn't say another word, but only because common sense prevailed as fear for her daughter suddenly consumed her. She closed and locked the door.

An hour later, the man returned with another backpack. In it was an additional $50,000.

"I talked to my bosses. They are really sympathetic and told me to let you know they vow to keep your daughter and you safe. The word is out: There will be hell to pay for anyone who might try and hurt you and your girl. Here's my card. My name is Sosa, but my friends call me Glasses, because of my eyeglasses. Don't hesitate to call me if you need anything."

Over time, Marisol came to understand that the man in the suit, nicknamed Glasses, was just doing his job. She knew the NW's treacherous reputation and realized they had to feel truly guilty to give her $100,000 in cash.

The Night Walkers became a constant presence in Gisele's life. They were everywhere, and as a kid and later teenager it became a running joke with her friends that an NW goon or bodyguard was always a stone's throw away when she was out in public. They helped Marisol raise her and even a few times intervened when her young high school daughter broke curfew or caught the attention of bad boys that Marisol didn't approve of. It was an act of rebellion to those phone calls to Glasses and the strict tension between her mother and herself that pushed Gisele to become a high-class prostitute. By age 16, she'd become a breathtaking beauty, five inches taller and much skinnier than her mom.

"You got your father's height and my face. And that wonderful body, I don't know whose that is," Marisol would often say. "And I see Humberto's big black eyes every time I look at your face. All I want to do is protect you the way no one was there to protect him. That's what mothers do, Baby Girl. One day, you will know what I am talking about."

Now, on the outskirts of Rio, Gisele's handsome, mysterious client had her wallet in his hand. This man fit the bill for what she was seeking. She was bitter for all those years feeling suffocated by her over-protective mother and guardians. Whenever she engaged in bad behavior, the NW would apprehend her, and she would throw tantrums when they would throw her in the back seat of an SUV to take her home, or a team on motor scooters would surround her and force her to hop on.

"Get on the bike voluntarily, or your mom told us we can handcuff and force you to go home," they'd tell her.

Jefferson Painter didn't know that being around the NW all those years had inured Gisele to fearing bad guys.

It also left her romantically deprived. No one in Rio, not even Glasses, knew that she was a call girl. She started a couple of weeks after she'd convinced her mother to call off the NW as her protectors.

"Mom, no one is ever going to bother me. Everyone knows now that I am protected. Just call them off. I want to be a normal college student without these guys lurking in the background. Let me date, meet new friends, and have fun."

Marisol reluctantly agreed.

"Okay, but you know Glasses is very fond of you. He sees himself as your godfather. I will tell him to give you your freedom, but remember: If you get out of hand or need help, I won't hesitate to call him."

Two weeks later, Gisele became Jasmine or Sophia. They were the two aliases she used in her new life. To remain discreet and avoid embarrassing her mother, she maintained a small, select client base, limited to well-to-do tourists and businessmen who visited Brazil. Her $10,000 per night fee ensured an elite clientele willing to maintain her secrecy. Her agency, Covert Events, screened them carefully and ensured that her identity would be protected.

Painter traveled to Brazil under a fake name, Tom Henry.

The first time they met, Jasmine sauntered across his studio, her ass rhythmically harnessed inside a tight black miniskirt worn below a white tube top glued to her to chest.

"You don't look like a Tom Henry."

"Okay. What's a Tom Henry, look like?"

"I dunno, a candy bar, maybe," she answered and cut her eyes at him flirtatiously. "But I'm the candy bar, at least tonight. Okay, Tom Henry?"

At that moment, Jefferson Painter realized he could like her. There was a sweetness, confidence, and control in her voice that relaxed him and that he needed.

Brazil was one of three places he traveled after big contract hits. The other two were London and Montreal. There was a method to his choice of hideouts. If he did a job in London or Western Europe, he'd hide out in Montreal. If he did job in Canada or Mexico, he'd hide out in London. And if he did a job in the U.S., he'd hide out in Brazil.

He watched as she inspected his small flat. Painter knew the drill. It's what high-class prostitutes did. They'd walk in, put their purse or bag down, and then look in every part of the house to make sure everything was square.

Jasmine always wore a six-inch steel hair clip. It pulled her long hair off her face and funneled it down her back, and it doubled as protection. She was trained to disassemble it in seconds to turn it into a two-handed weapon. Its fork and six-inch steel spike could ward off any client who might have bad intentions. She'd never had to use the weapon.

"We have no tolerance for clients who come here and think they will negotiate after the fact or harm our girls in any way," her agency told prospective johns. "If you want to leave here in one piece, you must abide by three simple rules. Number one: Treat your date with respect and dignity. Number two: Provide her with safe environments. Number three: Pay us in advance and tip generously. If you follow these three rules, we promise you satisfaction and an experience that will be worth every dollar.

"Stand up, please," Jasmine had told Tom Henry.

The whites in her large black eyes glistened like ivory. The artist was struck by her beauty.

He unfolded himself from his chair. The artist was a tad over six feet and weighed just under 200 pounds.

Jasmine stood next to him. She was an inch shorter, and her breast rubbed on his chest. She inhaled deeply to take in his scent.

Hers had already overcome him. He knew then that he wanted her for more than one night.

She turned around, took his hand, and led him across the room to the sofa.

"Come here, Tom Henry. I'm your candy bar. Are you ready for something that tastes so good? Come on now, Darling."

That was five years ago. Today, he looked at her with even more reverence than ever. Getting away safely from Teddy Walker had done that.

He hadn't thought it through before he said, using her real name, "Gisele, would you give up this life and come back to the States with me?"

Neither had ever used the other's real name, but he wasn't surprised by her response.

"We have something special, I think, Jefferson Painter. I know what you do and what I do for you. How do you think I would be safe as your woman?"

Chapter 25

The Farmstand Elder

Two days after spotting Whit Smart at the farmstand he returned for more groceries. The owner's eyes lit up.

"*Amigo, o gajo de alguns dias atrás!*"

Painter shrugged and raised his hands, palms upward, to communicate that he didn't know what he meant.

The elderly man, whom Painter guessed might be in his late 60s to early 70s, switched from Portuguese and said in halting, thickly accented English, "Apologies, my friend. My English is really bad. I'm out of practice."

Painter stared at him uncomfortably. He sensed an urgency in the farmstand owner's speech, but could only make out every fourth and fifth word. Finally, the man calmed down.

"The man whom you spoke to here, a couple days ago, remember?"

"Yes," Painter said.

"Ah, my friend," the man said. "He stopped by afterwards and wanted me to give you this number."

The man reached into the pocket of his green apron and retrieved a slip of paper.

"He said please call him. It is serious."

He handed it to Painter and the Artist Hitman's heartbeat picked up. His assassin's instincts went to Code Red. Instinctively, he spun in a circle, scanning the inside of the farmstand, the one-lane road outside to the left and right, as well as the wooded area across the street. The roads and woods were silent and empty. No enemy threat was apparent. He moved the backpack he carried from his back and slid his hand inside.

"Thank you, sir. I need a dozen fresh eggs, three batches of spinach, and two-pounds of tomatoes, onions, and potatoes. Can you put them in the backpack please?"

"*Claro, Amigo*," the farmstand owner said and then switched back to English.

"Just one second," Painter said. He pulled two semi-automatic handguns out of the backpack, along with the weapons' cartridges. He stuck one weapon in his waistband and handed him the backpack.

"Ah, I see," the man said. The emptied-out backpack was heavier than it should have been. The farmstand owner peered into the bag, and his face froze. He turned to Painter with a confused look.

"That is for you, Sir," Painter said. "In that backpack is $20,000 American. I'm paying you not to know me. *Você entende?* Do You understand?"

The farmstand owner twisted his head from side to side.

"*Você entende?*" Painter asked again.

"*Sí.* I mean yes, I understand. I don't know you. I've never seen you before. Is that what you want me to say to anyone who asks if I know you?"

"*Sí. Obrigado,*" Painter said.

The farmstand owner continued to speak in English, his accent suddenly less thick. For Painter, it seemed as if he had removed a restrictor on his voice.

"Pardon me for the bad accent. I was educated in America. Spent fifteen years there in my youth and had a career there in big corporations. I retired here ten years back. Nowadays, I don't speak English too much, but I know what you want me to do. Are you sure you want to give me all this money? I don't need it."

The man was Caucasian Brazilian, white-haired and paunchy. Painter imagined, based upon his own words, that he was a retired white collar worker who'd moved back home to be close to family.

"No, you keep it. I'll feel better if you have it. This is a big favor. It's better that way."

"Young man, is that why you showed me your guns? I'm a smart man. At least my late wife, Dalia, thought so. You seem like a person in the midst of an adventure I'm too old for."

The man was suddenly interesting to Painter. Painter didn't have any friends nor talk to anyone in Rio except for Jasmine, but he had met many people like the farmstand owner over the course of his life on the run. There were countless happy-go-lucky types just looking to talk and who wouldn't betray his request for discretion. But for everyone who would be honorable, there were equal numbers of nosy sorts and gossips he knew couldn't be trusted. Even worse were the wannabe big-timers, the people who loved to tell stories and name drop. They were the dangerous ones and for easy money, or even a cocktail, would gladly sell him out.

The $20,000 and show of guns was a test. If he was looking for easy money, Painter would see to it that the farmstand owner would be dead in an hour. It was a fate the old man knew instinctively and readily shared with his customer.

"I'll tell you what I do know, and that is how to mind my own business. I live up here on the outskirts of the big city for a reason. I don't want the limelight or drama. That's why I don't need your money or any more stress other than making sure my chickens lay enough eggs to serve my customers. Do you know what I mean?"

Painter nodded.

"Thank you for saying that," Painter said. "But I do have a question."

"*É claro*," the farmstand owner said, slipping back into Portuguese. "I mean sure, what is it?"

"What is your name?"

"Ah, my mysterious American friend."

A half smile followed.

"I thought you were going to ask me how fresh the eggs are, or if I will get a new batch of avocados or tomatoes soon. I thought we agreed, I'm not interested in knowing your name. Or for that matter, sharing too much. If you must have a name for me, just call me Farmstand."

Painter stepped back and sized up the man. He was an inch shorter but looked and moved with a fluidity that belied his aged. . The name tag on his large green apron read: "Owner."

"How about Owner?" Painter said and flashed his best easy smile.

"Oh, that's cheating."

His eyes widened as his face livened.

"My late wife made me wear the name tag so customers would respect me. People always try and haggle on prices. She was convinced they'd be nicer if they knew they were speaking to the owner."

"Smart lady. That makes great sense."

"I miss her," he shifted his eyes skyward. "You know that old expression: 'Behind every great man is an even greater woman.' That's gospel, *meu novo amigo*."

Painter nodded. Farmstand's reflection made him think about Gisele at home waiting for him to return. He followed Farmstand around as he filled the backpack with spinach, tomatoes, onions, and potatoes. After Farmstand finished the rounds, he handed Painter two cartons of eggs.

"Put these eggs on the back of your cart, okay?"

It was then that Painter realized the man hadn't dumped the money out of the backpack. He'd slyly put the vegetables on top.

"You know I saw that."

"Trust me, Son. I don't need it. Can I tell you why? It's actually what you would call in America, a cautionary tale or story."

Painter nodded.

He continued, "What if I told you a story of an international businessman who was accused of insider trading? It's illegal buying or selling of stock, if you don't know, my friend."

"Yes, I do," Painter said.

"Well, this guy that I am referring to, he didn't commit a crime, but he knew something was going on and looked the other way. Later on, the authorities came in, conducted an investigation, and a lot of powerful people end up in jail. A new management team comes in to the company, and the guy who looked the other way was able to keep his job. The new managers turn the company around, and five years later the stock rebounds. Then for another stroke of good luck, as a token of appreciation they decide to give him a golden parachute when he retires to live happily ever after."

"Is that you?" Painter asked.

"I didn't say that. I'm just telling you a story, the cautionary tale of the guy who minded his own business" he said.

This man, whom Painter had come to warn, maybe even kill, was suddenly even more mysterious than he. Maybe the old man was living on the outskirts of Rio for the same reason: to remain anonymous.

The main continued, "I told you my name is Farmstand. Owner is okay, too. Bottom line, I'm not in need of money. Once again, I thank you for the kind offer but politely decline with sincere gratitude."

The Artist Hitman nodded and bowed slightly in deference to Farmstand.

"Thank you, Sir," Painter said. "I enjoyed this conversation. I'll see you when I see you again."

"I look forward to that visit."

The Artist Hitman walked outside to his motor scooter and, with the backpack full of money and vegetables, and eggs in his cart, smiled as he thought about the conversation. He was relieved that he would not have to return to kill the old man. Doing so would jeopardize his Rio hideout. Painter wondered if some of the people Farmstand had referred to, now likely out of jail, might have him on a assassination list. He decided as he motored home it was a contract he'd never accept.

It was also the second time he'd heard an elder talk about love. Whit's long ago conversation about building a family, now the old man's about missing his late wife. Could they be signals? Gisele was at home waiting for him to return. He was 35; she was 23. He might need that $20,000 after all. It might be time for The Artist Hitman to consider retirement.

Chapter 26

Decision

For three days after his visit to the farmstand, Painter hadn't yet called Whit Sharp. Too much was on his mind. Gisele was still at his place. Their time together was perfect; as was the weather. The mornings were 65 degrees, and the mid-afternoons 85 degrees with low humidity. Cool breezes with scents of wildflowers from the nearby fields flowed throughout the loft. But Gisele's presence was the highlight for him. She made him happy.

On their third afternoon together she made a request. Until then, he had busied himself drawing a series of sketches.

"Make a portrait of me, Painter-man."

He shook his head and vehemently refused.

"I can't do it, I'm afraid I -+ wouldn't get it right. You're too beautiful to capture."

Gisele seemed to expect the objection, but it didn't deter her. Each day she'd ask again.

He'd issue the same response: "I'm afraid I wouldn't get it right."

And then, it became her mission to get him to paint her. She began with a teasing, delivered with her hands on her hips and her neck jutted out like a rooster crowing. But for The Artist, each Gisele crow revealed to him another interpretation of beauty. Her movements and posture engaged and tempted his artistic senses. But his cautious side was against it. He'd never painted anyone close to him, especially someone as beautiful.

The requests, the tempting and then demands, continued for four full days. Each coaxing attempt was more aggressive than the last.

He'd continue to answer, "I'm not that good, Gisele. You're too beautiful. I wouldn't get it right."

"No way," she'd say, her thick Portuguese accent slowly piercing his defenses.

Gisele also displayed her determined will.

"Let me tell you something, Jefferson Painter, if that is your name. You know that I always get my way. Always, and you will paint me."

"Oh, really? You seem very certain of your power, young lady."

Initially, he attempted to answer her with a Portuguese accent. It was a terrible mangled attempt, and she laughed uproariously. She grabbed her sides and threw her head back, her long dark hair dangling over her shoulders and white teeth glistening in the sunlit loft.

"What's terrible is your Portuguese accent. It is *fedor*. That means "stink," in English, my Americano lover man."

"*Bela menina, Eu sei*," he said. She smiled, and then he added, "*Minha namorada linda*. Do I have to have an accent to say that?"

"Oh, you have a way with words, *mi Americano*. Do you know what you just said?"

"Bela menina or namorada *linda?*

"Both. I just want to be sure."

"Yes, I called you a pretty girl, but then I realized it wasn't enough for what I really feel. Let me say this slowly, my beautiful girlfriend."

Gisele stood ten feet away. Painter watched her lose her balance and her smile blur. She grabbed a chair arm to steady herself, and her face began to flush. Her next response sold him on her. It was honest, without any pretense.

"I've never had a boyfriend. You are my first. I mean, if you are serious. Are you?"

The smile was gone. An intense stare replaced it.

"If you would have me."

"*Se você me quisesse?*" She repeated, "Se você me *quisesse?*

In English the translation if you would have me. Her English voice wasn't working because her heart was overwhelmed.

Gisele continued, "*Claro, eu gostaria de tê-lo. De boa vontade!* Of course, I would have you. Gladly."

Jefferson, relieved and elated, just gazed at her.

"I remember meeting you five years ago. You were so handsome, strong, and certain. Clear about what you wanted from me. Yet, you were so gentle and never rude. But in the midst of all that strength I was able to see that you were with me for a reason.

I liked your face, your patience, and the way you treated me afterwards. Your mother raised a gentleman."

"Thank you, Gisele."

"The second time you visited, I began to wish you were my only client. After the third visit, I quit for six months. I told my handler that I was done. I had made good money and had enough for college. That drove my rate up astronomically. I've only had nine other men, all international businessmen, much older than you."

"You don't have to explain that to me, Gisele."

"Yes, I do. I'm an open book with you, Jefferson."

Each admission weakened him, and he liked it.

"You really know how to work a guy, young lady."

She moved behind him and began to kiss his left earlobe as they stood in the center of the small, two-room loft's living room. He could feel her breast on his back as she used her hips to steer his body to the left and near the racks of canvases on the floor.

"Are you going to paint me now, *meu namorado?*"

"How could I not, now that I am your boyfriend? I guess you do get what you want, after all."

"Yes, I do, my love," she whispered.

Jefferson painted her three times. It was three different looks. The first took the most time to complete. As he feared, he was nervous about it. His steely assassin's nerves allowed him to be dispassionate about killing someone; they also served him well as an artist. But now, he needed to focus differently for the woman in his life.

In the first portrait, Gisele wore a yellow sundress that clung lightly to her long, slender body. Her breasts protruded slightly. She sat in an arm chair with her right arm slung on the back. In her left hand, she held a wine glass half filled with red wine. Gisele looked ahead, smiled, and winked. Half of her long curly mane flowed over her right shoulder. The rest of the locks draped over her left shoulder and fell down to her breasts.

In her second portrait, she stood behind a simple wooden chair. She rested both arms on the chair back, which had three horizontal slats. Her left hand held the same half-filled wine glass. Her tresses fell over both shoulders and rested on the straps of her yellow sundress and on her butter-colored shoulders. Her lips were puckered. Her hollowed cheeks hid her dimples, and her eyebrows were arched to show that she had just tasted the wine as a connoisseur might and enjoyed it.

In the last painting, Jefferson captured Gisele from the back. She stood behind the chair with her svelte back facing him. The skirt of her sundress and her long mane flowed to the left, as if a breeze had rushed through the room. Her head was turned as she looked behind her, revealing her bright smile, one dimple, and eyes that sparkled.

She loved the works, and after she did, so did the nervous Jefferson.

He said to her afterwards, "I'm calling these, *Three Looks of Beauty*, Gisele."

Gisele had never been a model but had always been told that she could be. The completed portraits made her blush. Because she had cajoled him to do the works, she didn't complain as she sat for three days. He feared that she would lose patience, but it never became an issue. That was largely because she didn't have to sit still for long stretches. It was the way Painter's mind worked. All he needed was for her to wear the yellow dress and be in his presence. During the initial pose, he captured what he would later tell her was the essence of the works. There were a few moments when he asked her to sit or pose again. It was the same way that a Hollywood director or a fashion photographer would direct an actor or model to get the best shot.

He'd interrupt her from reading, napping, or listening to music and ask, "Gisele, can you sit in the chair? Can you push your hair to the left? Now to the right?"

The second day, he'd asked, "Let me see you lean on the chair? Smile big for me, please."

On the third day, he'd issued a similar request, "Stand tall and pretty, please."

Once the staging was clear in his head, he'd resume painting. It was that way for all three days.

In the late afternoon, he'd stop for the day. They'd spend the rest of the day drinking wine and cooking. It was also time spent listening to American jazz, loudly. Painter was a fan of songs from the Great American Songbook and had a growing fondness for Brazilian jazz, particularly Antonio Carlos Jobim's Bossa Nova. For him it was all classic stuff, but the American jazz was new to Gisele. She had an affinity for American hip hop, but loved the romance of the classic tunes Painter enjoyed and the mood it set. They danced slowly, kissed long and softly, and made love passionately to the music. When they would listen to newer Brazilian jazz artists whose lyrics in Portuguese and slang he didn't know, she would interpret in whispers during lovemaking and afterward in a love-drunk voice.

By the end of the third day, they needed more tomatoes, onions, and eggs. Painter hadn't called Whit yet and wasn't anxious to do so. Everything he needed or wanted in life was right in front of him. Gisele was perfect, and she fit him well in ways that were a surprise. She was even more of a neat freak than he was. In his line of work, cleaning up after himself was imperative to not leave incriminating clues. For her part, Gisele couldn't let dishes sit for more than a half hour after they finished a meal. She'd don a headscarf, wrap one of his painter's aprons around her body, and wash the dishes by hand.

She said, "The sight of dirty dishes bugs me, *Amante*. And I hate dishwashers. They don't really get all the stuff out, or rinse all the chemicals off the plates and utensils."

Painter felt a tingle each time she called him *Amante*. It meant "lover" in Portuguese, and he loved that she said it more regularly. Before, she'd called him just Jefferson or Painter.

Each day, he learned more about her past and realized that he'd only been exposed to a part of her over their five years together. It excited him as he considered what would come if they had a future together.

Gisele wasn't clingy or over the top with her passion. She'd leave him alone to work through the day. To busy herself, she'd take walks daily in the fields. She found there edible treasures, and foraging for them excited her and gave the long walks purpose. The first day, she came back with wild herbs. On other outings, she found a wild blueberry orchard and a raspberry vine. She also happened on fields of wild mustard greens, spinach, and dandelions. She'd return and make amazing meals and snacks with the pickings.

On the second day of Gisele's travels, Painter looked at Whit's number. He realized that his guard was down.

"If my enemies were after me, I would be done," he thought.

Teddy Walker's face flashed in his head. The Gotham Chief of Detectives was one of a few people he'd had a showdown with and not bested. Every other person he'd been assigned to kill was dead. Contract killers could not be plagued by guilt. A moment spent thinking too long could be all the foe needed to escape or attack.

That had happened with Walker in the Bronx. Painter had an opportunity to take a kill shot from a rooftop but chose to wait another day. As he was escaping, Walker spotted him trying to get away and had him running for his life. Anxiety coursed through his body as he recalled the life-and-death chase, which he'd barely escaped.

He closed his eyes and recalled the details out loud as chills ran up his spine. It was a habit he'd developed when he reviewed his work on contracts.

"Walker was a foe unlike any I've ever faced, but there was that moment when I could have, should have, killed him. What a crowning achievement that would have been. Because I didn't take the shot when I had it, he spotted me on the streets afterwards, chased me to an alley, and had me hiding behind a cement pillar. All I needed was for him to show himself. But he was too smart for that; he slid into the alley on his ass with his gun poised, and I missed the only shot I would get. That's why Teddy Walker is who he is: a super cop who is as deadly and even more calculating than I. I was lucky to get out of the Bronx alive that day."

The door opened and snapped him out of his reverie. Gisele smiled brightly and excitedly flashed a thumbs up. "I had a great day out there. We could eat off these fields for months. How's your day going, *Amante?*"

Suddenly, the thought of killing Walker wasn't good. Had the assassin taken out the famed Chief of Detectives, this simple peace wouldn't be. This restful domicile would likely be under attack, and he'd likely be the subject of an international manhunt. Instead of enjoying his hobby as a painter, he'd be in hiding, probably somewhere dark, dingy, and cold.

He stood at his easel. Gisele walked to him, oblivious to his thoughts, and kissed his cheek. Her face rubbed against his as she moved away. He smelled the scents of the wildflowers she'd picked. It heightened his desires to both love and protect her. She had no idea what ran through his head as she moved from him to the kitchen sink. She wrapped an apron around her waist, arranged the flowers in a vase, and began to wash the field greens.

"My day was wonderful. Glad you had a good time, Gisele."

He mustered a fake smile as a wave of misery washed over him.

"I've known that woman for five years, now. I always liked her. Now I'm certain that I love her. But with Walker and all his forces after me, I can't promise her a happy life."

The realization didn't stop his involuntary outburst.

"Gisele," he blurted out.

The beautiful Brazilian spun around, turned off the water, and picked up a towel. She fluffed it by tossing it in the air lightly, and it fell back into her palms. She winked at him and smiled as she dried her hands. Her looks and movements melted him.

"I love you, and I need you," he said. "You are perfect in my life. Are you willing to give up your single life to be with me and spend the rest of our lives together?"

Gisele's happy, innocent smile gave way to an expression of panic and shock. She wrung the towel in her hands. Her lips moved soundlessly. Portuguese utterances followed that he couldn't interpret.

Finally, she said, "Jefferson. Are you serious?"

Her voice now was high-pitched with a nervous tone he hadn't heard before.

"Yes, I am, Gisele."

Her eyes moistened.

"I made a deal with God, yesterday. I realized that I was in love with you then. Look at me, I'm out here with my *amante*, playing housewife, picking greens from gardens, wearing an apron like a *hausfrau*, and loving every minute of it. But I can't be the only person who gives up something. I know who you are. Will you give up your life as The Artist Hitman?"

That response wasn't a total surprise. Jefferson closed his eyes. His mentally flashed back over his kills, with the last image in the sequence the dozen bodies he'd dropped and ended with the sniper assassination at the Long Island golf club, with Walker's friend, Travis Pfaff.

"How do you know about The Artist Hitman?"

"I have a protector, a guardian. He heard, years ago, that I was seeing you. He told me about you and advised me to proceed carefully. As I got to know you and our relationship grew, he blessed it. He is a top guy in the Rio underworld. He also told me how, if I were to do this kind of sex work, I should do it to get paid handsomely and pick safe clientele. I run all my clients by him."

She walked across the room and stood in front of him. "I will give up my current life gladly, if you give up yours."

Gisele turned and pointed at the canvases. "You can be a world-famous artist tomorrow. Look at all these paintings. They are wonderful, *Amante*. So, do we have a deal? I love you, Jefferson Painter, but in order for this to work, you have to retire and become the *former* Artist Hitman."

Her words took his breath away. He had to inhale deeply before he could respond. His hesitation wasn't about whether he loved her. It was about her safety.

"It's not that easy, Honey."

She frowned and cocked her head.

"Tell me, why not?"

She stared at him and said, "I'm only 23 *Amante*, but not a fool. I've lived a hard life on one hand, a sheltered life on the other, and I know that if you want to leave this life of yours, you can. If you love something strong enough, long enough, hard enough you can make a way."

"I'm wanted by the law, Gisele."

She rolled her eyes dismissively.

"So what. Are you wanted here?"

"No. But…"

She cut him off and waved her hands to prevent him from continuing.

"So we'll stay here. Stop dramatizing things."

Before he could respond, she leaned forward and passionately kissed him. He felt comfort and a relief in the kiss. Her love, he realized at that moment, had pierced a force-field that he'd built. The constant running, hiding, and being a cold-blooded killer had hardened his heart, and she had smashed right through it.

Her kiss conjured a warm rush and sudden flush of emotion. It caused him to gasp for air while beads of sweat formed on his brow. Painter knew everything she said was correct. It was just new.

It was now clear. This was love.

"You're right, *minha linda namorada*. I have money," he said. "Three apartments in places where I'm not wanted. If we lay low, maybe I can beat this."

"Sure, and I have my own money, too. This $10,000 a night stuff works out well. I have a half million U.S. dollars in interest-bearing accounts. I have an accountant's brain, got it from my mother. It'll grow to a million in six years and by the time I'm 35 to $2 million. I can live off the interest then for the rest of my life."

"I have $2 million in interest-bearing accounts in the Bahamas and Switzerland," he said with his eyebrow raised.

Gisele's accountant's brain calculated the numbers.

"We have more than enough. There it is. Let's get married," she said.

"Yes, let's get married."

He looked again at the slip of paper with Whit Smart's name and number on it and said, "I need to call this guy and tell him I am retired."

Chapter 27

The Eighth of Nine Lives

"Whit, I got your message from the farmstand owner. What can I do for you?"

"Painter, it appears that you have cut off all communications with the States. They are looking for you."

"Who?"

"The Before Emancipation guys. They sent word to me. They know I'm retired but threw a big number at me. I told them I'm out of the game. They then asked if I knew you and if you are down here. Pretty much the first-degree interrogation of your whereabouts."

"What did you tell them?"

"Exactly what I told you I'd say. I am out of the game, and I didn't see you."

"Who is 'they' specifically? Whom did you talk to?"

Painter knew the answer but checked to see if there was another man in charge. He had the manifesto from The General and the notice that The Confederate was free. The news was also out about the abduction and savage death of The General. The Voice handcuffed him to a chair and in the midst of an interrogation, erupted in a rage and shot him in the forehead at point blank range. The fit of anger was leaked to let Before Emancipation members know that no BE member or associate was safe. What Painter didn't know was: The Voice intentionally freed The Confederate from the fake Society of Protectors prison, under the guise that The Confederate would work as a double agent and pull the Before Emancipation troops in line and help prevent a race war. A fate similar to The General's awaited him if he failed.

Even with death as the consequence, The Confederate chose to try and rally his forces to make another valiant stand against the Society of Protectors and continue their quest to kill the Black Camelots. Painter did not know that top assassins who learned of the casualties suffered by their peers were turning down significant paydays to work for the Before Emancipation team.

Smart answered Painter, "I talked to the Confederate himself. He offered me $2 million to get back in the game. I'm 65 years old, man. I've lived eight of my nine lives as a paid assassin. I'm not pitting number nine against the Society of Protectors. I've never gone up against those guys and never will. I had a few friends in our game who tried, and it went badly for them."

Painter understood and asked if Whit had heard a story that had made the rounds.

"You hear what they did to Billy One-Shot's team in New Jersey?"

"Yes, that story got down here in hours. It made the Society of Protectors more feared than ever."

Whit had no interest in getting back in the game but liked reminiscing about the old days. He told Painter the story as if he'd witnessed it. Painter knew the story, too, but let him tell it.

"Best deception ever. Bronson Pagent was a scurrilous character and deserved it. Paid Billy One-Shot a million dollars to rescue him after a Society of Protectors team abducted him from his home. Pagent contacted Billy from his cellphone, and Billy sent a hit team to chase down his abductors. Mistake was, Billy didn't know the guys he was chasing were members of the Society of Protectors."

"That changes everything, or at least it would for me," Painter interrupted.

"Me, too. It seemed like a simple enough plan. Except that it's never simple. Billy-One Shot's rescue team didn't know they were being followed by a second group of Society guys. The really ruthless ones. At the same time, Billy sent a backup team to support his first squad. He was sending messages to his troops with the coordinates of Bronson's whereabouts made trackable by Bronson's cellphone. Pagent had the phone in his pocket, and a beacon was sending signals to Billy with his coordinates.

Painter's anxiety rose as he listened. But this was entertainment for Whit Smart. He couldn't pass up telling a story

"Finally, Bronson's abductors were within reach of One-Shot's team. It was then that Billy learned that his team's fate was not good. It was too late to back out without being labelled as having reneged on the million-dollar contract. Bronson wired the cash to Billy before he accepted the contract. One-Shot had to fulfill it then, being a professional and all. That's what you would have done, right Painter?"

"Our name is all we've got in this game, Whit. We can't fink out on contracts. That's the code. If we balk once we're paid, we end up with a bounty on our head. So yes, he had to fulfill."

"Yep, One-Shot didn't have a way to back out," Whit nodded.

"It sucks when you get stuck like that, but you're right," The Artist added. "The code is the code."

Sharp continued, "On that day, the Society guys were one step ahead. They pulled off the highway in New Jersey and headed down the access road of a state park. They are on a two-lane road with wooded areas to the left and right. Billy's team followed in a high-speed sports car. They said it was one of those $100,000 plus rare European types. It was then that they learned they were being followed by the second team of Protectors. Billy's guys downshifted, turned around, and left the park to reassess. They probably should have left well enough alone, but they couldn't fink on the paid contract. Anyway, they got away without incident as they awaited their backup."

Whit took a deep breath, and Painter interrupted him.

"You like telling these stories, don't you?"

"I do, young man, and I tell them to you for a reason: because I lived long enough to tell them. So let me get back to it."

Whit's response was tinged with attitude. Painter wondered if Whit thought he was being a smart-ass. He didn't comment further as Smart continued.

"Billy's team returned in just minutes, now with guns blazing. But they had no idea what was waiting for them. They riddled the Society of Protectors' SUVs, which had been positioned across the two lanes as a barricade. But it was a trap. As soon as they got too far in to be able to turn around, a Society member emerged from behind one of the SUV's with a rocket launcher and blew both of One-Shot's team's cars to hell. Boom! Their cars exploded in a fantastic mushroom fireball.

Whit paused for dramatic effect and yelled again, "Boom! The fireball sent smoldering debris everywhere. The leader of the Society team then got on Bronson's phone. Bronson had no idea that the Society guys knew his phone was live and luring Billy's team. He asked, 'How much did he pay you?' "

"Billy, they say, was shocked, but he did not equivocate. 'A million dollars.' "

" 'You collected it, right?' "

" 'Yes, I have the money.' "

" 'Then, my suggestion is that you take that money and get out of town for a long time. Your guys are dead. Bronson$s future is up in the air.' "

Whit was drinking his afternoon cocktail, a glass of white wine, as he told the story. He refilled the glass. Painter chimed in during the silence.

"I'm gonna ask again. You enjoyed telling that story, didn't you?"

"It's a fabulous story and a cautionary tale. The caution is that it left Billy One-Shot on their watch list."

"Whose?"

"The Society's"

"How do you know?"

"I have my sources."

"What about me?"

Painter figured he was on the list because of the Teddy Walker showdown in the Bronx.

"Oh, they want you dead. You killed Walker's friend, Travis Pfaff, at the golf course on Long Island, and then there was the showdown in the Bronx. You don't know this, but Walker is a retired Society member."

"What are you saying, Whit?"

Smart took another swig of his cocktail.

"Are you afraid yet?"

"What?" Painter snapped. He didn't like the cloak and dagger taunt of Smart.

"Apologies, Painter. Let me rephrase that question. I quit the game fifteen years ago, when I realized I'd spent eight of my nine lives in this work. I needed to save my last one for one reason only

- to protect my family- and not use it executing someone else's vendetta or solving their issue. Right now, the Society has bigger fish to fry, and you ain't on the top of the list. Walker has his hands full keeping the peace in New York. He hasn't put a notice on you for the Rosario shooting, but he's pissed off at you for shooting at him in the alley. He's keeping it professional."

"How do you know all this? And for the record, I didn't shoot Rosario. I was just there."

"It doesn't matter. You still killed Travis Pfaff. That one was personal for Walker."

Whit took a long chug of his wine.

"Let me tell you another story. I was on Gray Wall's team fifteen years ago when The Voice killed Grayson. That man beat the crap out of all of us. We were lucky; that was all. He was there to take Wall in, not kill anyone. As I lay there, bloodied and bruised, he took my ID, which was fake. They still tracked me down later and took me in. Those were five of the worst days of my life. They subjected me to waterboarding, electric shock torture, sleep deprivation, pulling the nails off all my toes, and making me eat dirty snails raw, just to give me enough protein and energy to withstand the next day of torture."

"That's the business we are in. Right, Whit?"

Painter's response was an instinctive one. He knew Smart was trying to scare him and his response was to let him know he understood the risks of the job.

"I guess, but then they showed me pictures of twenty guys from our world. Top assassins we thought were killed in the line of duty or in retaliation for executing their contracts. But no, all those deaths were at the hands of the Society. They'd staged the photos and used their contacts in the press to plant news stories to make it seem as if those assassins had been victims of revenge killings. I saw five people I knew personally in those picture files."

"That still doesn't answer the question. How do you know all of this?"

"The Voice. I wouldn't say we are friends, especially after my torture at his hands. But he contacts me from time to time. When they let me go fifteen years ago, he was the one who told me that my days as an assassin were over. That I'd used eight of my nine lives."

But there was a fact that Whit didn't tell Painter: Ten years before he was tortured, The Voice had contracted him to talk with Hardwick Bivens. It was the only reason he wasn't killed in the takedown and murder of the notorious Gray Wall.

Whit continued, "In case you want to know, The Voice contacted me with a message for you, just yesterday. 'We hear that Painter is in Rio,' he said. 'Tell him he's off our radar for now. We don't want him in this fight. Otherwise, we will send our Project Maim team for him, and they will break his hands and feet, and then we'll kill him. We hear that he really is a talented painter. He should use his hands to wield paint brushes, not pull triggers. Tell him what I told you: that, like you, he has lived eight of his nine lives."

The words sent chills through Painter. He had more questions but couldn't think clearly. Piercing his throughts was that Gisele could be collateral damage now, and fearing for her caused his palms to sweat.

"I've got to go, Whit. You've laid a lot on me. I need to hang up and process it all."

"Do that, Painter. The BE guys want you to help in their fight. They're desperate. Don't take their calls or jobs. It would be a death sentence. I'll have nothing to do with them, and you shouldn't, either.

Painter knew his elder buddy was right.

"Thanks, Whit."

"My pleasure. I have one final parting gift. I have my ear to the ground here. Billy One-Shot is here. You should meet him."

"Why? I'm on hiatus. Don't know when I'm going back to work."

"He's probably here for the same reason you are."

"You mean he's hot?"

"Yep. I don't know what he was working on, but if he's here, you guys should meet, anyhow."

"I don't go into town, Whit."

"How about meeting him at the same place where I bumped into you?"

"The farmstand?"

"It's as good a place as any."

"Okay, Whit. Set it up for tomorrow. I want to do it before you head out of town."

"Fine, tomorrow noon it will be. See you then."

Chapter 28

Rio Meeting

"Giselle, I need to go to the farmstand this morning. Is there anything you need?"

"Maybe. If he has a fresh chicken, it would be nice. I found a nice patch of rosemary and sage to pair with it."

"Okay, my love. I'll see what he has."

"Thank you. my dear."

Jefferson didn't tell Gisele that he was also going to meet with Whit and Billy One-Shot. Telling her that he was going to meet with two hitmen, one retired and another as hot as he, might not sit well. Especially after he just declared his love for her and vowed to retire from that dark profession. He didn't know much about Billy One-Shot, except that he was known to be as elite as he.

Today, he wanted to tell Whit and Billy that Rio was his safe place. He wasn't wanted here, and he planned to live quietly just like Whit Smart and the mysterious man he agreed to refer to as Farmstand. He hoped Billy One-Shot felt the same way. Rio had its corruption and underworld, but he had no intention of being part of that life.

This could be his place of retirement; at least that's what he and Gisele talked about yesterday. They had enough money and an exciting, passion-filled love for each other.

His new life with Gisele he would not share with them. That could be a detriment. Especially to this group of assassins. She could become a target if the talks went badly.

Smart arrived before Painter. Not surprisingly, he was engaged in a smile-filled conversation with Farmstand. Painter watched them approvingly as he parked his motor scooter directly in front of a large wooden cart of apples and melons outside the front entrance. It was where he always parked.

"Good afternoon, my friend," Farmstand said in Portuguese-accented English. He flashed a warm smile that made Painter think, "He's a good man. I'm glad to have met him. This is the right place to have this meet and greet."

"Greetings to you and my friend, Whit. It's good to see you both."

"Hello, Artist," Whit said.

"Artist? Is that your nickname?" Farmstand asked.

Painter nodded. He could hear chickens clucking in the rear of the store.

"Yes, it is. It is my professional name. I hear chickens out back. My -" he stopped as he almost said, "My lady."

"I need a fresh chicken today. How long will that take?"

"I just finished plucking four this morning. How many do you need?"

"Only one."

"Okay. I'll wrap it up for you."

As Farmstand turned to walk to the back, One-Shot pulled up in an old Jeep. Painter guessed it had to be twenty years old. It looked official, as if he'd purchased it from a military base. One-Shot jumped out of it and entered the store, wearing a relaxed smile.

"How'd you get that Jeep and where?" Whit asked.

'I know people," Billy said.

He flashed a deceitful wink that both knew meant he would not divulge the true story.

"Don't worry, I didn't steal it. That's not my line of work."

He stuck his hand out to Painter.

"Billy One-Shot. William Turner is my government name. A great honor to meet you today."

Painter grabbed his hand and shook it. Billy's grip was strong, and his hands powerful. It's what Painter expected from a world class assassin who killed people in a multitude of ways.

He stared coldly into Billy's eyes. There would be no warmth in this greeting or their relationship until Painter decided whether they would be friends or foes.

"Jefferson Painter. I am known in the trade as "The Artist Hitman." Pleasure to meet you, too."

Painter turned his cold gaze to the vehicle. The Jeep didn't have a top. It had clanked noisily and gasped after Billy turned off the ignition. It didn't make for a discreet entrance, and that bothered

Painter. The vehicle invited attention and was not one he'd drive to relax and enjoy himself. The assassin had to be very secure to drive that type of vehicle down here. Billy sensed Painter's thoughts and the code of discretion violations.

"I have a place in London and another in Montreal. I also have my Hoboken home in the States. I can't have a toy like this anywhere else. This is my safe place, Painter. Just in case you think that I'm crazy driving an Army surplus vehicle."

Billy paused, scratched his head and continued, "I guess in our line of work, we all are a little crazy."

"Yes," Whit replied.

Painter nodded.

"I suppose you're right. But I don't like attention."

"I respect that," Billy answered. "You never know who's in the wings."

"Indeed," Smart said. "You both know that I'm retired, and this is my safe place, too. We have to keep it that way."

"How do you propose doing that?" Billy asked.

Farmstand reappeared, holding a whole chicken wrapped in butcher paper.

"Gentleman," he said, "discretion is invaluable. Some of us kill, some of us steal, some of us cheat, and then there are some of us who know how to keep our mouths shut."

The three assassins looked at him. An air of reverence permeated the atmosphere, and his words validated that impression as he spoke slowly and with a measured thoughtfulness.

"I know the line of work you guys are in. You're highly respected and have been paid well. There are risks, and there are rewards. Being able to live here is a reward. And now you must honor the elite status you've obtained. And it is a status shared by all of us in this special place."

He stared at Billy. "That, my friend, is minimizing risk."

As the men looked at each other, Farmstand continued, "I believe in keeping my mouth shut. So, you will never learn about what I've done to live here on the outskirts of Rio, but I will share that it is my safe place. Even the gangsters and crooked cops in Rio don't come here. Let's keep it that way. I hope you can agree."

Billy lowered his head. He had broken the rule for discreetness. Everyone knew that downtown Rio, just twenty-five miles away, had an underworld as dark and evil as any American big city. There were countless gangsters and corrupt cops who would gladly come to the hills if it were known that three notorious assassins were up there, hiding in plain sight. Contracts on their heads would turn into instant combat.

"I apologize. I'll get rid of the Jeep tomorrow. I can't say it is a safe place by making it unsafe for everyone else."

"Thank you," Farmstand said. "Y'all continue your chat now. Don't mind me. I need to move some melons that were delivered this morning to the carts in front of the store."

Part Five

Chapter 29

Two Years Ago

"No one in Washington owes Digby Yates a favor nor feels obligated to support him. He's radioactive," W.T. Hill said to Jones Rivera.

"Yeah, but that's why he could win, W.T."

"He's a criminal, and common sense will prevail. It has to, Jones."

That conversation between the Managing Editor and his second in command at *The Beltways News* took place two years ago, after Yates announced his candidacy. Neither Hill nor Jones gave him any hope. Both thought his Tax Liberty Con would kill his campaign, but to their dismay, that scam that he pulled a dozen years ago had been forgotten by many. Without a meaningful censure or congressional rebuke, the GOP Presidential Committee had welcomed his addition to the field of contenders. In hushed circles, Yates's candidacy was permitted because the top two contenders lacked Yates's brand of charisma.

Yates had started out in the primaries a distant third to two incumbent governors: Stone Prosper from Nevada and Dilbert Seymour from Missouri. They were measured and scripted politicians, with every word and act controlled by teams of handlers. Yates, on the other hand, was a carnival barker and a racial alarmist. Those in the inner circles of politics and high information voters dismissed him as a crook with no political future. The penalty he faced for his Tax Liberty Con was a Senate censure that led to a self-imposed decision to not run for a fourth term. Twelve years later and despite his weaknesses, the GOP Presidential Committee welcomed him.

"We've got three unappealing candidates on the GOP side. I'd much rather watch paint dry than listen to any of them," Hill added. "The only one with any retail political skills is Yates, and he is a scoundrel and enemy of the state. I might move to Canada if he wins."

"Costa Rica for me, *Papi*," Jones said.

Neither smiled at their quips. They knew how dangerous Yates could be with presidential power. Jones attempted to forecast a silver lining. She believed in the greater good and wanted to put her trust in people's ability to recognize a con artist.

"I know you hate him because of your family ties that go back to how you grew up, but the American people are smart. They'll be able to see through him. I'll bet good money that he won't make it through the primaries."

"I pray that you're right, Jones."

Jones could read her boss and had a huge fear for Yates's skills as a campaigner and his ruthlessness. She tried to make a case against him.

"He is running against two governors, W.T. It's true they are far less charismatic, but both were two-term governors and now have pre-election approval ratings ten and twelve points higher than Yates's. Prosper also has a wonderful backstory. He's an honest-to-goodness war hero. A Viet Nam vet and combat team captain who suffered a hip wound in battle that ended his combat tenure."

Hill nodded in acceptance of the facts. But he was nervous that those great qualities and achievements would not translate to votes, especially to voting blocks that were motivated by intangibles those governors didn't have. What they were, Hill didn't know. What he did know was that they weren't the usual policy promises for lower taxes and more money in the pocket.

"War heroes always get love with voters these days," she said.

Hill shrugged and hoped Jones was right.

Jones read aloud the details of Prosper's war battle.

"His injury came from bomb shrapnel after he and his first lieutenant were leading a small team on a mission in Hanoi. The first lieutenant was killed by the blast. Prosper suffered a hip fracture so severe it was feared he would never walk again. After his tour, he returned home a war hero. Prosper's aspiration up to that point was to return to his job at the local bank. He was an Army Reservist and attended college under the Army Reserve Officers' Training Corps (aka "ROTC"). It was the VFW in his hometown of Elko that pushed him into a career in local politics. It turned out to be his calling, and he ended up at the Nevada governor's mansion."

"Prosper sounds like a good guy who has overachieved and is being rewarded because of his war-time heroics."

"He's not a bad guy. There's nothing dirty about him, W.T. The man's just not a guy who is a world-changer, and he's sorely lacking the charisma to convince people he should be the most powerful man in the world."

"How about Seymour? Is he any more inspiring?"

"Nope. Not at all. Worse for him is he's stuck under his family's thumb. His great grandpop is the megachurch pastor, R.C. Seymour. The Seymours are a legendary white evangelist family in Missouri. Dilbert ran the church's statewide food ministry. That work gave him positive exposure across all ends of the state and inner cities. As a result, he has a bigger profile in the state than his grandfather, father, and brother."

"What else do you know about the family?"

"Not much at all. Trying to follow all these political dynastic families and their shenanigans is a full-time job. White evangelists are not exactly my thing."

She continued, "However, they are a big deal in Missouri, but not household name outside of the religious right. The Seymours are a multi-generation family of evangelists who traveled the world teaching, preaching the word of God, and saving souls. Dilbert Seymour was not a trained minister and had never delivered a sermon from the pulpit of the home church in Lake of the Ozarks.

However, he grew the donation base of the family ministry, known across the country and globe as American Christian Ministries, to $100 million dollars from corporate, not-for-profit, and individual donations. The success of the program led him to run for governor. His work and high profile propelled him to a landslide win in his first election, against two-term Democratic governor Ben McKinley. He defeated McKinley again even more soundly by forty points in the second race."

"His father, J.C III, and older brother, J.C. IV, are the caretakers of the ministry. Unlike SCTV, which focuses mostly on bringing talented Christian preachers, singers, and choirs to communicate the gospel through television, ACM was a boots-on-the-ground ministry. The leaders of each ministry, Detrick Damon I and J.C. Seymour Jr., the eldest Seymour, did not get along. Seymour Sr. died twenty years earlier.

Publicly, they supported each other, but privately bickered about how the other served God. The Seymours believed the SCTV music and news information format did not meet their pious standards of humble Christian servitude and scholarly devotion. They also had a hardline commitment to the King James Bible. No other translation was acceptable. The Seymours believed and taught that interpretation of the Word could only be made through scholarly dedication, not the music ministries and charismatic preaching often found at SCTV."

"Oh, this is deep. A good ol' fashioned family feud, like the Hatfields vs the McCoys. Any shots fired?" Hill asked.

He adjusted himself in his chair and sat up at attention.

"No, Boss. These are church guys, not street guys. There are good people on both sides, save what I suspect is a bit of racial intolerance. Both permit too much white evangelical noise for my liking, for which neither side is fully held to account. That aside, the family leaders just were not in agreement on some key matters."

"Okay, then. Go on, Jones," Hill said.

"DD1, the Southern Christian Church, and his SCTV network did not ascribe to Seymour's hardline doctrinal teaching strictures. He believed that God had opened the doors for him, and made him and his ministry leaders the faces and voices of a 21st century discipleship that was needed to bring people closer to God. Eventually, the hardline adherence to the King James Bible and opposition to the Southern Christian Church's style led to SCTV's blocking ACM ministers from appearing in their programming, and further grew the gulf between the patriarchs of both ministries."

"That's a pretty big rift."

"Yeah, and a gap that could be filled by Yates."

Hill's nose crinkled, as if he'd smelled something rotten. It might be just what Yates needed to emerge victorious in the GOP horse race.

Chapter 30

One Governor Down

"Boss, we talked about this two years ago. I didn't believe he had a chance. I'd have bet good money that there'd be no way we'd see him take down Prosper in the way he did. Prosper is a Silver Star honoree, a true public servant. And yet..."

Jones Rivera sat across from Hill in his office. She was shocked by Yates's overwhelming annihilation of Governor Stone Prosper.

"That snake Yates was able to confuse the electorate and make Prosper look like a man leading a sex-crazed double life. Yates destroyed him."

Yates had Tommy Tubbs plant stories in underground right-wing websites that portrayed Prosper as the head of a unit of youthful sexual offenders while in the Viet Nam war theater. Prosper and his team were branded as a group of rapists having their way with underage girls. The stories were later proven to have been written by Tubbs and circulated by Southern Rights, a BE offshoot headquartered in Marshtown, a community an hour west of Yates, Tennessee.

The fabrication reminded Hill of the character assassination of his cousin, Bruiser Jackson.

"He's just evil, Jones," Hill said. It's the kind of stuff that they'd do all the time in Yates to black people. That one comes right out of the Digby Yates and Sheriff Johnnie Tumult playbook."

"Well, it worked," Jones said. "He took one of our country's best, a literal Boy Scout, and painted him as a sexual molester for adopting a little boy and girl that he met in Hanoi."

The right-wing group, Southern Rights, planted the stories nationally. Tommy Tubbs, Yates's Chief of Staff, placed in the *Jeffersonville Standard* and the *Yates Dispatch* a story titled, "America's Perverted Boy Scout." The story maligned Prosper and his late first lieutenant, Barry Bright, who was killed in action when he stepped on a twig that activated a land mine. Bright was five feet in front of his commander when the mine was triggered. Any closer, and Prosper would have been killed as well. The explosion wounded two others in their elite seven-person Rangers team. The article alleged that over the span of an eight-year tour of duty, while embedded in Hanoi, the team fathered ten to fifteen children by underage girls.

The sensation of the false stories spread virally from third-rate underground news sites to a national news story overnight. As a result, Pentagon officials requested a Judge Advocate General's Corps (aka "JAG"), investigation. Prosper supported the inquiry.

"We see how Digby Yates has entered the race," the governor said. "This is a man who has stolen from the working class across

America with his Tax Con scam that filtered contracts to his company and earned him tens of millions of dollars. I'm lauded as a war hero. Service is something he never had the mental or physical discipline for. His smear campaign is an attempt to hurt me in this race, and it's a dastardly political move. A savvy play, those who believe the ends justify the means, might say. But remember, I had family men on my team. Some who paid the ultimate sacrifice. How dare he defame their names and legacies."

"My service as the captain and leader of Team Save is not one to be tarnished by an accusation that would bring into question their moral character. The men who served under my command are America's best and brightest. I was honored to lead them and for them to follow me as their leader. Losing First Lieutenant Bright was one of the darkest days of my life. He was as fine as any man and officer I've ever known. How dare these accusations be uttered to muddy the memory and integrity of Lt. Bright and the members of my command. The two young children that I am proud to have adopted and who now refer to me as Papa and my wife, Chrissy, as Mama should not have their names or future blemished by this reckless reporting and these false accusations. I ask that the Judge Advocate General immediately begin an inquiry into these allegations to clear the names of Lt. Bright, the other members of my team, my kids, and me. I will suspend my campaign at their request and submit to any court proceedings as ordered."

The candidate made the request after the allegations suggested that two adopted Vietnamese kids were not orphans he'd adopted, but were rather Lt. Bright's offspring by rape. The article indicated that a member of Prosper's team was an unidentified confidential source who'd confirmed the accusations.

According to the alleged source, Bright, as he lay dying, begged Prosper to find his kids and bring them back to America to "Save them from this Hell."

The account, while dramatic, was debunked. DNA from the two kids did not match Bright, Prosper, nor any of the other five men in the elite unit. However, the scandal rocked Prosper's campaign, and the allegations about his adopted kids, now adults, gained traction with the low-information voter base, particularly with Midwesterners who were loyal to Seymour and with Southerners loyal to the pork king of Tennessee.

The day after the story was planted, Prosper polled at 44% with Republicans, two points in front of Seymour and twelve points in front of Yates. A month later, he polled at 36%. Two months later, the JAG issued their report refuting all the allegations. By then, Prosper had dropped sixteen points to 20%. Three weeks later, two megadonors had defected to support Seymour. The next day, Prosper dropped out of the race.

W.T.'s star reporter and friend, Ronald "R.L." Lawson, had entered Hill's office to discuss the news. Prosper's leaving the race was the biggest news in the Beltway.

"Poor guy didn't know what hit him." Lawson's nose flared and he hissed in anger. "He didn't fight back the right way. Hell, he's a war hero. He should have gone straight to Yates and smacked him in the jaw, and punched Tubbs in the gut. He tried to be a good guy, but he didn't know how to talk to low-information voters. Yates's team killed his campaign with a chapter straight out of a trashy novel."

"Sure did," Jones said. "Trashy worked against him."

Now with a heightened anger laced voice, Lawson suggested another pugilistic response.

"Look, let me say it again, and I don't mean this as a first response, but Prosper needed to kick both Yates's and Tubbs's fat asses."

"Stop it," Hill said.

"Hell yeah, W.T. etiquette-wise, it's maybe not what people expect from a presidential candidate, but for campaigning - in this rare instance - hell yeah, it's right. Prosper should have punched Yates in the nose, in public, and threatened him for dirtying his name."

Hill and Jones both shook their heads in disagreement.

Lawson continued, "I'm telling you, the low-information voters get that stuff. It would have gotten more television replays and more Internet views, and then when the backstory came out about him being a war hero, defending the honor of his fallen comrade, the team under his command, and his adopted children, those same folks would have liked him, and branded him as a man of honor and a strongman. It's what men and women expect from a wartime field commander. Someone who gets dirty when it is required. Tell me if you think I am wrong."

Hill grimaced and lowered his head as he considered the street tough response, "I can't argue that there are times that men must be men, but it's not good behavior. It could backfire."

"Definitely what my late husband would have done," Jones added. "But it's not presidential. He's supposed to set the right example."

"Against whom?" Lawson continued, "We know what kills a campaign and what doesn't. That's all I'm saying. Dirt kills it every time. A right cross to the jaw is the best antidote to a lie. It may not kill it, but makes you feel better. And Prosper could have said after the fact, 'I'm fighting for the truth.' "

"Part of what you said is right, R.L." Hill said. "Low-information voters remain so because politics don't interest them. A good sound bite stays with them much longer than it does with a high-information voter. Low-information voters only get interested in the home stretch of a campaign, and they don't learn all the issues. Most importantly, some never learn what's fact versus fiction. But six months, a year from now, when they head to the polls, they'll remember the guy who stood up for his friend. I really can't argue the point. You make sense R.L. "

"Well, I must add," Lawson's face took on a sullen look that forecasted his fear of defeat, "it appears to be Yates's time.

Seymour looked like he was a great candidate, too. Except that SCTV flashed its ugly teeth. I guess we know who has more power in the religious community. That boy went out with a whimper."

"The Prosper scandal scared the Seymour family," Lawson continued. "They had their ears to the ground and were fully aware of the power and influence of low-information voters. They also knew that their long-time rivalry with SCTV meant that they would have to ask for favors from their dreaded rival."

"Egos, huh?" Hill said.

"Cain slew Abel, so we shouldn't have been surprised," Jones said.

"You're right, Jonessa," Lawson said. "Just like a Cain vs. Abel battle, someone had to perish. DD1 and J.C. Seymour Jr. couldn't negotiate an agreement."

"Neither put God first," Jones quipped.

"You're right, Jonessa," Lawson said. "I think the stakes were just too high."

Everyone nodded as they remembered the battle of wills between the two mighty ministries. It came to a head when Seymour Jr. assumed SCTV was already in bed with Yates. He made an accusation that DD1 interpreted as another slight to the integrity of his ministry. Accusations of such in their feud had occurred time and time again.

Hill had received a transcript delivered to him by an anonymous source. It had a Lake of the Ozarks postmark. The postmark implied it came from Seymour's camp. After elements of the meeting were aired on *SCTV News*, Hill released the story in *The Beltway News*.

DD1 didn't care. He didn't want to work with the Seymours and publicly dismissed their stance as sour grapes. Privately, though, he seethed and wondered if he was failing God. The final conversation he had with J.C. Seymour would bother him for his remaining days.

"God forgive me," he prayed. Months later, he sent a private note to J.C. It was handwritten on a small card embossed with DD1's name. On it, he had written four words, "Please forgive me, J.C. Your friend in Christ, DD1!"

Chapter 31

The Old Bulls Battle: Another Governor Down

DD1's spirit was bothered, and their final conversation tormented him.

"He's not of God," Seymour Jr. barked into the phone. "You're giving him a platform that such an unrighteous man doesn't deserve. What's more, there are two sides here, good and evil. We know what side we are on, DD1. We believed, despite our differences, that we agreed on this basic truth."

DD1 breathed deeply. There was truth to Seymour's rant. Despite their differences, he did respect Seymour and the work they were doing with ACM. But he despised Seymour for his superior attitude. It had grated on him for years, but he knew Seymour was right. Yates was a significantly flawed man.

"We? Whom are you speaking about when you say, 'we'?" DD1 asked.

"You know, the people of God. Yates is a con man and has stolen from the taxpayers. And you guys give him so much airtime."

"He pays for it. Just like you do. It's no secret that you and I have our issues, but I'll accept your money. That's just business, J.C. I'll accept money from Democrats, too."

"Well, we have higher standards out here in Missouri, I guess," J.C. responded.

Seymour's comment was intended to irk DD1 and, given the tension between the two leaders, succeeded.

"I don't know what that means, but in case you have forgotten, I run the television network that has the most Christian viewers in the nation. We reach across all demographics and political affiliations. Yes, we believe that our conservative Christian values are more aligned with Republicans, politically that is, but we seek to serve all of God's people here at Southern Christian Television. I think you would say the same for your ministry. Am I right, J.C.?"

"I suppose you're right, Detrick," Seymour answered. "But as I said, we have higher standards here in Missouri, I guess."

DD1 gritted his teeth. He needed to suppress his anger before he responded. Finally, he spoke.

"J.C. I'm taking the gloves off, and I'm going to do this as a man of God. I've been led by Him to build SCTV to what it is. And let's not forget that, because this call - I thought - was to be about business. Let's talk about how you can use SCTV to support your grandson's campaign. Not to fight over our differences."

"You are correct, Detrick," Seymour responded.

"But you sound like you want me to accept your advertising and let you dictate more than where your ad placements appear. As if you think it entitles you to run our business. If that is your goal in this negotiation, we can stop right now."

Seymour's response was immediate.

The statement backed the eldest Seymour into a corner, and his ego took charge again.

"This doesn't sound like the right place for us, Detrick."

Seymour made the call from the conference room at ACM's Lake of the Ozarks headquarters. His grandson, the presidential candidate, sat across from him. Governor Seymour's jaw dropped, and he raised his hand in defiance of his grandfather's declaration.

The governor was aware of the longstanding feud and agreed to have his grandfather on the call after his father suggested the two old bulls should clear the air.

"I guess they still have to show who has the bigger horns," J.C. III said. "Let your grandfather have his moment here."

Now, the conversation that Dilbert had hoped would be an olive branch between America's two most prominent evangelists had gone sideways.

"Grandad!" Governor Seymour yelled.

"Did I just hear your grandson, the Governor? Sounds like the presidential candidate you represent wants you to think more before you speak," DD1 said, dripping sarcasm and clearly angered by his rival's comment.

Seymour Jr. ignored his grandson.

"I would have thought you would have done more research on Yates and would be welcoming us with open arms, Detrick."

"No man is perfect, J.C. You know better than that. We teach and live by that in our trade: 'Let he who is without sin cast the first stone.' That scripture is readily available in the KJV, New KJV, New International Version, and all the other interpretations I read. If you need some help, my scholarly friend, I can advise you."

"Grandad!" Dilbert yelled again.

He was six foot five, with dark hair and a muscularly cut upper body that was gym-built. The governor had spent six months weight training to look strong and imposing on the campaign trail. He stood up and glared at his grandfather. His father, J.C. III, was in the room, as well. He also stood up and glared at the eldest Seymour.

The patriarch ignored them both and slammed his fist on the conference room table. The loud thud reverberated throughout the room. The olive branch negotiation had failed.

"Okay," Seymour said.

Sorrow and confusion filled his voice. He knew he had messed up and made a final volley. He thought it was a power move but only added more fuel to the fire.

"I see where this is going. Just send us a rate card. We've got $100 million to spend, and I'm guessing it will be elsewhere."

"Grandad!" Dilbert yelled a third time. The governor knew no other network could deliver SCTV's access.

There was also limited inventory for advertising, and SCTV was a direct line to the Christian right. Seymour's campaign needed as much time on SCTV as they could buy. Seymour Jr. showed his hand when he said $100 million. It was the clue that DD1 needed, and he pounced.

"As I said, there's Yates, Prosper, you guys, and two other Republicans who are long shots. Plus, there's a lot of senate and state race money for both Republicans and Democrats that we are courting, as well. Nobody else is telling us what to do, not even Digby. So, J.C., I'll tell you the same thing we told Yates."

"What is that?" The ACM leader asked glumly.

"We are building our election platform now. We've got a couple of new shows that will air during the campaign season, but there are only twenty-four hours in a day, and our inventory will be sold out in a week. Act now, or get locked out."

The Governor took a step back and fell into his chair. A dejected scowl covered his face. J.C. III's face bore the same expression. The elder Seymour suddenly realized his error, and his face turned an angry red.

In Jeffersonville, DD2 and DD3 sat in DD1's office and listened. He was telling the truth. Digby Yates had been planning this run for four years. Even though the Pre-1860 had voted against the $500 million he wanted to raise from the membership, he had $50 million coming from them. He also had a super PAC that was two years old. The super PAC provided the $100 million he needed to buy the advertising he wanted at SCTV.

As he realized the gravity of his ego-driven mistake, Seymour Jr. relented, "We'll call you tomorrow. We're going to get our team together and go over this. I'll have them call and ready to make an order."

DD1 sat back. A confident, smug smile on his face. He had won, and his voice was rich with arrogance.

"We'll await your call, J.C. It was a pleasure saying hello. We look forward to doing business with you and supporting your grandson's campaign in any way we can. Have a blessed remainder of the day."

DD1 hung up the phone and turned to his son.

"Let Yates know that he needs his super PAC to come up with $150 million to secure 50% of the airtime in the Morning and Prime Time day-parts. We need a hard guarantee by the end of the day."

"What's that going to leave for the other four candidates?"

"They'll have time in the Mid-Afternoon day-part, and the other four candidates can fight it out for the remaining 50% of Prime Time. But the best we can do is offer 25% to the first person to come after Yates."

"You shouldn't be picking a dog in this fight, Dad," DD2 said. "He's not wrong about Yates."

"This isn't about Yates. I really don't like the guy, but Seymour is dangerous to us. Did you listen to him? He's unbendable. I will work with anyone, but that guy would push his grandson to get the FCC to hurt us in some way. They'd take away our broadcast licenses and our not-for-profit status, and create new rules for how we would operate as a religious organization. No, in this moment, we need to render unto Caesar what is Caesar's and talk to God directly. Trust me on this, DD2 and DD3. We can serve God and so can ACM, but I've prayed on it, and God is telling me that this is the best way for us to move forward."

Chapter 32

"Let's Return to What We Should Be"

When Stone Prosper dropped out of the race, Dilbert Seymour got a jump in the polls to 45%. Yates was second at 39%, and the campaign became a race of advertising spending. Seymour ended up spending $150 million on SCTV, with most of the media buy channeled to the Midday and Late Evening day-parts. Yates also spent significantly in the Midday and Late Evening day-parts. The impact of the senator's heavy spending coupled with his carnival barker's charisma began to win over those who identified as members of the religious right, evangelicals, and Christian nationalists.

Seymour was touting fiscal conservatism and family values as the linchpin of his program, while Yates was promoting his campaign mantra: "Let's Return America to What We Should Be." For the left and political moderates, it was a thinly coded dog whistle that quickly became a rallying cry for white supremacists, hate groups, and low-information voters.

"They don't care about fiscal conservatism. Many of these people don't have a pot to piss in, but they can be exploited because they are broke, busted, and disgusted without hope," Tubbs told Yates when they introduced the campaign to the public. "But they do know that black and brown people are living better than they in too many places across America. That's a sacrilege, and for the voter base we seek, enough to get you back to Washington, D.C."

Yates looked at the most recent billboard ad treatments for the campaign. They focused on resentment and anger. Tubbs described their intent to his boss.

"This billboard shows a prosperous black man and his wife. They are driving a fancy black sports car and stopping at a gas station in a rural county. The setting is anywhere in America, in a day gone by. Fifty years ago, this couple couldn't have taken a drive in such parts. That's part of the messaging. Worse yet, they have a grown white Southern Christian American, Bo is his name, waiting on them. Bo's the gas station attendant forced to pump their gas. He fills their gas tank, but with disdain; his eyes are angry slits, his teeth are grinding. One hand holds the gas pump. The other is perched on the pistol holstered on his hip. The black couple look ahead, totally oblivious to the pistol packing Bo glaring at them with envy. They are seated in the car, the man ruggedly handsome, his lifetime of accomplishment materialized in multiple ways besides the car: he's content, smiling, wearing designer sunglasses. His pretty wife, her hair covered with an expensive silk scarf, is flipping through the pages of a magazine titled, *Life Is Good*."

Yates points to the tagline on the bottom of the billboard, "Life Is Good for Whom? Let's Return to What We Should Be. Vote For Digby."

"This is spot on," Digby said. "I like it. The hand on the hip-holstered gun says everything. We can't have these people forgetting their place. We've let them think it's okay, up until now. But from now on, if they step out of line, there will be consequences."

"Exactly, Digby. I'm glad you like it."

In similar vein, TV ads were created featuring an Hispanic couple. Bo, the gas station attendant, looking angrily at the couple as he pumps their gas. As they drive off on a long, quiet road flanked by cornfields, Bo is shown unlocking his gun, and the screen turns black as the words flash on the screen, "America, Let's Return to What We Should Be. Vote for Digby." The voiceover is followed by the sounds of two gunshots, tires screeching, and a car crashing.

The ads did not pass the standards and practices regulations at the four major networks. The big outdoor company, Mercury Advertising, however, posted the billboards in the top fifty markets across the country. The billboards were criticized from coast to coast for their overtness, but they never accrued a fine.

DD1 ran the ads on his SCTV network and said to his son, "Well, we picked a dog in this fight."

"Yes, you did, Dad. These ads are a long way from the regular policies and issues-oriented creative we usually receive from politicians. The people will certainly understand where Yates stands."

"I must admit, Son, I'm not certain this is what I want. And the advertising billboards and TV ads certainly surprised me. Yates is paying us a lot of money to be his voice to the people, and I can get why the networks wouldn't carry those commercials. As a not-for-profit we can run stuff that is a little more out there."

"It's not that simple, Dad," DD2 said.

They both knew there was a lot more on the line than the $150 million they stood to gain from the ad buy.

"What will happen if our audience rejects it, Dad? What will we do?"

"Already covered that with Yates and Tubbs. They have a backup. I told them that if we receive negative feedback on the ads from 5% of our audience, we're pulling them. They know the spots and billboards are controversial, but have decided to be outrageous to distinguish themselves from Seymour."

"Who told you that?" DD2 asked.

"Yates himself. He told me that he gets it. He said, 'I'm in third place. I am running against two governors. They are good men, both of them. And I have this awful Tax Liberty issue always chasing me.' "

"He did enrich himself from that, Dad. Yates deliberately betrayed the trust of the American voters and enlisted his fellow members of Congress to support the scam."

"Well, he told me it wasn't a con. Yates contends that it is how big business operates. He said, 'We didn't have our ducks in order, and the big box companies that benefitted used their lobbying power and lawyers to find the loopholes that allowed them to walk away from the deal.' "

"Does he have any remorse? This bill made him rich, or I should say even more wealthy, and left those communities without the jobs they were promised. It's that simple, Dad. He ripped the taxpayers off."

"I agree with you, Son. Whether or not he will admit to it, this was a bad thing and the American people paid for it."

"Thank you for agreeing," DD2 said.

He was pleased that his Father understood that Yates was a risky bet for SCTV and that he put a caveat in the contract: the 5% kill clause if SCTV viewers complained about the campaign. He then challenged DD1 about Yates's Christian sobriety.

."Now, that brings me back to my original concern. Do you realize whom we are dealing with? This man is not of God."

DD2 glared at his dad. This moment was a first for the father and son. DD2 had never before attempted to overrule his father's decisions. It was DD1's company. DD2 would run it after him, but this decision risked putting their good name in peril.

"I know what I am doing here, Son."

The answer came too quickly for DD2. He pushed back, this time his voice stern, all the subservience gone.

"Do you, Dad? Because I don't understand. This is your life's work. Mine, too. We could be throwing it all away for this man."

"Just pray, Son. It might not be our place to make this decision. Let's allow the people to decide. Even if Yates wins the primaries, he is not assured a general election victory."

DD2 sat stunned. His father was across from him, separated by a table. DD2 got up and stared in his eyes.

"Are you okay? This is not of God, Dad." DD2's

voice was now even more stern and dark.

"I trust God and the people of God, my son. Our flock will not fail us. I know; I have faith far greater than a mustard seed, and I ask that you employ it now. Say 'amen' with me, Son."

DD2 grimaced and took a deep breath. They had all the power to stop Yates in this moment. The big networks had turned down Yates, and if SCTV did the same, they would protect the nation from the narcissism that was sure to be unleashed during the campaign and beyond.

As DD2 expected, the ads worked to Yates's advantage. He won forty out of the fifty states in the primaries, including the GOP mega-states of Texas, Florida, and South Carolina.

DD1 called his son after the primaries. A gulf had grown between them as the campaign's impact took effect.

He said, "Don't doubt God, Son. That's not our place. HE has a plan. Just call on your faith. It's still greater than a mustard seed, right?"

"Yes, Dad. Of course; I am a man of God."

"Then that's all you need. Give it to God. Just like I did."

Part Six

Chapter 33

Give Me Permission

Donald Alexander said to his wife, "Honey what if I told you that I think the best way for Yates to be defeated is for me to buy back Harris Simmons?"

Carrie Sinclair was sitting across from him, drinking tea. She put the cup down slowly, sat back in her chair, and crossed her arms. He guessed by her response that she wanted to give the idea measured, thoughtful deliberation. He was wrong. She hated the idea.

"No, Donald. You don't want to do that. Absolutely not. What do you think you'd achieve?"

Carrie wanted her hubby out of the rough and tumble industry that he once ruled. He knew that and had a ready answer to her objection.

"Baby, can't you see what's going on here? SCTV is behind Yates. He wants a race war. He's going to push for it either way, so let him have it with me. Bivens is great and will be a wonderful president. But she ain't prepared to run a race war. We'll galvanize all of the forces that want to be about the greater good. Stuff that sounds maybe even a little corny, at the same time calling out cheating, deception, and racism, and, she'll lead the fight on the policy and legislative front. I'll win the battle of the hearts and minds of America, and direct them to her with my new media company idea."

Donald's face was aglow and his hand gestures rapid. He was fired up. Carrie could tell it wasn't a new idea.

"How are you gonna do that? And more importantly, a new media idea? How long have you been thinking about this, Baby?"

"For a while now. That's why I couldn't give the answer the people wanted from me in the Hamptons. My heart says this is what I do best."

"Okay, but what will Bivens do for a VP?"

"How about Susan? She's ready. Besides the only person who doesn't want me to run more than I is you."

Carrie sighed and flashed a forced smile.

"I'll definitely sleep easier if you don't run. But Susan? I think she'd strongly object to being on the ticket."

. Carrie knew her dear friend would be hard-pressed to hit the campaign trail again.

"Really? You don't think she'd be willing?"

"Susan is tired. The senate race took a lot out of her. And she hates campaigning."

Donald smirked at his wife. Her response about Susan being tired wasn't a winner.

"You've gotta do better than that, Baby. I'm coming out of retirement, risking my wealth on this."

Carrie's eyes bulged. She turned the cynical stare back on him.

"Wait, hold on, Mr. Moneybags. You need to slow your roll. Don't you think you should talk to your wife about stuff related to risking 'our' wealth? How is that part going to work?"

He stuttered his next response.

"Uh, well, that's what I'm doing right now."

His voice had turned sheepish. Technically, the riches were his, but if he was going to fund any big business idea, he knew it was best to consult his wife beforehand.

She glared at him. Her eyes burned through him, and her jaws had tightened.

Finally, she said, "Sell me, then, Media Man."

He took a deep breath. She crossed her arms and continued the intense stare. Her face was stoic, her unblinking eyes pierced him like lasers. Carrie was a tough audience. He deeply inhaled, then exhaled.

"Okay, here you go. Here's how the money will work. I own 25% of Harris Simmons stock. It's where 30% of my -" he stopped, winked, and corrected himself, "- our fortune is invested. Kwame owns 10%, Sammie has a 5% position. That represents 40% stock ownership of the company. The other members of the Guiding Force collectively hold more than 11%. Collectively, those stocks will give me control."

Carrie walked to a chair a few feet away and sat down. "How much do they own exactly?"

"Yeah, Kurt Wimer has 10% and Zell Mulliken, 4% as do J.S.P. Curtin and Mauldin Daniels. Most of the heavy lifting on the stock has been done by Guiding Force members."

"Will we lose money? I know you are doing this to save the world, but how much is it going to cost us?"

"Nothing. The audience click projections are that we can get a low double digit, 12 to 14% growth rate: 7 to 9% on the low side, 18 to 20% on the high side. It's very safe, even with a low rate of return.

Carrie had no reason to like the idea. But she hadn't seen him fired up in this way in a while, and he was buttoned up on the risk of the venture.

"Okay, Mr. Alexander" she said. Her voice had changed and was now teasing. "I see this idea has really got you going. Is there anything more I need to know?"

"Carrie, after the shooting seven years ago, I knew I wanted to have a legacy that was different than Harris Simmons. When Oliver told me to go change the world, I thought running his foundation might be the way to do it, but this is idea much more meaningful and important than anything I've ever done."

"Even running for office?"

"Politics suck, Carrie. You know it as well as I do. It is controlled by big money and bad characters. We've got a chance to fix that. I've taken on big jobs before. This one might be the most important."

Chapter 34

Political News Network

Kwame Mills knew of the plan. It was his idea. The only others who knew about it were Sammie Rivers and Ron Cherry, the Black Camelots' consigliere.

An text pinged his phone. It echoed throughout his 4,000-square foot penthouse. He and his bride, Michelle Nubani, were sleeping in this Saturday, and their apartment was otherwise silent. It was the first time in weeks.

Since their return from the Hamptons with the other Black Camelots and their friends, they'd had a Society of Protectors team stationed at their place 24/7. They also had building contractors there every weekday constructing a panic room. It was silent because the contractors had the weekends off.

Normally, two Society of Protectors bodyguards were stationed inside the apartment. This morning, they stood guard outside the apartment's entrance. Still another secured the downstairs lobby at The Oscar.

"This is a nice break from all the noise, and dust, and the construction crews," Michelle thought as she lay in bed.

She appreciated the silence of the weekend morning and wished for more of it.

Michelle still hadn't told Kwame about murdering the two men in the park. It was six weeks ago when she had lured two assassins to an empty area at the reservoir and savagely killed them. Since the murders, there'd only been one minor news report, headlined: "Two Men Found Murdered in Central Park."

The lack of coverage and the barbarity of the murders had her on edge. There were multiple ways she could be identified. She feared there were multiple video recorders at the reservoir. There was also the male jogger she passed afterwards. And then there were the homeless people. They were everywhere in Gotham and always in the Park. One or many could have watched from the wooded areas around the reservoir. She lived with a rapid heartbeat now, fearing being identified, arrested, and breaking the heart of the man she loved.

"Millions of people visit the park daily. I killed these guys with my bare hands, slowly. Somebody had to see it," she thought. It was a recurring thought she had twenty to thirty times daily.

A second text to Kwame's phone interrupted her anxious ruminations. Kwame turned to his nightstand, and as he read the text his face lit up.

"Well, Michelle, I've got some news," he said.

She turned to him and smiled. He didn't wait for her to respond.

"Donald - I mean - Donald and I - are coming out of retirement."

Unlike her, Kwame didn't keep secrets from his spouse. Or so she'd always thought. At least until now. Still, it was business-related and not nearly as devastating as the secret she was keeping.

"What do you mean?"

She sat up in bed and faced him.

"Let me explain," he said. Kwame sat up and closed his eyes.

She could see he was measuring his thoughts.

"Along with Sammie, we still own 40% of Harris Simmons. Over the last several weeks, with all the talk about what Donald should do in politics. He doesn't want to do it, so I came up with another idea. We both hate the fact that political campaigning has gotten away from the truth. There are too many liars winning seats based upon deception and manipulation of facts. I suggested that although Donald might be ideal for a public office seat, we should both consider, instead, doing what we do best."

"I'm not sure I follow, Sweetie."

"This presidential campaign is going to be a war of what America will become. Digby Yates is a con man, and although not branded nationally as a racial arsonist, he is, and that makes a race war a factor in his candidacy.

Michelle nodded.

"Okay, but that's the book on Yates, Honey. He's not a very complicated man. He's a bit of an outlaw if you ask me. I don't know why the world is blind to him. Tell me more."

"Exactly, Michelle, that's exactly how we see it. As you know, my life's work has been providing news and information to the masses. The same is true for Donald."

"Yes, you guys were very good at running media companies, that part I follow," she said.

"And, that's the essence of this new opportunity. There are 150 to 170 million people who will vote in the next election, but there are about 40 million more on the sidelines. Since Yates wants a race war, Donald's being on the ticket would present a face for what Yates wants to abolish. That's *no bueno*. And as a candidate, the ticket might not gain steam with audiences that are aligned with Yates, irrespective of the candidates' policy positions. In other words, Donald can't afford to spend every minute of every day defending or talking about race."

Michelle's eyebrows lowered. He understood the look: She was not sold.

She asked, "So not being on the ticket will avoid that? Won't people get tired of hearing about race from Harris Simmons? Also, hardcore politics is not what Harris Simmons is known for. Harris Simmons owns a bunch of lifestyle magazines. They have no political magazines or a web presence in that space."

"Yes, but Harris Simmons properties reach people in fifty states and has a database of nearly 200 million names from all of its media properties, 110 million that are active."

As an economist, Michelle loved numbers. The size of Harris Simmons's database surprised her.

"One hundred ten million? That's a third of the American population. But you still have to connect with them. How do you plan to do it?"

"The company we want to build will be called Political News Network. We'll hire some of the top names in the news business as anchors, and some of the most brilliant statisticians and top Harlowe quant jocks to do all of the analysis. We're going to market the heck out of this, with a focus on two deliverables for the American people: easing and increasing voter registration, and fact-checking."

Michelle nodded.

"Ooh, this is interesting, honey. Let's take this to the kitchen. This ain't pillow talk. I want to hear more while I have my tea and you drink your coffee."

Five minutes later, they sat across from each other at their kitchen island. It's where they shared small talk most mornings.

Michelle knew by then that she couldn't deter Kwame from the idea. She was pleased for him and stopped asking hard questions.

"Well, this is a different conversation than we've had in a while. I'm happy for Donald and for you. Now, our discussions in the morning will be a little bit heavier than those since our honeymoon."

She was on sabbatical from Sheraton University in Chicago and had recently started teaching a class as a Visiting Professor at

Harlowe. Most of their conversations had been about her work and transition, and about the Oliver Harris foundation.

"Yes, Honey. This is a big election. It's really important that the good guys win."

She walked around the island and gave him a bear hug. She kissed his ear and then his cheek, and then rested her chin on his right shoulder.

"You miss working, huh, Kwame?"

"I do, Baby. The Oliver Harris gig is great. We've done a lot of good over the last seven years, and this will be a really good next step. Donald's heart isn't that of a politician's, it is that of another kind of leader, and I find that I'm still learning from him. This is the best next step for both of us. And I'm enjoying public service work."

"What you said is true for him, but what about you as a politician? You know your favorables are right below his in New York. And you're right: Your accomplishments at Oliver Harris position you well. But you could be a force in public office, as well. Mayor Kwame Mills. Governor Mills. Those positions could be in your future, too."

In the past Kwame defiantly objected to the idea of running for office.

"You know the answer to that. It's not my thing, Honey. I have no interest."

She locked eyes with him. For the next ten seconds, neither blinked.

Finally, she said, "I thought you just needed some time to think about it. You really don't want to be Mayor? Governor? President?"

He shook his head emphatically.

"Nope. Not at all. I would have considered Lt. Mayor if Donald were elected, and later maybe found my way to being the lead candidate, but I really believe that we are kindred spirits on this Political News Network idea. We have a chance to change politics behind the scenes in a big way. One hundred ten million people in the active database as well as the other 90 million who are inactive is a great way to stay connected and inform voters. Donald and I could be the change agents for American politics for at least a generation.

"It's really important work, Kwame. And it could strengthen our economy, way more than Digby Yates's them vs. us platform. His will ruin domestic peace and the economy. And, as our economy goes, so goes America, and..."

Kwame finished her sentence, "...so goes the world."

She released him from the hug and said, "Exactly, my beautiful man. This is serious stuff. Do you know what it would mean to global currencies, international trade, and worldwide alliances?"

Michelle's teaching focused on global markets sensitivity, and tracing the impact of political strongmen, particularly autocratic governmental leaders, in her home continent of Africa and several Eastern European countries.

"Kwame, I agree, Honey. These kinds of governments create oligarchies and socioeconomic hegemonies that decimate the vital middle class, replacing society's haves with have-nots. Study after study shows how authoritarians, including those elected fairly as well as those who've seized power unlawfully, share a singular intent: to gain individual wealth and everlasting power. Once in power, such strongman leaders use any means necessary to keep it. Electing such autocrats should be recognized as a threat to democratically controlled countries. Research conducted over a fifty-year period indicates that when governments of democratic countries are overtaken by strongmen, they impose import and export trade policies and control market prices in ways that invariably lock out middle and lower income earners from obtaining staple items at affordable prices, and they then price comfort and luxury goods out of their reach.

"That's why this work is so important, Michelle. Your work contributes to why I know we should be doing this. By the way, what does hegemony mean? That's a five dollar word, right there!"

He often kidded Michelle when she talked like an economist and found himself searching for his dictionary for definitions to follow her thoughts.

She pinched him on the cheek for being a smart aleck and then kissed it. She also had more to say on the topic.

"Honey, think for a second. Digby Yates is a tyrant. There's no question. He hates black and brown people. He's gotta be piping hot about the headlines publicizing his wife leaving him and humiliated by the photos of her in a lip lock with a black man. But Sweetheart," she paused.

Michelle had begun to walk back to her chair opposite him. Kwame imagined her in front of a classroom full of doctoral students having the same conversation. His wife's intellectual brilliance matched her beauty, and both were on display right now. She closed her eyes and lifted her hands in prayer.

"Digby Yates already showed us who he is when unchecked. That Liberty Tax con tipped his hand. And he only had the power of a senator back then. He deceived the taxpayers, lied to his peers in Congress, and consciously deceived American working and lower class citizens. He knows that black, brown, and poor white people can't touch him. With the absolute power he'd have as president, he'd go after the white middle class next, and then there'd surely be chaos. If Donald's and your new media venture could revolutionize fact-checking and convincingly teach the electorate to distinguish between truth and lies, then you could change the world. I salute you, Baby. That is revolutionary work."

She lowered her head, and after a few seconds lifted it and said, "America can't have Yates in charge. He'd ruin us. There'd be chaos, civil war, and abandonment of the Constitution and rule of law. And when it was over, the people who were fighting for him would wake up to an America broken into itty bitty pieces. Some would realize that they played a part in its demise. Others, suffering from cognitive dissonance or slavishly enthralled by the cult of

Digby would continue to believe they were right. We must not allow this guy to win."

"But what if he does, Michelle?" Kwame asked.

"Then it's biblical, Honey. This democratic republic, as we know it, would be over."

Chapter 35

Let's Make News Credible Again

"There's way too much news that's not checked for accuracy. The term 'fake news' has been hijacked by politicians, pundits, provocateurs, writers, and opinion web pages disguised as verified news sources. Way too much trash has been allowed to enter into the marketplace. We aim to fix that," Donald Alexander told the audience of political, news, financial, and gossip reporters.

Behind him were the other Black Camelots, Kwame Mills and Sammie Rivers. Also on the dais were Richard (Rick) James, CEO of Harris Simmons's competitor Spring Media, and Wilson Dallas, CEO of Trident Media.

"What is he talking about?" W.T. Hill whispered to R.L. Lawson. *The Beltway News* editor and his top field reporter had flown in this morning on the D.C.-to-N.Y. shuttle. "I thought he would be here with Bivens to announce that he would be her VP or maybe for some spiciness announce his own run."

Luke McFlemming, who didn't hold back his fabled attitude, yelled from the back of the room, "What is this all about, Alexander? You're supposed to be running for VP on Biven's ticket."

McFlemming was sitting with the other Celebrity Hacks.

Usually, Kung and Desanctis would chastise him. They didn't this morning. Even they were confused by the start of the presser.

"Luke, Luke, Luke," Donald said, a wide smile creasing his face; his perfect white teeth glowing against the darkness of his skin. "Haven't we been here before, you and I? You yelling at me like you forgot your manners. Me, still wondering if you'll ever learn how to act better in public. Kwame would always warn me about you during those pressers in the past. And he did again, today."

Alexander turned to Kwame.

"First thing I said, when we walked up here: McFlemming is in the crowd, watch out," Kwame barked.

The audience broke into a roar of laughter.

There were fifty reporters in the audience and another thirty representatives from Harris Simmons, Spring, and Trident. Also on hand were NYC notables: management consultant Marianne Michaels, the Black Camelots' consigliere Ron Cherry, investment banker "Big Stan" Ralph, wealthy real estate mogul Yancey Stuart Sr., and Guiding Force member, Kurt Wimer. Standing against the rear wall were the Celebrity Hacks's bosses – the managing editors at Gotham's top daily newspapers: Pete Colon of *The Post*, Pattie Cunningham of *The Ledger*, and Zach Goldberg of *The News*.

Alexander was a gentleman's gentleman to the public and the press. While at Harris Simmons and at The Oliver Harris Jr. Foundation, he never broke from the script of the handsome, sophisticated, erudite front man. This was the first time the press or anyone outside his circle had seen him respond with a wisecrack. Luke didn't see it coming, and his jaw dropped with astonishment.

Never to be outdone, Luke bowed in a gesture of defeat and then yelled over the laughter, "I guess I had that coming. You've taken a lot of incoming grenades from me over the years."

Donald's and Kwame's smiles were as big as the those in the audience. When they nodded and bowed back at Luke, the crowd laughed harder.

Seconds after the din subsided, Zach Goldberg yelled from the back of the room, his face still red from laughter, "You've done the impossible, Alexander. I've been trying to humble Luke for more than a decade. This was worth taking time out from the newsroom, even if you announce today that you are not going to run for office."

Luke blushed a darker shade of red as the New York press witnessed his boss chip in with another dig.

"By the way, Alexander," Zach continued, "semi-retirement looks good on you. My question, when you start taking questions, is: Why come back to the fire and brimstone of the workplace?"

"Thanks Zach. I appreciate the kind words and am happy to be of service with Luke. That crack from me was well overdue. Your question is a great one. And it leads right into what I am called to do, at least for now."

Donald scanned the room. The reporters held their tape recorders over their heads, set to record his words. All eyes were locked on him.

"As many of you know, I survived being shot in the workplace. Statistics say that the majority of Americans support gun regulations. Gun rights is a forever policy issue. I also live in a blue state, where there is little controversy over voter suppression. But there are many states in this great republic where that is not the case. Like guns, it's a major national policy issue."

His bass tone deepened when he said, "great republic." His voice instantly took on the cadence of a black preacher, not as pronounced as Rev Joseph Frank Hall's, but one uniquely his, and the audience didn't find fake.

"I know I am supposed to do something, especially with all the good turns that my life has taken. I am a Black Camelot. To be clear, I never asked for that label. Nor did Kwame or Sammie. It was given to us by Jennifer Kung, Luke McFlemming, and Mike Desanctis, and the title stuck. The world loves it. They also know that we are privileged. But we three know that we are supposed to do more than be celebrated. The great Oliver Harris, in one of his final requests, asked us to go be world-changers. That is a mission we choose to accept."

The crowd of reporters and invited guests listened anxiously, the former still holding their tape recorders high. Donald slowly panned their anxious eyes. They were captivated and waiting to hear more. He pointed to a group of people sitting in front of him.

"In the first row, here are Deidre Francis, Sheri McCready, and Steve Ryan, the top three executives at Harris Simmons. The big news today is that Kwame, Sammie, and I are returning to Harris Simmons."

Loud whispers and mumbled conversations erupted throughout the room. Many of the reporters dropped their tape recorders, flipped out their notepads and pens, and began writing furiously.

"Now…" he said loudly.

The tape recorders popped back into the air as if choreographed.

"…they are not stepping down. You can also see here my one-time peers and competitors, Rick James of Spring Media and Wilson Dallas of Trident Media. I've asked them to partner with me on a resource that can impact politics, voting, and most importantly truth in political campaigning. We're going to accomplish those goals via a political news source and web destination named the Political News Network, PNN for short."

The reporters' faces filled with surprise, and they once again lowered their tape recorders and returned to note-taking. W.T. Hill's hand shot up in the air.

"What are you talking about, Man?" Hill yelled. "Is this a polling site, a news site? What gives, Alexander?"

Alexander had slipped back into the unflappable persona he was noted for during his Harris Simmons reign.

"W.T., my dear friend. So good to see you."

He smiled at Hill, the grin's intent was to disarm the highly respected political editor.

Tape recorders popped back into the air, "Hill, reporters, and other friends, let me finish introducing this new media entity to you. Rest assured," he said, returning his eyes to Hill, "we are not a news organization. We are not building this to compete with you for news, information, or storytelling. Our entity is a fact verification and voter registration destination. And let me say it again clearly to end any confusion, we will not be in competition with you."

Alexander paused dramatically as the grumbling continued. On cue, tape recorders dropped as writers wrote again furiously.

"What we have designed," the recorders again popped in the air, "is a destination that will combine the databases of these three media companies: Harris Simmons, which has 110 million American active subscribers, Spring Media, with sixty million in America, and Trident Media, with fifty-five million in America. This combined database of over 200 million comprises subscribers to properties that are focused on lifestyle pursuits and give users of our resource the opportunity to connect with these folks in their special interest areas, be they cooking, fishing, sewing, home repair, mechanics, gardening, sports, movies, games, fashion, music, travel, etc. Research shows that most people who are not involved with politics treat it like a hobby. Or for comparable understanding, most people can cook a meal but they would never watch a cooking show, just as others have fished but would find watching a fishing show boring. Politics is similar, most voters only bore in when the election season is upon them. And why? Because people have learned to be wary of politicians."

"We're bringing our best quantitative analysts and researchers together, from all three companies, to create some fast-turn analysis that will fact-check claims, confirm truths, and expose lies and misstatements from all candidates in all races, such as those for state and federal congressional seats, for state governorships, for attorney general roles, and of course for the big ones, Vice President and President of the United States."

Grumbles came from the audience as the reporters processed the Political News Networks' mission.

"Will this destination grow voter registration?" Hill yelled, his voice boomed over the crowd noise

"You are getting to be as bad as Luke, W.T.," Alexander responded.

"Well, I flew up here thinking that I was going to get some news about you joining Bivens's campaign as a VP, or maybe for some real spiciness: you running against her."

Hill's announcement drew more rumblings from the crowd. Many in the audience nodded. It was also one Alexander was ready for.

"Well, not today, Hill. It's good to see that those hard news fingernails of yours are as sharp as ever. That's not on my list of things to do. There are some wonderful people across our great country. Political leaders who are proven. The Democratic party has a bench of talent, and Janet knows them all. But the first thing we must do is protect our right to vote. Another is to grow our voter base. We can do that through the PNN. One hundred fifty million people voted in the last presidential election. Imagine if we could engage higher percentages of young people, old folks, and those in between. Our goal is to grow the audience 25% and get the voting audience to 200 million."

The tape recorders dropped again. Some reporters still wrote furiously. Others spoke into their phones or tape recorders.

As the journos documented their notes, Donald nodded to the energized faces of a crew of 20-somethings who appeared at a doorway to his right. There were five of them. Each had a bundle of press kit folders.

"Our PR team from the new company that will operate here at Harris Simmons has packets of all the relevant information on the new company and our mission. We're going to break now. Instead of participating in a Q and A, you can meet with me or with Wilson, Rick, Kwame, Sammie, Deidre, Sheri, or Steve for a one on one. I'll end my prepared comments by reiterating this statement," Donald said in his preacher-like cadence: "I am not running for office. There is no con or skullduggery of any sort with me. This next project will be the most important work of my lifetime. I do believe that our political system is in peril, and one candidate will not save it. What will save American politics will be a better informed, larger, and more engaged electorate. A better informed electorate will ultimately become a better government of the people and for the people. That is the purpose of Political News Network. I appreciate you listening and your support."

As Donald turned away, a throng of reporters jostled towards him.

As they hustled forward, he turned quickly to Kwame and whispered in an anxious voice, "How did I do?"

"This was perfect. We still have to pray that it works, though. The accusation will come that it's a backhanded way to defeat Yates."

"Well, if we can protect the notion that we are independent and just giving the facts. We can beat the nonsense that is certain to come out of SCTV News."

"Agreed," Kwame said. "W.T. Hill came at you hard. Hopefully, the $100 million will calm him down. I see Sammie whispering in his ear now."

They looked at *The Beltway News* editor and saw the angry glare on his face transform into a stare of confusion.

Donald lipread Hill's response to Sammie, "Does he want to give me an exclusive on this?"

"No," Sammie responded. "Meet the three of us on the 38th Floor in a half hour. We'll explain then."

Sammie didn't say another word. She just walked away. Hill watched her, befuddled, then looked at Kwame and Donald, and at his watch. He wanted to get the next hourly shuttle back to D.C.

He had a paper to close this afternoon. Making him wait further pissed him off.

Chapter 36

The 38th Floor

The 38th Floor of the Harris Simmons headquarters had offices for Donald, Kwame, and Sammie. The spaces were holdovers, perqs from the time when the Harris elders, Oliver Jr. and Cornwall, used them as headquarters from which they ran their charities. They were places to beat the boredom of retirement, and most importantly, to walk the halls of Harris Simmons to feel like Kings of Business again.

The Black Camelots very rarely used the spaces, even though Donald, Kwame, and Sammie remained the largest shareholders of the company. Donald purposely stayed away to give the new leaders space and freedom to run the business without fear of interference. Kwame did the same.

They also wanted to cut the cord from the company's dark past. Gill Harris was killed one floor above, on the 39th Floor. The same place where Donald was wounded and nearly died.

The tragic memories of the shooting, seven years ago, remained fresh in Donald's mind, and he'd had the 38th Floor reconstructed. Before, it had been a shrine to the Harris Dynasty as well as Cornwall's and Oliver's accomplishments. Now, the floor-to-ceiling windows that provided hypnotizing views of Central Park remained. But Donald's office was in the far right corner, thirty yards from the elevator. A conference room was in the corner between his and Kwame's corner offices. The offices of Donald's Chief of Staff, Wanda Howard, Kwame's office was on the other side of the conference room. A small office for Donald's Chief of Staff, Wanda Howard was next to Kwame's office. Sammie had the other corner office, right across from the elevator. Donald's secretary, Selma Jones and Kwame's secretary, Sheila Duncan, had desks on the floor. Sheila doubled as Sammie's secretary. Besides Wanda Howard, the secretaries were the only holdovers from the Harris Simmons days. Wanda managed the day-to-day affairs of the Oliver Harris Foundation as its chief of staff. The secretaries were busier than ever with the Foundation's work, especially as its fundraising arm was non-stop with events around the country.

Sammie would come to the space often. Portraits of the Harris men and James Horace Simmons, Sr., hung on the walls. For her it was a way to reconnect with a past she had been denied. They were people she barely or never knew. Oliver Jr. did his best to give her a coming out to his powerful friends in New York. She found the 38th Floor to be a sanctuary since his passing seven years back. There were large oil paintings of her family members that hung on cherry wood paneled walls. Many days, she would come and hang out, and talk to Wanda and the secretaries. Some days she'd wander down to the lobby and visit with Abe Spann, the shoeshine guy. Sammie was still getting accustomed to her new bon vivant existence and on occasion would bring in friends and show off.

"These are my family" she would brag. Sammie took great joy in showing the oil portraits of each Harris man. "I lost them, but they found me at the end of their lives and they turned out to be the best people ever."

Sammie also used her money to pamper Wanda and the secretaries. She treated them as elder aunts and bought them expensive gifts. The treats became so excessive that eventually the women begged her to stop. Sammie would argue back, wearing them down by claiming the cathartic joy the gifts gave her.

"Please you must accept. These walls connect me to an entire side of me. It's all I have. I don't have memories. And you all make me welcome. You guys know more about them than I may ever, so please accept."

Like the 39th Floor, the 38th Floor was the only other stop for the private elevator. It was the same elevator Cornwall and Sammie used to escape the building after he shot Gill and Donald. The stock of the company that Donald took public was selling at $125 per share, up $70 over the IPO price that made Donald $4 billion. Kwame's hold on the stock and the growth since the IPO and sale had increased his net worth to $1.2 billion. Sammie was not far behind at $750 million. It had remained steady between $124-$126 over the last year and was rated as a AAAA buy by all of the top stock rating agencies because of its best-in-class properties and seasoned and highly regarded management team of Deirdre Francis, Sheri McCready and Steve Ryan.

Sammie had called Wanda and the secretaries on the 38th Floor immediately after the press conference to announce the Political Network News, "We are having W.T. Hill and R.L. Lawson from *The Beltway News* up for a visit. Seat them in the conference room but invite them to tour the 38th Floor lobby and see all the oil paintings on the wall."

The oil paintings by noted African-American artist Neal Webster were representative of the artist's use of bold colors. Even though the men sat for their photos in blue suits, white shirts and red ties, Webster would place them in the settings that each favored. Oliver Sr.'s was a standing photo of him in ski chalet, James Simmons' was a standing photo of him in front of a hospital in Key West, Florida that bore his name. Cornwall's was seated with his loyal dog Rusty by his side in the den of his luxurious Vermont summer home. Oliver Jr.'s was him in the lobby of the Harris Simmons headquarters, a silhouette of people moving about in the background. Gill's was him standing in the center of the 39th Floor conference room, the legendary room where he would tear executives to shreds and once famously annihilated his cousin Wynne Shields. He stood with his back to the window arms crossed, looking very much like the blue-blood titan of business that he was, with fully bloomed colors of Central Park to his back.

Hill and Lawson entered the floor and Wanda greeted them. "Gentleman is this your first time to the Harris Simmons headquarters, and this floor, the headquarters of the Oliver Harris Foundation? It is your first visit, am I correct?"

"Yes, it is for me," Hill said.

"Me too," Lawson added, with a nod.

On the shuttle flight coming up, Hill warned Lawson. "Need I remind you that the only reason you have a job is that we are best friends."

"Why are you bringing this up? Do I need to apologize again? I'm sorry for messing up with Susan. And, I lost my way with those young girls. I know that less of a friend would have fired me. You could've blasted my actions to the world so I would lose my reputation. You did what no else would do. I'm in counseling and have sworn off dating, at least for another year. Part of my recovery is to apologize and try to understand the pain of my ways on my suitors. I've finally been able to connect with Susan. She says she has forgiven me and has moved on."

Hill had a reason for bringing the subject up again.

"Good, do you think she has?"

"Has what, forgiven me? I hope so. I'm a creep. You don't know how bad I feel. I was in love with the woman and she was my best friend. I broke her heart and could have put you out of business. I needed help. Thank you again for standing by me."

"Okay, then R.L. but don't leave my sight today, not even for a minute. No excuses. If you do and break my rule this time, friend or no friend, you will be fired."

"Come on W.T. stop it with the parenting, I'm a grown man. I told you that the womanizing is behind me."

Hours later as they rode the elevator to the 38th Floor, Sammie's face was stuck in R.L.'s head. The beautiful, exquisitely-dressed Black Camelot princess mesmerized him. Hill said, "You saw Sammie, right?"

"Yes, I did," Lawson said. He took a long deep breath, and exhaled slowly. "I read stories about how beautiful she is, but wow."

"Now, I am talking to you as a friend. Just stand by me. She's off limits, think of her as your daughter, or a niece. I need you to be one of the faces for what we want to do if we move this digital platform to cable television. The private equity guys we have lined up have you on a short lease too. Before you cost me a few million. Another mistake of the same kind would cost us their $75 million investment. Or they may demand that I fire you as a term of agreement. I don't want to face that decision. Net, net, a lot of money is on the line. Have I made the stakes clear?"

"What do you want me to do, pluck my eye out?"

Hill responded to the sarcastic comment with a tilt of his head.

"Since you bring it up, Matthew 18:9 said, 'If thine eye offend, pluck it out and cast it from thee.' "

Hill stared at his buddy and locked his glare on his left eye.

"Forget that, I ain't. I'm keeping both my eyes."

Hill burst out in laughter. "Had you there for a second, didn't I?"

Lawson snarled, nodded in admission to Hill's gamesmanship and said, "Point made. I'll behave."

"Good now, R.L.. Let's go see what this is all about."

Chapter 37

This Revolution Will Be Televised

As they entered the conference room, a cool, soulful voice rang out over a jazz tinged melody. *The Beltway News* men recognized it immediately.

"The late great poet and voice artist, Gill Scott Heron, the revolution will not be televised," Hill said.

"Oh yeah, that takes me back, W.T. Our college days and a whole lot of other shenanigans," Lawson quipped.

Both smiled and shook their heads. The recollections were enough for Hill to wisecrack, "Remember Matthew 18:9, R.L.".

"Don't be kill joy. Let a brother have his memories."

Hill ignored the whine. The song was a surprise and had him wondering if there was a meaning to it. Only people in the know played Gil Scott Heron. Critics and fans alike called him a rabble rouser, his lyrics were not for the faint of heart.

"Doesn't seem to quite fit the Harris Simmons settings. Maybe Donald is giving us some kind of deep reveal into the true spirit of the Black Camelots."

Lawson agreed with the idea of a hint.

"Civil rights, revolutionary? Are you saying? Could it be that the counter-culture, rebellious Donald Alexander and Kwame Mills are coming out? "

"Maybe, you never know," Hill said.

As the song continued, *The Beltways News* duo heads bopped rhythmically. By the fourth stanza they began to sing along in a whisper. The song was an anthem during college and young adulthood and for those who'd had enough with white supremacy.

"There will be no pictures of you and Willie Mays

Pushing that shopping cart down the block on the dead run

Or trying to slide that color TV into a stolen ambulance

NBC will not be able predict the winner at 8:32

Or report from 29 districts

The revolution will not be televised"

By the fifth stanza Hill wondered if they know about their private equity meetings? Their hopes to extend their platform to cable?

"There will be no pictures of pigs shooting down Brothers on the instant replay

There will be no pictures of pigs shooting down

Brothers on the instant replay"

"Does he know what we are up to, R.L.?"

"They are pretty powerful. I wouldn't be surprised, boss."

They listened on until the final stanza. Their heads no longer bopped and they had stopped singing along. Everyone told them that Donald Alexander was a genius, a man with wonderful people skills, an imaginative leader and an amazing problem solver. It's why he emerged as one of Gotham's premiere business executives. Republicans feared that Bivens would win in a landslide if he joined her ticket as her VP. Pundits forecasted it would lead to 16 years of Democratic control of the White House as he would succeed her as President. Powerful people begged him to run, including several prominent senators. When Alexander showed reticence a whisper campaign began. Hill and his staffers at *The Beltway News* were targeted to make the whispers legitimate.

The first proponent was Pernell Brown, the four-term senator from Michigan. He told Hill, "He's it, but not eight years from now. Alexander is the man right now. The guy came to Detroit visited our plants and sat down with the shift workers. He met them at 4:30 when they punched out. They wanted to see him. Kwame Mills was with him. The shift workers were curious about the Black Camelot phenomena. Alexander wanted to hear how the union was working for them and get their points of view on a proper living wage. It turned into a two hour discussion. 25 people were there when he started talking, after 15 minutes the shop steward began to call workers on their way home and asked them to turn around and get their asses back to listen to this guy. First thing Alexander said was 'I am union friendly, I negotiated with the newspaper guild for our writers, truckers, sellers, print machine operators while at Harris Simmons and got the other major media companies to let me cut a fair deal.' A call was made to the newspaper Guild head in New York to verify because, you know, the union guys hate liars and con men. He would've been in for some hell if he lied to their faces. The Guild head in New York said, 'Alexander is as good as they come. I'm sorry he left, but happy that he has all the success he has. That guy earned it.'"

Brown continued, "Don't know if you understand what it means to have the guys come back to hear some smart guy talk. They loved him and led a cheer as he finished, Black Ca-ma-lot, Black Ca-ma-lot.' They made it up on the spot. Alexander and Mills laughed hysterically. If he ran for President, he's got the auto and news guilds. The others would follow because of this endorsement. You should start a whispering campaign for him in your pages."

The second came from Dorsey Calabro, the Ambassador to Italy. For over two decades she was a high-powered lobbyist. She met Alexander as a favor to Marianne Michaels during his last year at Harris Simmons. She told Hill how Alexander became close friends with the former President of Italy, Fabio Mondino.

"Donald has all these acres of land at his Hamptons estate. He didn't know anything about making wine, or about grapes, or climate. He was spending a little time over in Italy, primarily for Harris Simmons business, and fell hard for Italian wines. He read that Mondino liked American baseball and had grown up on a vineyard. He sent him a care package of Harris Simmons magazines and a signed baseball glove by retired star Mays Bonds. In the care package was a card that read, "Mr. President, I am not a politician, just a modest American media company CEO. I do have a hobby and an interest similar to yours in American baseball. I also have 50 acres and am trying to build a vineyard on my land in the Hamptons. I'd love to visit you next time I am in Europe. I'll make a special visit to Italy to sit with you and learn from you about your family wine business. In turn, you have an open invitation to visit my homes in New York City or the Hamptons.' The two hit it off. Mondino, a notoriously private and quiet man outside of the rigors of being a public servant, called Alexander his brother from America. He attended all of the Black Camelot weddings after Donald had asked Kwame and Tom to add him to their guest lists. Donald wanted him to be a groomsman for his wedding, but Mondino had to decline. Mondino, knew the security detail of a head of state could have ruined the event. Alexander is special. His people skills are unique. All the ambassadors and diplomats envy him. He has a natural connectivity with people that we have to master in our job. You know, how we have to get people to like us? Listen and work with us? To answer our calls happily, if at all, even when they know the reason for the call may not always be good."

She shook her head in admiration.

"We all want to be like that guy. He has that special touch a president is supposed to have. You should put the word out that he's considering running. Create some buzz for him. Maybe it'll push him."

"I don't do that, Dorsey. You know that," Hill told the diplomat. The point, however, was made. Alexander could win at politics.

Hill's strenuous rejection of the ambassador's suggestion didn't dissuade her. She pushed the idea again.

"You should, W.T. No one will know. Except you and me."

Those endorsements ran through Hill's mind as Heron sang the final verse:

"There will be no pictures of pigs shooting down Brothers on the instant replay"

"That song scares me. I pray that it is not prophetic," Lawson said. "What's next on the playlist, Chuck D? Fight The Power?"

Donald, Kwame, and Sammie then walked in the door. Their faces glowed and they appeared energized. The presser to announce the Political News Network had gone as well as they had hoped.

"I heard that. Chuck D? You like Public Enemy?" Donald said and looked at Lawson. "That song has its place and time. But not for what you need."

He turned to Hill. "Thanks for coming in, W.T. You hit me with a couple of zingers out there. For a moment I thought that you and Luke had planned a double-team. But I know you're way smarter than he is."

Hill stared back at Donald. The stern, grizzled countenance of a hard news hound was baring itself. He wondered if Alexander's comment was a set up.

"What do you mean?" Hill said. The subdued growl of his voice matched his mean mug face. "That's just a normal question in the political news world, especially if you're running for office."

Alexander shrugged, "I guess you're right, that is your job. Ask the hard questions, get to the truth. Chuck D would ask it unapologetically. That is the only way to 'Fight the powers that be,' I suppose. Do the public some good with good hard questions, right? That is what you're saying?"

Hill shook his head. Lawson did also with a growl. "That's exactly what I'm saying."

The Black Camelots had not taken their seats yet. They stood next to each other at the doorway. W.T and R.L. had stood up when they entered, Donald said, "Well, let's shake hands to that."

The request confused the reporters as Donald, Kwame and Sammie walked to them. As guests they were placed on the side of the table with views of the park. After the handshake Kwame and Sammie walked to the non-view side. Hill and Lawson sat down, then Kwame and Sammie. Donald moved to the front of the table and pointed to the gigantic window and the fully bloomed Central Park .

"You guys got the best seat this morning. Gill Harris loved this so much. He swore it was the best perk of the job. He enjoyed it even more than meeting all the big corporate and heads of state, flying on private planes, the private club memberships that were part of the job as head of Harris Simmons. One of the things I've learned in my years of working with people is that the eyes don't lie. You would have love to see Gill's light up when he looked out that window. They came to life in special ways. Oh they were something."

Donald paused and turned his gaze outside. The *Beltway News* team took notice of the reverential reflection of his former boss and dear friend. The room fell silent.

Kwame and Sammie also turned their eyes to the window. W.T. and R.L. stared with admiring half smiles. Finally, Hill broke the silence, "It's hypnotizing for sure."

"Yes indeed," Lawson added.

Donald finally returned his attention to them. Hill turned his eyes to his watch. If they left in 10 minutes they might get to the airport in time for the next shuttle at 2 pm.

"You asked us to hang around. I got a paper to close this evening, and need to be back by 4:00 Alexander. I want to catch the 2 p.m. shuttle."

Donald nodded.

"Give me a second, will you W.T.? I want to do this right. First point I want to make it clear is that I am not running for President or V.P., so there is no exclusive coming about that."

Hill lifted his wrist up to his eyes, gazed at his watch once more, and then slowly dropped it to the table; and for dramatic effect folded his hands. Donald took note of the editor's movements, this time he pursed his lips. He locked eyes with Hill and his voice lowered.

"Okay Hill, it's clear that you want to get out of here to catch your plane, so let me get right to it. I hear you are trying to raise $75 million. And you've got two private equity groups interested, but you are balking at their terms. One you fear might try and take over your business; the other you know is not a kindred spirit. You are dealing with a devil and the deep blue sea decision. What I don't know for certain is: What is the reason you are seeking financing?"

Alexander blindsided the editor and Hill didn't have a ready answer. Responses crisscrossed in his mind, but he said nothing. All he could do was take a deep breath.

As he exhaled Alexander continued his bombardment: "What is this money for, W.T.? Are you trying to grow audience? Hire more talent for the election season? Open more editorial offices? Buy a building? Or," he raised his eyebrows and slowly asked, "are you trying to open a studio for *Beltway News TV*?"

He then winked and his pursed lips turned in a knowing smile.

Hill looked at Lawson. They sat up straight at the same time. Both had been seated with their hands folded. Hill unfolded his and scratched the inside of his right forearm. His forearm itched when he was stressed. Lawson breathed deeply and kept his hands folded. He didn't say a word. Sammie could have waved at him and tried any seductive taunt possible. It wouldn't have caught his attention.

"Y'all need to relax," Kwame said. Their shock and nervousness was obvious. They knew that Alexander had the money and power to put a competitor up against *The Beltway News* and put them out of business. Hill and Lawson had a network of insiders everywhere and there was no talk of such, nor were they rivals or enemies. It was all a surprise.

Donald flashed a joyful smile. Sammie did, too. Kwame spoke for them.

"This is all good gentlemen; no need to panic. We want to help you. For starters we understand that you are bound by oaths of confidentiality to not share anything with us by your prospective lending partners. That said, the Black Camelots have a lot of money, and *Political News Network* is only part of what we want to do. We know you are trying to raise $75 million to start a television network. We want to top that number and give you $100 million. And we will have our hands full with PNN, which means we will be hands off, giving you full independence"

Hill and Lawson exhaled loudly.

"I guess I should get Jones to close the paper today, huh?" Hill whispered to Lawson. "Never let it be said that W.T. Hill looked a gift horse in the mouth and declined."

He turned to Donald and then to Kwame before asking, "Kwame are you serious?"

"Yes, W.T. You're the only one we can trust to protect this venture. We didn't play Gil Scott-Heron for nothing. This time, the revolution must be televised."

Darius Myers

Part Seven

Chapter 38

Go Get Betty Blonde

D1 and DD2 sat in the large conference room at the SCTV campus. The presidential race was expected to be a financial bonanza, and they had already begun counting the money. The network was rated #1 with religious right and Southern Christian audiences, and they expected a 50% revenue spike during the campaign.

"Whom do you think we should send to lead the Yates coverage, DD2?" Damon1 asked his son.

He responded, "All the local stations in Tennessee will be there. I'm guessing Shawn Cooper will be there for Ch 2 Network News. We need someone she can't outshine."

DD2 gritted his teeth, "Cooper! That woman. She's a pain in the butt, Dad. Betty Blonde. Mega hard news stories like this are why we are paying her so well. We'll send her."

Betty Blonde's birthname was Nancy Kean. She was a newsreader who had flopped out in both Chicago and Detroit. Home for her was Jasper, Michigan, a middle of nowhere minor news market that fed to the local audience of 100,000 stories from state capitals of Illinois and Michigan, and the big cities of Chicago, its closest big city. It also provided stories from Detroit, where 85% of Jasper's residents worked in the town's steel plant and belonged to the steelworkers' union.

Blonde, just weeks earlier, was hired to be the lead anchor for SCTV Midwest, the political news bureau that was created to fill the heightened demand for election season political coverage. The other hire was Colt Maximus, a local Jeffersonville football star who'd played collegiately, with great fanfare, at Christian Southern. After college, Colt played a few years in the Canadian Football League. He wasn't quite good enough to make it in the American pro league. Maximus was also DD3's childhood best friend.

The youngest Damon had walked in the door and overheard DD2 tell DD1 that they would be sending Betty Blonde to Yates.

DD3 was in the doghouse with his grandfather. The old lion had still not forgiven him for the embarrassing interview a year back with Shawn Cooper. Cooper had exposed a special payment made by the family to help him gain acceptance into Harlowe's #1 ranked divinity school. It was an embarrassing moment for the religious dynasty after DD3 was exposed as an intellectual lightweight.

Undeterred by his grandfather's anger, DD3 weighed in on the decision.

"We should send Colt. He's right here and itching to get some action."

DD1 shot the suggestion down.

"Colt is a rube, just like you. He's okay as our man on the street, and that's about it," DD1 snapped. "We'll use him to chase down stories in D.C., knock on doors, and be a pain in the butt. He's not ready to be the face that our network needs on stories of this magnitude. Your buddy is an ambulance chaser, a former jock with a handsome face. Nothing more."

The rebuke was the first exchange between the grandfather and DD3 in weeks. The last time he threatened to throw Damon off the campus if he didn't get out of his sight. Fearing more was to come, DD3 glared at his father and grandfather, and without another word bolted from the room.

His father yelled, "DD3, get back in here."

Damon 3 returned, a scowl covering his face.

"You are still on probation," his father snapped. "That means you don't have a voice. You don't speak unless you are asked to, and your functions around here will be behind the camera: operations and production."

"And grunt work," DD1 barked.

"Yes, lots of grunt work," DD2 added. "Are we clear? If there is any misunderstanding, let it be known right here, right now."

The youngest Damon's eyes had turned to cold, dead glares. His jaw was tight. DD3 didn't speak; he just nodded.

"Okay, then. Call Betty Blonde and tell her that we want her in Yates, Tennessee. Let her know we will send the private plane, SC Air 2 to pick her up in…" DD2 looked at his watch, "…five hours at the Jasper airport. So, she needs to pack and be ready. Tell her your grandfather and I will call her in an hour. After you call her, gather together the senior remote crew and tell them they are going to camp out in Yates. They'll be there for next three days, minimum. Let's get moving."

DD3 continued scowling. He glared downward at the floor like an unrepentant child but didn't dare lift his eyes to his father or grandfather. He also didn't respond.

The non-response angered DD2.

"Do you understand, Son? Am I clear?"

"Yes, Dad. I mean, DD2."

"Good. Then get moving. There's lots to do."

DD3 walked out the door. Seconds later, the arrogant bark DD3 displayed before and during his failed PR tour echoed in the hallways. He was bullying the staffers as he relayed his father's orders.

DD1 shook his head as his thoughts shifted to the new hire.

"Son, let's talk a minute about Betty Blonde. She is expensive, isn't she?"

"Yep. A million a year. I know we usually don't pay that much. But if we wanted an anchor or a newsreader from a bigger network or a bigger market, the ask was $1.5 to $2. Plus, those people don't want to give up their seats to come to a religious network. It's just the way it works, DD1"

"Well, she's still expensive for us, Son. You made sure she knows that we are paying her to be a world-class reporter, not a local yokel, right son?"

"It's a big deal for her. She understands."

"And as for DD3," the eldest Damon said and shook his head.

DD2 stared at his dad. He remained glad DD1 hadn't ordered his son to be fired.

"You hear him yelling. My grandson's out there acting like an entitled fool. I need you to be a father to your son. Give him a really good verbal lashing. If you need to, suspend him for a month. He's not close to being ready to be the face of this company."

"I have talked to him, Dad," DD2 said. There was a whiny resignation that tore at him, as he was stuck between the demands of his father and the chaos of his son..

"Do you want me to step in, Son? I won't suspend him; I'll fire him. I won't hesitate. That boy will never be poor, but we don't need any more of his entitled heir apparent stuff. The pregnancy, the strip clubs, all the prodigal son stuff is an embarrassment. Let's not forget that we are doing God's work here. He's got to try to be a better servant, not a ruler."

DD2 couldn't, nor did he want to, argue on his son's behalf. His father was right. They'd had the discussion countless times and he agreed with his father: his son was acting very much like an entitled, prodigal brat. He had yet to comprehend that his father and grandfather would only take so much, and once that line was crossed, they'd banish him from the grounds. DD1 was not going to let his grandson destroy his legacy.

"Okay, DD1. I got it."

"Good. Last thing, DD2. Make it clear to Nancy, I mean Betty Blonde, that she is the managing editor. She's the boss. DD3's a nepo hire, not her boss. I don't want her to be fearful of doing her job."

"Gotcha, DD1."

"Good, now get out of here. Call him into your office and give him a lesson on leadership. Tell him that what we heard when he left this office is not leading the troops. He needs to circle back and apologize. We've got a great team of producers, editors, and camera people. Tell him that I've had enough, and he's far from being out of my doghouse. He must talk to the team respectfully and treat them as the talented professionals they are."

"You're right, DD2. I'm on it. I'll do that right now."

* * *

DD1 understood the stakes. The Cooper fiasco had forced them to open their pocketbooks. Until then, they had gotten by on homegrown talent for decades. DD1 started the network fifty years ago. Back then it was Sunday sermons from local preachers Monday-Sunday. In those early days, they often played the same sermons for a full week straight. It aired from sign-on at 7 am to sign-off at 9 pm. DD1 himself would sign off for the evening with, "Time to pray and go to bed."

It took five years before he generated advertising for his shows. In year five, the local free station that gave him the channel on public access got hit with a tax bill of $1,000. They told him they might lose their license if they couldn't pay the thousand dollars. That same day, DD1 went live on the air and made an appeal to his audience.

"People of God, the local government has imposed a $1,000 tax bill on us. As you know, we are a small operation and bring the word of God to you as God directs us. I hope you can find it in your hearts to support us so we can continue to be God's voice to the people."

DD1's appeal brought in $10,000. At that time, he was a full-time dairy farmer, and delivering the gospel on the local free television station was a hobby. He attempted to return the donations received after the first $1000, but the supporters refused to take the money back.

To show his gratitude, he thanked them for their support by calling out their names during broadcasts at the beginning, middle, and end of each day.

Thanking supporters in this way continued for the next ten years. At the same time, the channel's bandwidth expanded to a 50 mile-radius, then 100 miles, and finally 200 miles outside of Jeffersonville; and so did the radius of donors. Eventually, Damon created a Donor Book with names of the supporters of Jeffersonville Gospel Shows, the network's name at the time. The donor group continues to this day. Now, in addition to the books, donors receive tee-shirts, pins, mugs, plaques, and a variety of other mementoes that identify them as supporters of the local station that after fifteen years became SCTV. The mementos were an extreme source of pride for those early partners, as DD1 called them.

DD1 regarded the early donors as "simple people supporting a simple man of God." A small barn on the family dairy farm was converted into a television studio. The 150-acre farm had since become the main street of Jeffersonville. It is now a modern, sprawling campus that includes a megachurch, day school, television station, and 200-room hotel with a four-star rating. Humbled by it all, DD1 took great joy in reminding and thanking the original donors for what they helped build.

"Only God and God's people can do this," he'd say. He kept a keen reverence for the multitude of white-haired elders that would come and visit with pride knowing that their hard-earned $10 and

$20 donations had built something special. That history was also another reason why it wasn't just DD1 that his grandson embarrassed when he took on Cooper. It was those long-term friends and partners, DD1 maintained, that he embarrassed, too.

As DD2 walked to the door to chastise his son, his father stopped him.

"My grandson still has no idea how badly he messed up. I can't leave this to him, and that's going to be in my will. He's a grown man and should have known better. We are in the business of God first, and then the information and news business. How do you go into the lion's den like that unprepared? Shawn Cooper is the best in the business. There's no one better. It was a David vs Goliath match, Son. He struts in there with Goliath's confidence and swagger, and she cuts him down, bit by bit. Our audience, the religious right, will never forget that. He will be infamous for it. They'll forgive you and me. But he's not a front man. And not the man whom I will leave my life's work to."

"You're right, Dad, I understand. It pains me to agree. Anyhow, that's years from now. You're not going anywhere. Maybe before God calls us home, he'll have a son or daughter who can assume the throne."

"Anyone but him," DD1 said.

Chapter 39

These Are the Rules

DD2 walked into his son's office and closed the door. His son, seated at his desk, glared at him with rage-filled eyes.

As DD3 opened his mouth, his father raised his hand and barked, "Don't say a word. Let me speak."

"But, Dad."

.DD3 stopped when his father took a deep breath and raised his hand. A menacing stare followed that punked the third generation Damon.

DD2 walked closer to the front of his son's desk.

"I am talking to you as a father now. You are Detrick Damon, the third, my son and grandson of that old man down the hall. This is a company that was started on a dairy farm. We are now a multimedia company with reach to people of faith in markets across the world. That is our core mission and will always be. But we are also a business, generating $$2 billion annually, and we have chosen a side."

DD2 took another deep breath and closed his eyes. His son had seen the look before. DD2 was trying to reach him, kindly.

"Son, I'm not even sure the old man down the hall knows what side he has chosen. He still thinks romantically of yesteryear when he started this place."

"When he got the free television channel?" DD3 asked.

"Yes. He loves what he's built, and I admire him for it. Only a true man of God could be blessed to do so well. But I'm going to tell you that he made a mistake. This stays between you and me, and if you betray me, you will suffer unimaginable consequences."

The tension in his dad's voice scared DD3 and they made his father's words believable. Up until the Shawn Cooper fiasco, DD3 had never feared or faced any consequences. He was the crowned prince waiting to be king, and everyone treated him as such.

"Listen to me carefully. Your grandfather betrayed God when he began to take donations from certain people in those early days. Like I said, he romanticizes it all. But he knew who they were."

"You mean Before Emancipation people?"

"Before Emancipation, Southern Values, White Ways, and many more groups, as well as individual Christian nationalists. Before Emancipation, especially, has always been about violence. The fact is, we bear responsibility for giving them a religious home. They come to us after they commit their acts of hate against God's people. We never called them out and told them that their acts are not works of God."

DD3 looked at his father, his eyes narrowed. He wasn't in agreement with DD2.

"God's people? The people they target are not of God. They're devil worshippers, sinful reprobates, the enemy of goodness, Dad."

"Where did you hear that, Son? You never heard that from me, or your grandfather. Certainly not in God's word."

DD3 had an answer, but it wasn't one he was prepared to tell his father. He didn't say anything more. DD2 began to quiz him on his source. Anger tinged his voice.

"Did you hear it at that strip club where you caused the car accident? Or was it the demon that was in your head when you impregnated that beautiful church worker, and her husband nearly beat you to death."

DD3 sat up straight. His eyes shifted nervously.

"He should have gone to jail, Dad. We should have prosecuted him."

"Don't try to change the subject, Son. Where'd you hear it?"

DD3 didn't answer.

"I'm guessing it was at the strip club where the locals, probably some hate-filled rednecks that envy you, the wealthy man about town, but can't be you. So they choose to blame their plight in life on black and brown people. I'm guessing it was them. Am I wrong?"

DD3 still refused to answer. Each second of insolence further incensed his dad.

*　*　*

DD2 was by far the most charismatic of the three Damon men. He was also a loyal family man, and once had a burgeoning talent that his father suppressed.

Besides cows, the dairy farm included a handful of bulls and fast Thoroughbred horses. The animals became a natural training ground. DD2's childhood dream had been to join the competitive rodeo circuit. At a stout 5 foot 11 and 210 pounds, he had the frame and strength to handle the tough animals and a sufficiently buoyant back to pop up and not feel any pain after falling or being trampled. At 16, the first year he was eligible, DD2 competed in the Carolina Regionals for the Texas Big Show. For up-and-comers, it was the biggest rodeo event of the year. He won second prize overall and an invitation to compete in the Texas Big Show.

After he qualified his father told him, "I will support this dream of yours until you are 18, but I can't after that. You've been called by God." DD1 cited 1 Corinthians 13:11, "When I was a child, I spoke as a child, I understood as a child, I thought as a child: but when I became a man, I put away childish things."

DD2's rodeo aspirations and his memory of the discussion that dashed them flashed in his head as he spoke to his son, "Those men who fill your ears with such things are the demons you face son, not black or brown people. Ask me how I know."

"How Dad? How do you know?"

"Because I have friends that are black people. Dear friends."

He lowered his head and tightly closed his eyes. His face

contorted painfully as he thought about his son's darkness and the embarrassment that would threaten his friendships.

"Well, I had them before you went across the country acting a fool. Bessie Ann, Freddie James, and Rosalie, you know who they are. They've been coming down here for years, and they are my good friends. Your mother's, too. We sneak out a couple, three times a year to see them while they are on the road and even when they perform in New York, where Bessie Ann and Rosalie live. Freddie James lives in Phoenix. He has a few horses. Freddie's a country boy, and we go riding. Bessie Ann and Rosalie have had me to their homes, as well. I've met their husbands and kids. All three have wonderful family lives, and there are no drug dealers circling around, no gangster stuff, or demon-possessed people darkening their doorways like the morons you count as friends tell you."

Damon 3 didn't know this part of his father's life. He wanted to feel anger, even betrayal, because ever since the Shawn Cooper incident, all he had heard from his father and grandfather was that he was a shame to the family. Why was his father telling him this story now?

"Son, the reason I so desperately wanted you to go to Harlowe was to help you see the world as I see it. You could sit side by side with blacks, Latinos, Asians, Native Americans, Africans or Europeans and see that God don't make mistakes. Instead, I have no idea what you did up there, except graduate. I fear that when we bought the building there, Harlowe admitted you just so they could take the money and rid themselves of the burden of having to reject you constantly, and then gave you a diploma just to rid themselves of you."

DD3 lowered his head. His anger was morphing into shame, but it was fleeting.

"Did you learn anything about other people, other races, other cultures up there, Son?"

DD3 didn't answer. Harlowe was a decade ago. He was a grown man being dressed down by his father. The humiliation caused him to bristle.

Damon 2 could see his son steaming. DD3's brewing was another act of defiance and angered him more. His jaw tightened. The teaching moment that he'd hoped for was over.

"You've jeopardized your grandfather's life's work. He may never forgive you. He's furious and is still working through it. You act as if you built this thing, son. Just moments ago, he didn't ask for your opinion on the Yates deal. You interjected as if your voice matters or as if you were in charge. Of course, he was going to put you in your place."

DD3 lowered his head and remained silent.

"And for your next act you demean the people who help us succeed. You took out your frustration on the staffers. Why? Because your grandfather did not agree to put Colt on this story. We don't treat the people who work with us here that way."

"But…" DD3 started.

Damon 2 raised his hand, his palm facing his son to stop him from talking.

"No buts, Son. I don't think you fully understand."

"What are you talking about, Dad?"

"There've been too many mistakes. DD1 is adamant, and I'm in agreement with him. We're never going to give you the keys to this place."

The news was a blindside. Damon 3's lips shook. His mind blanked as he searched for words.

DD2 raised his hand again and continued, "He doesn't want you to have it, and frankly I don't give a damn. You've both put me in a spot that I don't like. But if I had to choose a side, I pick my dad's. The way you are right now, you'd destroy this place."

DD3's brows furrowed as his back straightened. His sense of entitlement kicked in, and he responded angrily.

"No, Dad? This belongs to me. It's my inheritance, my destiny."

The response made DD2 furious.

"Shut up, you idiot!"

DD2 slammed his fist on the desk. He now weighed close to 240 pounds. He stood up, and it was clear that he'd been spending time in the gym and was far more fit than his son. DD3's eyes turned downward as cowardice overcame him.

"My father allowed things to happen that were not of God. I sat at the wheel and did my best, but I lost my way, too. We saw

Digby Yates as a cash cow, a golden goose that we could profit from after losing so much money from your failed New York escapade. Between your mistake and my father's decision to support Yates, we've gone down a path that this network may not be able to come back from."

"What do you mean, Dad?"

"Don't you understand what's going on here, Son?"

"Sure do, Dad," DD3 snapped. "Digby Yates is a son of the South. He represents Christian nationalism overtly, BE covertly, and all that that represents. Yates is a proud ambassador of Southern values. He was shot, and his wife has embarrassed him and the Southern elite."

Damon 3 had given his father the summary of all the news stories SCTV News had written and distributed about the Yates shooting across its cable network and online. Views on SCTV.com had generated $7 million in its first two hours and another $20 million in revenue on the first day. There was one truth to his summary. Digby Yates was good for business.

The father shook his head. An embarrassed frown covered his face.

"Son, you only know what you want to know, see what you choose to see."

"What do you mean, Dad?"

"Do you know that Yates consorted with four to five prostitutes, regularly?"

DD3 shot back.

"Why should that matter? He's not perfect. I never said he was."

"Okay, Son. Does it matter that Yates wants a race war and that, if he were to win, our country as we know it would be changed forever?"

Damon 3 looked up at his father and shrugged. He then issued an answer that shook DD2.

"That might not be so bad, as long as the good guys win."

DD2 loosened his tie and undid the top button on his shirt. His son's answers had raised his blood pressure.

"I guess you think we are the good guys?"

"Yessir, Dad."

DD2's face froze.

"Son, you will not be allowed to use God that way in my presence anymore. That ends now, as does this conversation. Get the team ready to go to Yates, and we will talk again upon your return."

"What about my inheritance, Dad? I've worked hard. I'm entitled. This is mine-"

DD2 cut him off.

"Shut up," DD2 snapped.

"But Dad."

"I said shut up."

He gritted his teeth and puffed his chest menacingly.

"Right now, you need to think about getting this story covered and about your relationship with God. Pray, Son, that He reveals what your true calling is. I guarantee you that it won't be using this network as a leading voice in a race war. And let me be clear, I am second in charge to your grandfather. As of this moment, you are just a worker. If you don't like it, you are free to leave the campus now, and we'll send the team to Yates without you. Are we on the same page about what you are going to do today?"

DD2 was screaming now. His voice bellowed in the hallway. The workers that moved about had stopped in their tracks. They hadn't heard him yell, ever. Many smiled when they heard the threats, especially the words, 'you are just a worker.' It was a comeuppance they'd never expected, but one that lifted their spirits."

"Yes, Dad. We are clear," DD3 whispered.

DD3 spoke in a hush. His ego did not want his father to be heard by the captivated audience in the hallway.

"Good, now get going. I'll be in my office the rest of the day. If there are any issues once you guys get to Yates, make sure I know."

DD2 turned and walked out the door. He didn't bother to say goodbye.

Chapter 40

Advice

"**I** tried to take him down a peg," Damon 2 muttered under his breath as he walked to his office, "but I know my boy. He's as stubborn as a mule. God, please soften his heart."

His assistant, Bonnie, sat at her desk. Like most of the staffers she heard the shouting from the showdown.

"I'll be in my office for the next twenty minutes, Bonnie."

DD2's voice was somber, the anger his son provoked broke his happy-go-lucky manner.

"Hold all calls from everyone. Especially my father and son. For any advertisers, tell them I'm in a meeting and will get back shortly."

"You okay, Mr. Damon?"

On days when DD2 felt like talking, he would share almost everything with her. Today, he responded with a riddle.

"This used to be a church business that started on a dairy farm. Now, we are a big business with our fingers in a lot of other things. Do you know what I mean?"

Bonnie didn't know, exactly. But she was in her late 50s widowed, with grown kids, and had enough experience to know the ups and downs of life.

"What I know, Mr. D, is that life is hard, and sometimes you just gotta let it go and pray."

"My friend, Bessie Ann, says the same thing all the time, 'Let go and let God,' she says."

Bonnie smiled.

"Oh, I like Bessie Ann. That woman is something special. When is she coming back? And Rosalie and F—F-Forest-."

She forgot his name.

"You mean Freddie James?"

"Freddie James, that's right. Good people of God they are. You have to get them back here. And I want the same concert tickets I had before."

"First row, center. You were smiling like a schoolgirl that night. I saw you."

"Sure was. Lovely people, too. You can tell. You must invite them back."

"I want to, Bonnie. But it's getting a bit crazy around here with these upcoming elections and all."

Bonnie knew about the family tensions and the busyness of the election season. She also knew about Digby Yates's drama. Everyone at SCTV was talking about it.

"Digby Yates, ugh, that story about him being shot and his wife. Lord have mercy, Pastor Damon," Bonnie said.

She sometimes called him "Pastor." He didn't preach but didn't mind her saying it.

"You like him, Bonnie?"

Damon trusted the smarts and character of his long-time assistant. Bonnie didn't have a mean bone or bad thought, ever. She took the job because she wanted to serve the Lord and never complained or made a fuss about long work hours, or DD3's temper tantrums, or angry callers who wanted free things, like tee-shirts or free tickets to concerts or show tapings.

She wore big, bright wigs in various shades of red and pant suits that she told DD2 were thirty years old. For her, they were a source of pride. She'd lost sixty pounds in the last two years and didn't want to buy new clothes to show off her weight loss. She claimed the red wings added some spice in her life. They always made DD2 smile.

"I don't know much about politics," she said, "but Digby Yates's shooting and that of his wife's sister, and the wife's new boyfriend in New York, that's a saucy scandal. Too much for a country girl like me. Frankly, I guess I'll learn more when the election gets nearer or as we cover the story."

She continued as Damon took one step inside his office and started to close the door, "But I guess I have, already. Adultery, coveting another man's wife, killing over love, it's all Old Testament stuff. I've read it all before. There's nothing new."

"Except it's on our watch, Bonnie. And might become our responsibility. What shall we do?"

"At this here Christian religious TV network that started on a dairy farm in the middle of nowhere? You already know the answer.

You go talk to God. Pray on it, as long as you need to. He'll give you the answer."

Her response made him smile.

"I love you, Bonnie."

"Not as much as God, my good man," she said. "Let Him know, and ask Him for guidance."

Chapter 41

Scoop Montgomery

Damon 3 sat in a private room at Pop's Palace. This would be his last night ever at the club. It was also the night before the shooting in Yates, Tennessee. The next day, the town would finally shut it down after forty years. The shutdown wasn't because the town and its elders had had enough. It was because of the story that was scheduled to air in a month but had been pushed up to an earlier date.

The national press was digging up every story it could on Yates and his supporters. For Shawn Cooper, any story about the family-owned SCTV franchise and its multiple generations of leaders was red-flagged. Her assistant found this story and made a bee-line to Cooper's office.

It was 3 pm, and during a brief lull in the chaos between the morning and the evening news broadcasts. Cooper anchored both.

Her assistant, Angie, had read the first eight chapters during her lunch break. She plunged into the book after reading the opening paragraph in the press release sent by the author's publishing company. It was excerpted from Chapter One.

"It was at the strip club, a couple years ago, that he'd fled the scene. The driver of the black European sports car had caused a dangerous, but non-fatal, car accident. His car hit the rear panel of the vehicle driven by an evening shift worker driving home in the small town where the biggest business was religion. The worker was driving home in a twenty-year-old SUV in the early morning. He had just clocked out after finishing the 5 pm to 1 am shift. The struck vehicle spun out of control and hit a utility pole. Damon 3, the prince of the town and heir apparent to the SCTV megachurch and Southern Christian Television Network owned and run by his family, was the driver of the black European sports car. He didn't bother to check on the condition of the SUV driver. The scion panicked and fled the scene.

The Damons paid the victim a million dollars, plus his medical fees. The man willingly signed an NDA to keep the story quiet. *The Jeffersonville Standard*, the town's only newspaper, suppressed the story. It was a known pattern of behavior in Jeffersonville and of the Damons', in particular, that the church paid for the sins of the son. I know this because I was the beat reporter for *The Jeffersonville Standard*, the only beat reporter on staff."

Cooper's light brown skin began to redden, and within seconds became a fiery red. The anchor typically didn't take a personal interest in story subjects, but Damon was different. He was, in her opinion, an entitled idiot---and if not taken down he would become a problem. The reporter did her part to neuter him during what had now become known as Yates's White Privilege PR campaign, but she feared that - if given the right opportunity - he would resurface, unrepentant and even more powerful, with an international television network behind him.

"That guy, Angie," she said after reading his name in the press release. Her lips closed into the tight pout Angie knew all too well. It meant Cooper was hot.

"I thought you assassinated him, Coop?"

"Me too, Angie, I did my best, but some pests have an uncanny capacity for resuscitation."

"Well, this book will give you every opportunity to finish the job. We got an advance copy, and I've read eight chapters. Ooh wee, it's a good one. Lots of spice in the beginning."

Angie was 24 years old, only a year out of the esteemed Harlowe graduate school where she'd graduated with honors. She smiled and handed Cooper the book.

"I want this one back after you finish it."

Cooper, who could tell from the exchange her young assistant's engagement with the book, said, "How about this, Angie? Read it and take notes. Provide me with the Cliff's Notes. Can you do that for me? I need it by tomorrow."

"Sure thing, Coop. Consider it done."

"Anything more on this one?"

She knew Angie was whip-smart and already had the answer.

"We need to get to the booking people and get him on the air. His tour is supposed to start in a month, but I say we get in front of this. The author is a reporter, and his tell-all about the local corruption in Jeffersonville will put him in great demand. We want that story first."

Cooper flashed a cynical half-smile.

"Good. Small towns can be beautiful places, Angie. But they are also like prisons when the wrong people get too much power. Is it that bad?"

"There are a lot of issues with the son. The father and grandfather are too busy with the dynasty. The son sounds demon-possessed, like he needs some good old-fashioned prayer oil..." Angie giggled at her punchline, "..and a jail sentence. Five to ten years, at least."

Cooper chuckled.

"And a butt-whipping by his pa and grandpa," Angie continued. "Seems to me that those ministers exempted their heir apparent from the 'spare the rod, spoil the child' sermon."

"Ooh, child! Remind me to not get on your bad side," Cooper said.

"You know how we black people do things, Coop."

The anchor's eyes shot to the ceiling, as she recalled her parents' threats.

"Momma Cooper's go-to line was, 'I brought you in this world, and I'll take you out.'"

Angie laughed, "Heard that one a thousand times. There's no comeback to that."

Cooper's gaze turned reflective

"Angie, in this seat, I've had encounters with some of the most charismatic people you'll ever meet. I'm sad to conclude that many of them are not good. Today's story about the attempt to assassinate Digby Yates is one of those. He has a following that I don't understand. He's corupt not very handsome, not an amazing speechmaker, not incredibly warm or charismatic. This guy has no IT factor at all. The same thing with Damon 3. I met him here two years ago. Rumors ran rampant that he wasn't special and was admitted into Harlowe because of his privilege, that in fact his family bought a building. That bothered me because he was going around the country tearing down black and brown people's accomplishments and suggesting they were being given handouts."

"'Anti-woke' is what enlightened people call his mindset."

"Well, you saw the interview. He wouldn't know the true definition of 'woke' if you spelled it to him using kindergarten alphabet blocks. What's worse, he is just the kind of fool that Digby Yates could use to build the coalition he wants."

"You mean the "Let's Return to What We Should Be" coalition that wants to take the country back to a time when this place was only great for wealthy white men. I'll pass on that."

"Yes, Angie. What a demeaning campaign slogan. But it has a ring to it. Let's hope it never gains traction."

Cooper continued, "The word in news world circles is that the grandfather and father got blinded by money. Their taste for cash just got too big, and they have looked the other way for so long that they can't tell the difference between right and wrong. They are also not connected to the streets anymore. They are superstars, so they don't know the truth about guys like Yates. Or if they do, they don't care. They started out on a dairy farm. Now they own the complete downtown. If Yates gets his hands on their network, he can win this election."

Angie frowned, "And Yates is a white Christian nationalist."

"That part seems to be certain, Angie. Our job is to find out if the father and grandfather are white nationalists, too. The grandson, we know, is an idiot. We've gotta get to the father and son."

"Well, we can start with Scoop's book. You'll enjoy it, but after I'm done," Angie said.

Chapter 42

These Things Happened

"*G*od's *Town, USA,* by Scoop Montgomery. I love that title," Cooper said as she looked at the book jacket.

It had a silhouette of a stripper pole and a half-nude woman with her back turned to hide her breasts.

"What a cover. The publisher is definitely putting it out there, Angie."

"You'll make it a best-seller, for sure, by the time you finish the interview," Cooper's assistant replied.

Scoop Montgomery had been the local newspaper reporter at *The Jeffersonville Standard.* He'd followed the typical career trajectory of a college journalism school graduate: work as a young reporter at a small newspaper, do all the dirty work, report on city hall, local corruption, town weddings, high school sports, etc. It was work for little to no money but provided exposure to all levels of news reporting. Most of the time, the assignments were those the senior writers did not want. It was a job cub reporters took for two to three years to accumulate a book of bylines, and then move on to a bigger market. It's what Scoop Montgomery had done. Except this town had a far bigger dark side and more juicy storylines than he expected, particularly as it was the home of the biggest Christian television ministry and broadcast network in America.

Angie was able to book Montgomery on Cooper's morning show two days after giving her his book.

The writer told Cooper, as they prepped for the interview, "I'm originally from Upstate New York. My plan was to do a couple of years in Jeffersonville, learn how a news organization worked, and write enough good stories to move on. Jeffersonville turned out to be different. These guys owned the town, the Damons. I don't know if they are good people or bad. I never met them. But I learned quickly that they were the most powerful family within 200 miles of Jeffersonville. Maybe even the state. I attended their church services once, and one of their concerts, and then I saw a hit-and-run accident in the red-light district outside a strip club frequented by Damon the Third."

The show had been renamed *Cooper's Morning On Channel 2*. The award-winning reporter was now the top face of the network, and she had been named managing editor. The rebranding of the morning show and Cooper's promotion to managing editor were carrots to keep the top-rated anchor happy. They were also acknowledgements that Channel 2 couldn't afford to lose her, especially with the election nearing.

She read an opening from the teleprompter:

"The strip club's owner was a redneck who favored cowboy hats, blue jeans, and well-polished cowboy boots. He alternated between two pairs, one black and another brown. Both had pointed toes that were reinforced with steel tips. Known as Pop Palace, his birth name was Pete John. He was in his mid-60s, and had slumped shoulders and a pot belly that revealed he hadn't worked out in decades. Pete John had owned the place for thirty plus years and was known for being crafty and a bit crazy. It was rumored that he made an annual payoff to the local police. The payoff was look-the-other-way money to ensure they ignored the red-light activity that took place in his club and the ten to fifteen roughed-up patrons that were admitted annually to the emergency room at Jeffersonville General Hospital."

She then did a second opening to introduce the author as the camera did a close-up of him. His flushed face was tense and revealed his nervousness.

"Author Scoop Montgomery's book is a tell-all about how Southern Christian Television Network owned the small town of Jeffersonville, North Carolina. It exposes the scandals that revolved around the son, and the suppression, by the local police and Montgomery's bosses at *The Jeffersonville Standard*, of Montgomery's planned expose that preceded the son's hit-and-run car accident."

The newscaster then turned and faced Montgomery.

"Thank you for coming in," she said. "My assistant read your book in one day. She gave it to me, and I read it overnight. It is an outstanding read, Scoop."

Montgomery smiled at Cooper. The camera panned his face and captured him shifting in his seat. That, and his red-tinged face, revealed his nervousness.

She continued, "I was reading this book last night in bed and kept saying out loud, 'Wow'! I said it so often my husband, Cal, got up and went to sleep in the family room. I need to apologize to him.

Smiling directly at the camera, she said, "Sorry, Calvin. I hope you got some sleep." Cooper then turned back to Montgomery and said. "Anyhow, this book reads like fiction, these stories are so sensational."

Montgomery blushed. He ran his hand through the dark blond curly tangle on his head and pushed it back.

"Thank you for having me. I'm a big fan of yours."

"Glad to have you. Now, tell me about yourself, Scoop, and how you came to write this story. Most importantly, and maybe a bit off-topic, will you ever work again as a newspaper reporter? You know ambition is an incentive in our business. We only get better when we get our teeth into the big story and don't let it go. We chase it without reservations. I'm curious, was this the right time to write this story?"

Montgomery straightened up in his chair and took a deep breath.

"There's a time and a place for everything, Ms. Cooper. For starters, the story might not have any relevance twenty to thirty years from now. For me, the time to tell it is now."

Cooper nodded and flashed an approving smile as she thumbed through a small sheaf of papers with her story questions.

"Well, you have a real talent for storytelling. Whether you stick to nonfiction or move to novels, this book indicates you'll have a bright future.

"Thank you, Ms. Cooper," he said.

The compliment helped him relax.

Scoop looked up to the sky and whispered what Cooper and the audience could see was a silent prayer. The camera guys and set producers looked at each other. Their faces lit up.

The lead producer, Baker Roberts, said, "He's wholesome and quite believable. That was humble. Our audience will love that."

Cooper nodded at Montgomery.

"I get it," she said. "So, tell me. Is Jeffersonville that bad? It's not a charlatan town, is it?"

"I'm not sure I understand the reference, Ma'am."

Montgomery waited for her to respond. It was a skill he'd learned as a reporter: Ask a question, and wait, even if an uncomfortable pause ensued. Cooper had the same training and knew the reference needed explanation.

"A charlatan town is just a town full of fake people, Scoop. Nothing more."

Cooper flashed a half-smile that she quickly replaced with a glaring side-eye.

"You said, Ma'am? Come on, now, Montgomery. First you gave me the Ms., and now you Ma'am me. Don't make me feel so old. My assistant Angie is 24, and straight out of Harlowe. You people have to stop old-folksing me," Cooper said with another half-smile. "I'm only 40."

Angie stood in the background, beaming. The camera turned to her, and the team of producers and camera crew around her. Some covered their smiles; others let theirs glow. It made the newsroom look like a fun, happy place.

"I'm sorry, Shawn. No offense meant," he said.

Scoop had taken a year-long sabbatical to write the book. He had received a $50,000 advance for the story idea. This national interview alone, based on past reports of Cooper's author interviews, was expected to generate as much as a half a million dollars in sales. Those projections came from his publicist, Seven Moore. She was standing next to Angie and the camera crew. Moore knew that Roadhouse Press, the book publisher, would be calling her and her client minutes after the interview, with both positive and negative comments. She winked at Montgomery.

When he stole a look at her, she mouthed, "You are doing great. Do your thing, Scoop."

Her encouragement steadied him as Cooper continued.

"When did you know you were someplace different?"

"Right away, honestly. On my first day in town, I was told to stay in my lane. It was strongly encouraged that I mind my own business, but for a person with the training to be a hard news ambulance chaser, that's a challenge."

Cooper interrupted him with a dramatic wave of her hand.

"Hold up, Mr. Journalism School. You need to explain what ambulance chaser means to our audience."

"My apologies, Shawn. I was trained at Harlowe, and the same way writers are taught at all journalism schools. That is: to be fearless and unashamed when chasing a story. We don't back down, nor deny our instincts and hunches. The job of a journalist is to ask tough questions, a lot of them, and at the same time dig for details. We must cover the who, what, when, where, how, and why to a story."

Montgomery took a deep breath. His facial features were now electrified. Gone were the tension and nervousness.

He continued, "In Jeffersonville, there were always a lot of situations when those six questions were never being asked. Superficially, it appeared to be a sleepy little town with a big church known worldwide, but in reality, that place was far from sleepy."

"I'd say," Cooper said. She peered again through her notes. "Now, tell the audience about the strip club, without of course giving too much away."

"Yes, Shawn. As I said, Jeffersonville is known to be a sleepy town, but as my book points out, it was not. There was a strip club on the outskirts of town, and I'm told it was the only one within a 200-mile radius. So naturally, I was curious. Remember where we are, the home of the largest religious television network in the country. The strip club's existence there didn't fit. Why was that club there? Who was permitting it to operate? What power did SCTV have to shut it down? It was a Gomorrah on the outskirts of the town. These were questions I wasn't permitted to ask at *The Jeffersonville Standard*. In this book, I investigate what I couldn't investigate then."

Cooper nodded.

"And you uncovered some doozies," she said.

She was getting the cue from the producer that the time for the segment was up.

"Scoop we could sit here all morning. Your book is first-rate work, a sure-fire best-seller. I encourage fans of the show to get a copy of *God's Town USA*. It is a must-read."

"Thank you, Shawn."

"And you, Scoop. Best of luck with the book. It's a great read. Audience, go out and buy it today."

Chapter 43

Pop Palace

Pop Palace was more than a strip club owner. He came from a long line of Southern gangsters and was said to be, although it was unproven, a distant cousin of Digby Yates's and also a descendant of Confederacy's President, Jefferson Davis. Palace's corrupt activities fostered a tense relationship with the elder Damons, and the legend was that the connections borne out of his political connections rendered him off-limits to prosecution. Scoop Montgomery was unable to document those connections.

However, he was able to prove that Palace had been successfully blackmailing the leaders of Jeffersonville: the owner of *The Jefferson Standard*, the District Attorney, Damon 1, and Damon 2. His blackmail evidence included countless photos of the leading men in town, state political leaders, and several noted guests of SCTV's, who made visits to Pop's strip club, The Palace Parlor. The most powerful evidence documented Damon 3 having sex with various women on several occasions, in a private room. Pop also had learned of DD3's sexual assault of a young parishioner at the Jeffersonville home church, and added that to his blackmail portfolio. Damon 1 and Damon 2 had never patronized the club, but were extorted because of the acts of Damon 3.

Scoop Montgomery's book had brought all of Jeffersonville's dark secrets to light. As a result, Pop Palace's Sodom and Gomorrah parlor would be shut down, and the truths of its thirty plus years in business would come out.

Chapter 44

The Pregnancy

An excerpt from Chapter Three of *God's Town USA* read:

The girl who sat at the table was a pretty Southern redhead from outside of Atlanta. Her cheeks were so freckled that, to some, she appeared cartoonish and childlike.

The freckled Georgian was the subject of a press conference.

She wasn't a child. She was a 23-year-old woman. Today, she wore makeup intended to accent her freckles and make her appear like the innocent young maiden she once was.

Marcie Jo Hicks was from Destiny, a small town thirty minutes east of Atlanta. She lived in a double-wide trailer with her mother, Lilly Jean; her brothers, Buck Barry and Jet Boy; and her baby girl, Anita Joy. There was another brother, Jimmy John, who was in the Army. He was a master sergeant stationed in Frankfurt, Germany.

Marcie Jo, had contracted a personal injury lawyer, Scott Gulp of Gulp Brothers LLP. The Gulp Brothers were shameless, self-promoting, public injury lawyers. Locally, and across the state with headquarters in Atlanta, they were feared by litigants for their wide variety of unsophisticated pre-trial public embarrassment tactics. They were especially known for their bully tactics and antics that humiliated their opponents into submitting to fast settlements.

There were four Gulp Brothers: Scott, Chip, Skip, and Riley. Scott had a law license in North Carolina and Georgia. The other brothers were only licensed in Georgia. Scott would be leading Marcie Jo Hicks's case. The Gulps, as per their reputation, decided to blindside SCTV and the Damon family.

Scott told Marcie Jo and Lilly Jean, "We'll have you come up to Atlanta and tell your story. We'll get it on TV and get you a nice settlement. Wear the nicest dresses you have. We don't want you to look like you need the money too much."

"But we do," Lilly Jean said. "This double-wide ain't built for no baby. We need a bigger place."

Marcie Jo was two months pregnant when she returned from her time in Jeffersonville. She was also skinny and malnourished. During the end of her first trimester, the doctors at the free clinic in Destiny had to send her to Atlanta via ambulance twice. Each time was for dehydration brought on by severe morning sickness.

"It's a stage. We've gotta get through the first trimester. Your body's adjusting to the miracle inside," her prenatal physician, Dr. Sylvia, said. "Your insides are confused and acting out because it's all new. It will settle down in a month or so, and you'll be fine."

After a few tough weeks, Marcie Joe adjusted. Six months later, Anita Joy, her miracle child, as Lily Jean called her, was born.

Marcie Jo grimaced as she recalled the pregnancy and the year she spent as a stripper in Jeffersonville. She was trying to reconcile the meaning of the word "miracle," as the baby would be a lifelong reminder of a bad stretch in her life.

"What is the miracle, and where is the joy?" she asked Scoop Montgomery. "Momma mean well when say that, but I was lost and wouldn't have minded if I was dead."

"That's why it is a Miracle, Baby Girl," Lilly Jean would always tell her. "You alive and so is this baby. God covered you through your darkest hour."

I was able to track her down after she returned to Destiny, and before she had contracted the Gulp Brothers

The series of events that dramatically changed Marcie Jo's life had started three years earlier. After two years of junior college, she was considering transferring to State College, just thirty miles from home. She'd earned straight A's in the junior college and won two merit-based scholarships to State College. One scholarship would cover her tuition; the other would pay for room and board. If she did well, she could leave Destiny for good and be off to a better life.

That same summer, she sat outside the double-wide in the late afternoon with Lilly Jean. She was helping her mother snap the ends of a couple pots of green beans picked from their backyard garden when Tim Wilder came by on a motorcycle. He was four years older and best friends with her older brother, Jimmy John. Marcie Jo adored Wild Tim, as they called him. He had been a wrestler on the Destiny High School team and won the county championships in the 185-pound weight class. Marcie Jo was fascinated by Wild Tim's muscles and his popularity. All the girls she knew always whispered about him, but they were late to the party. She'd liked him since she was 10 years old and first started liking boys, and at 20 after she had kissed a few.

"Close your mouth and act like you've had some home training," Lilly Jean whispered. "You've known Wild Tim all your life."

Tim went by the nickname Wild Tim because he lived life too fast. As a child, he was the kid that always jumped in the deep part of the lake and tried to outrun mean dogs. He even once tried to breathe fire. That time he burned the roof of his mouth and his lips, too. It left a mark that he'd still sometimes brag about. Wild Tim had always been the resident daredevil and still was, even as an adult in his mid-20s on leave from the Marines.

Today, Wild Tim pulled up to the double-wide on a souped-up motorcycle that he could run as fast as he wanted to in Destiny. There were only two cops in town. Both were relatives: his father, Tim Sr., and his Uncle Jake.

Tim had five more days left of a two-week leave and had emailed Jimmy John in Frankfurt to ask, "Do you mind if I date your sister?"

"Freckle-face? She's a hot mess," Jimmy John kidded. "Do it at your own risk."

Jimmy John knew his sister was a prize. Marcie Jo had a firecracker personality that matched her shock of red hair. It made her the perfect complement to her brothers. As a young girl, Marcie Jo had been a complete tomboy and "country tough," as he'd say. Jimmy John adored her then because she wouldn't cry when she fell down and scraped her elbow or knee. But he knew she was still a girl. As a young adult, she had grown into a fetching doll with a glowing smile, spirited personality, and freckled cheeks.

"I like Freckle-face, Jimmy John. She's a sweet girl. What do you say?"

Jimmy John was pleased. He knew of his little sister's long crush on his best friend.

"Go for it. Treat her nicely, Tim. Otherwise, you know the consequences."

"Of course, Jimmy John. We're best friends. I wouldn't treat her any other way."

Having received Jimmy John's blessings, Wild Tim got off the motorcycle, arched his back, took a long, exaggerated inhale that made Marcie Jo wonder if he, in classic Wild Tim fashion, was going to demonstrate to them how long he could hold his breath.

Instead, he exhaled, and in a bold, bass-filled, grown man's voice said, "Ms. Lilly Jean, I come a courting. May I court your little girl?"

Lilly Jean face turned pale white. Marcie Jo's burned red.

"Oh, Lord," Lilly Jean said. "Not a chance, Wild Tim. You still jumping into the deep end of the lake and burning your mouth up, trying to eat fire?"

"No, Ma'am. Them days are over. I've fully grown up. I've put away childish things."

"Where'd you learn about putting away childish things? We been praying for you to put away them childish things forever, but look at that motorbike you just pulled up here on. We heard you burning rubber a mile away."

"Ma'am I learned it from the Bible, First Corinthians 13:11. And that bike; it's the last vestiges of my youth, Ma'am. I'm going back to Iraq next week, got two more years. I'm selling that bike before I leave."

"Vestiges, that's a learned man's word, Wild Tim.   You come here spouting Bible verses and words of a learned man. I must say I am impressed."

His interest in courting her was a surprise to Marcie Jo. Her face continued to burn as she watched Wild Tim ask Lilly Jean's permission.

"I still don't know, Wild Tim," Lilly Jean said. "Let me think on it a second."

Wild Tim stood at the beginning of the walkway, with his back arched. He bit his lower lip and rubbed his hands together. Marcie Jo sat with a bowl of green beans in her lap and her mouth dry from nervousness.

"Finally, he said. Okay, Ma'am. I respect that. You want me to come back after you think on it?"

Lilly Jean knew she would never hear the end of it from her daughter if she sent him away, especially as he was going back to Iraq the next week. She quizzed him briefly.

"So, you say you are reading your Bible? You sure you putting away childish things?"

"Yes, Ma'am."

Lilly Jean nodded and quietly continued her contemplation for another thirty seconds. The silence had paralyzed both Wild Tim and Marcie Jo. Lilly Jean had a poker face, and neither could guess if she'd bless their dating.

Finally she yelled to Tim, who remained ten yards away at the beginning of her small gravel walkway, "Well, come in here then and start a-courting. This girl here been liking you since she was 10. Y'all both legal now, anyways. My opinion don't matter much, but I appreciate you for showing some home training and asking my permission. Now get to it, Boy."

Lilly Jean talked tough and gruff. Her voice and manner made her seem like a Southern backwoods mama fifty pounds heavier who'd greet you with a lip full of snuff, and the firm handshake of an arm wrestler, but she was the opposite. She was beautiful and, when she wanted to be, charming, even more than her daughter was. But she was a tigress when it came to protecting her tribe. Lily Jean was more full-figured and, at 155 pounds, thirty pounds heavier than Marcie Joe. And her thick hair was brownish red, with no gray roots. She had a bright perfect smile, too.

For both mother and daughter, this was one of the best days of their lives. When Wild Tim left that night, they talked for hours.

The next five days straight, Tim came courting, bringing flowers and candy, and he and Marcie Jo took rides on his motorcycle.

He didn't speed and told her, "I've got precious cargo. Can't go too fast."

Marcie Joe giggled and hugged Wild Tim tight around the mid-section. She rubbed her hands across the ripples of his six-pack and imagined a future with passionate lovemaking that would produce beautiful kids.

He left on a Saturday, headed first to D.C. and then to Iraq. By then, they'd made plans. Wild Tim would be done with his enlistment in two years, and if he could get a job on a base Stateside, he'd re-enlist and make a career out of it. She'd go to college, and they would build a life together, wherever Tim was stationed.

Two weeks later, Wild Tim was killed by a roadside bomb, an improvised explosive device, while on a patrol mission. Marcie Jo didn't enroll at State. She fell into a depression and one day, while Lilly Jean was at work, she left. Her mother found a note on the table at the entrance of the double-wide.

"I've gotta go. Don't worry about me. I'll let you know where I land and where I'll be. It may take a while before you hear from me, but I must go."

Chapter 45

He's a Monster

"It was a blur. I'd be lying if I told you I understood how I ended up at the Palace Parlor. I know there was a girl named Candy that sat across from me on the bus. She got on in Atlanta with me. My plan was to go New York, maybe even Canada. Next thing you know, I'm in a private room with Candy and this guy. A big fat, ugly, mean man. The brute told me and Candy that we needed to be nice to this other man. He told us the man was one of the most powerful men in the South. We had sex with him that night, and the next night again. After that, the mean man told me that the powerful man didn't want Candy anymore. He said that he liked me more, way more. That confused me, because Candy is way prettier than me. But he said I was sweet, and he liked my rosy red cheeks. It was all I needed to hear. I became his only customer for a couple of weeks. I didn't care much. The man I loved was dead, and that made me oblivious to anything else. That's how I ended up pregnant."

Marcie Jo continued, "I was an honors student. I don't come from some rich family. I embarrassed my momma and my brothers, I know. My family lives in a double-wide, but we have a lot of love for each other. My oldest brother is a master sergeant, and now that I have my wits about me and I have a child, I want the world to know the story. The man who impregnated me is a monster. He refuses to acknowledge me and my daughter, his daughter. I was told that he has done this before, and so I am doing what I need to do."

She stepped back from the lectern. The horde of photographers ran to the front of the room, the flashes of their cameras temporarily blinded her. She was highly photographic, maybe even model pretty, and the photos and interview would certainly go viral online.

Scott Gulp jumped in front of Marcie Jo.

His said, his face filled with fake fury, "My client is 23 years old. Look at her, she's still a baby. The man she is talking about is Detrick Damon 3rd, heir to the SCTV fortune."

Gulp was right. Marcie Jo looked like she could be 18. Her face still had the glow of innocence.

"She's been on her own for three years," Gulp said. "Damon refused to submit to a DNA test, but we've got him, ladies and gentlemen. We've got him."

Gulp was living up to the reputation his family law practice had as shakedown litigators. They were renowned for making outrageous statements at press conferences and then backtracking after opposing counsel threatened them with defamation lawsuits.

A collective groan arose from the crowd.

A reporter wearing an *Atlanta Daily Times* hat yelled, "Don't be playing us, Gulp. Or I'll never come to a press conference again."

"Me too," the *Columbus Journal* reporter shouted.

"You'd better not be lying to us!" a short, pretty blonde from the *Athens Press* added.

Several other reporters in the crush of press yelled threats as well.

"Trust me. We did our homework," Gulp answered. "He refused to submit to a DNA test, but as they say in the world of liars, thieves, and criminals, 'A zebra doesn't change his stripes.' Damon is still a regular at the strip club in question. We sent someone there undercover and got a water glass that he drank from. His DNA is a 99.9 percent match to that of the child. She is a girl, and the mother has already chosen a name, Anita Joy. There is no doubt he is the father, and it is time he take responsibility."

"What do you want? Is this about money?" the *Atlanta Daily Times* reporter asked.

"Yes, the child is a descendant of the family that owns the world's most powerful religious network. That makes her Southern religious royalty. We want her taken care of and acknowledged. We tried dealing quietly with Damon. We couldn't get through to him, or his father, or his grandfather, so now we are taking it to the people. The child deserves better, and the world needs to know the truth."

"Do you want to take down the Damons? They may be the world's most powerful religious force outside of the Vatican," a reporter asked.

"Not at all. Jesus died on the cross for the sinner. He told the high priests if they were without sin to cast the first stone. This case has very little to do with religion. I'm in the business of fighting for people against bigger forces. My client and her baby are the David vs. the Damons' Goliath power, if you will. This case is all about personal responsibility. My client made a mistake, but so did Damon. Let them both share in the responsibility for their mistake, and take care of this innocent child."

Three hours later, Marcie Jo and Lilly Jean returned to Destiny from the press conference. They sat in the front yard on used lawn furniture drinking sweet tea in the dress clothes they'd worn to the press conference. The loud sound of propellers broke through the quietness of the late country afternoon. The helicopter instantly became a curiosity as it landed on an empty, two-acre lot across the street from the double-wide. Scott Gulp emerged from the chopper with Damon 1 and Damon 2. The son was not there. Damon 1 carried a huge pink teddy bear. Damon 2, a briefcase. In the briefcase was $10,000 cash and a check for $2 million. The solemn-faced men entered the walkway and stood in front of Marcie Jo and Lilly Jean. The women overcome by the moment, sat stone-faced

Damon 1 saw the baby girl, and tears welled up in his eyes. He didn't bother to introduce himself or his son. He just turned to Marcie Jo and said, "You are a beautiful young lady. Your baby, my great-granddaughter, is a sight to behold. Is it true that he denied you for three years?"

"Yes sir."

"Why didn't you come to us before? We would've helped you."

He then turned to Gulp and glared. Gulp had lied when he said that DD1 and DD2 had been made aware of the pregnancy.

"We were told that bad things could happen," Lilly Jean interrupted. Her voice was strong and clear. The Damons took a step back and nodded deferentially. Lilly Jean had made it clear that she was a mama bear.

The old man put his head down and clasped his hands in silent prayer.

Afterwards, he turned to Lilly Jean and asked, "Do you want him as part of her life?"

"He's got some apologies to make, but we don't want or need to see him now. We are not going to let him fix his reputation that easily."

The dramatic helicopter entrance by the powerful Damon men intimidated Marcie Jo. Both women had stood up during the spectacular entrance. Now, she moved behind her mother and peeked at them from behind Lilly Jean's shoulder.

The Damon men nodded.

The noise of the helicopter with the big SCTV logo on its side caught the neighbors' attention. The community gathered to see what the commotion was all about.

"How about us? We'd love to be a part of your lives," Damon 2 said. His face was more eager than his father's.

"We need to think about that. This was a lot to deal with, and we are just little people that don't want any limelight," Lilly Jean said.

"I understand," Damon 2 said. "You are protective, and strong. I like this for our grandchild. I want to be involved in any way you suggest. We'll earn your trust. Let me start by letting you know that you have our deepest apologies. We will do our part, anything you ask to make you feel welcome by us."

Scott Gulp had taken the Teddy Bear from Damon 1 and handed it to the baby, Anita Joy. She was taken by it immediately.

Damon 2 looked at the child as she played with the fuzzy teddy bear. She smiled and hugged it, and it brought a glow to his face. With shocking red hair and freckles, she was the spitting image of her mother.

"I'm willing to do what it takes. Money will never be a problem," DD2 said.

He then turned his attention to Marcie Jo.

"I can't imagine the grief and pain that you had to endure. First, losing the love of your life. Then, having to deal with the pain my son put you through. I can't apologize for what he did. What's clear is that he's a grown man and needs a lot of help. I will never lobby to justify his errant ways. Just count on me and my dad to never do that with you or the child. We are committed to being here for you for whatever you need. This check will start you off."

He handed it to her.

Marcie Jo moved from behind her mother and took the check. Her eyes bulged as she looked at the words "two million" spelled out. She grabbed her mom. Both women lost the strength in their legs. They held onto each other and stumbled back to their lawn chairs.

"Thanks. Thank you," Marcie Joe said.

She didn't know what else to say. DD1 and DD2 were older versions of the man she had had sex with, but she didn't know much else about them except that everyone, especially the Gulp Brothers, said they were powerful.

They looked at her and nodded encouragingly with eyes that pleaded for forgiveness and acceptance. But she was grown now, and it wouldn't be so easy.

Finally, she said, her voice weak and nervous, barely louder than a whisper, "I don't know what else to say. As Mama said, we just want what's best for the baby."

Chapter 46

Status Revoked

"Son, I need you to come back here immediately," DD2 said. He and a team of reporters had been encamped in Yates for a week to follow the Digby Yates shooting."

"DD1 wants you to go away, and given what we just learned, that is best. You fathered a child with a woman who's practically a child herself. We found that out from a story broken by your nemesis, Shawn Cooper, and the *God's Town USA* book that has become an instant best-seller. Then there's the salacious press conference led by scurrilous lawyers renowned for defaming their opponents. These last transgressions are beyond embarrassing. Unfortunately, some of our members might agree with the idiocy of your fight with Shawn Cooper, but they won't side with you this time. This one is a real test of our faith, Son. You need to go to the wilderness for a while—that's Toronto—and think about building a life outside of Southern Christian Church and the network."

DD3's heart sunk. He wasn't equipped with a fast mind, so a witty retort was not forthcoming.

The response he mustered was barely audible, but DD2 made out the last part, and it angered him.

"I am not leaving, Dad."

"What did you say?"

"I said, I'm not leaving. This is my inheritance, my destiny. I am not going to the wilderness. No way I'm going to Toronto."

"Are you delusional? We are a religious television network, and your grandfather and I lead one of the most respected churches in the South. At least, we used to before this news."

DD2's voice dropped several octaves. Suddenly he was no longer the peaceful man of God or a gentle soul, or even the tough disciplinarian of just a few days earlier. His disposition switched to that of the many rugged, ill-tempered unrepentant criminals and street toughs that he visited as part of the church's prison ministry.

"Son, the private jet in the Yates Airfield is warming up. You need to come home, get what you need, and get back on that plane. We own a two-bedroom apartment in Toronto. That's where you are going, today. We'll have the rest of your clothes and furnishings sent to you there in a couple of weeks. And, don't try to come back here. Your access to the campus has been revoked."

"But Dad," DD3 whined.

"Don't make me come to get you, son. It won't be pretty. Just get on the plane and feel lucky you have a place to go."

"I'm not getting on the plane."

"Oh yes, you are. Your credit cards and bank account are frozen. You have no money or credit to access. The only way they will be unfrozen is if you get on that plane and follow my instructions. The old man wants you out of his sight. He has disowned you. Maybe in time, he and I will come to forgive you. You've failed us. Just go, Son, work on becoming a better human, and repair your relationship with God. Seek forgiveness from Him and then the beautiful little girl and her mother, and then me and your grandfather. That's going to take time. Just go, Son. I don't want to see you or hear from you for a while."

Chapter 47

Now Untouchable

Yates had recovered and was back on the campaign trail. He now travelled with a government-assigned security team but because of his injury was still under travel restrictions. His travel was limited to the Southern corridor, and he was hitting all the big cities from Virginia down to Florida.

Four days after Blaine's death, Flower buried her sister quietly in the backyard of Skylar and Blaine's home, as Skylar had requested. He was still on the run and called her afterwards on his burner.

"I'm in Canada. Can't tell you where exactly, but I appreciate your taking care of my request."

Skylar had video cameras across his estate. He didn't tell Flower, but he was able to watch the private service and burial remotely from his hideout. Hiding out in Canada was also a lie; he was in a small cabin outside of Savanah, Georgia. It was family property owned by his great grandfather, Washington Andrews. Skylar was the caretaker of the land deep in the woods, and it was perfect place for him to stay under the radar. He told her the Canada ruse because she would eventually be interrogated by the authorities.

"How'd you know, Skylar? It was supposed to be a private ceremony. I didn't want Digby to know I was in town. He's recuperating. I'm going to go into hiding, too. I'll be up North somewhere. I don't know where, yet. Tyrone and I. Juju and their mom want to stay in New York City. They like it and have reconnected with some folks from Yates and Waterside who had left and are now happily living in Harlem, the Bronx, and Brooklyn. We are staying under protection from this underground force of sorts and staying at a safe house. It's actually a five star resort-style place that is impenetrable. Oh my God, Blaine would love it, the food, the service. We will be staying here until everything calms down. The guys that are responsible for us say we can stay here for as long as necessary."

Skylar assumed that Flower was under the protection of The Voice and Society of Protectors. The Voice had recruited him years back. Skylar knew that Flower was safe, and it warmed him. He didn't let on that he knew about the Society.

"That's a good idea. Stay underground and safe. Digby can get to you, and I'm sure he'll try again at some point. But I'm not done. I promised him what I would do if my wife died."

"Skylar, be careful Please You haven't been named as a suspect yet. I'm wondering why? What do you think that is all about?"

"Oh, that's totally strategic. He knows it was me. I told him I was going to kill him. You see who he is blaming?"

Flower bristled as she thought of her husband's sinister plotting.

"Yes, that man's evil nature has no bounds. Digby tried to implicate Rev. Hall and black civil rights groups. By blaming them, he is trying to capitalize on this situation and incite the white supremacist hate groups to wage a revenge campaign. It will get Digby closer to the race war he craves."

She continued, "If he can get the public to believe that civil rights groups came after him, then he's got not only the white racist but, more importantly, the white moderate vote locked up."

"That's right, Flower."

Contemplating Digby's schemes intensified her anger.

"I want Digby dead as much you, Skylar. My dear sister is gone. She's all I had for family. I'll never get over her loss. And I know he wants my new man, Tyrone, dead. I hate him for that, too. He may even want me dead now."

She continued, "He's so delusional that he's probably thinking he can get me back because of the agreement we made to help him win the election. That is over. I can't allow Digby to go unchecked. Black leadership played no part in this at all. But if we don't call that out, and loudly, he could win the election, maybe by a landslide. The religious right voting block will definitely support him, and the moderates will be confused and vote for him. If he gets enough inertia, the political left will concede and not come out to vote."

"And a landslide will give him a mandate, Flower. Jesus, help me. What did I do?"

"Don't you dare, Skylar. Don't you dare regret your decision. You'd better believe that your choice was what Blaine would expect from you. You were her valiant protector."

Flower could hear him choke up.

"I bet she's pissed that I missed," he said. His voice caromed between glee and pain.

"You know my sister," Flower began to cry softly and giggled through her tears. "But you had to see her defending me and Tyrone. She was so fierce. My protective little sister. Oh, my dear Blaine. God knows I'm going to miss her."

"Me too, she was my heart," he said. His voice then picked up. "Flower, I have a chit to play. It could help get the truth out, and I can remain on the run. Let me play my hand. I'll be in touch. Thanks again for burying Blaine."

He hung up.

"Wait, Skylar! What are you going to do?"

It was too late, he was gone. She called back and then texted him.

She got no response and hung her head, exasperated. While Blaine was alive, Skylar was the epitome of the strong, silent type, her sister the free spirit who danced on tables. But when he said, "Enough is enough," she stopped. Blaine was obedient to him in a way that she never had been with any other boyfriend.

Flower had once asked, "What is it about this guy for you, little sister?"

"His heart is pure, Flower. The man loves me more than life itself. I mean everything to him, and he shows me in countless ways every day. I've dated sensational men, but no one comes close. I'm blessed by his love, and so if he tells me that I need to get off some gosh darn table and stop making a fool of myself, it's not too much to listen to my man. My Daddy Woo-Woo."

Flower smiled as she recalled her sister's girlish nickname for Skylar. He fulfilled her romantically, intellectually, and sexually. Women in Yates and Sidrow, where they met, fantasized over him and his lean muscular frame and ruggedly handsome looks.

The couple had met when he was a junior and she a freshmen at Sidrow. He made her blush as they were buying books the first day of school in the campus bookstore.

"Calculus 10. I have that book. You want to borrow it from me?" he asked.

"I'm okay," she answered awkwardly. Her first look at his handsome face and long, athletic frame made her guarded. Many guys had approached her in her first days as a co-ed but this guy had a twinkle and it made her anxious.

Flower had warned her to be wary of fast-talking upperclassmen.

"You should accept my offer. I got an A in the class. The book comes with my notes."

He winked at her, and when her face flushed, he smiled again to let her know he caught her nervousness.

"Tell you what, I'll keep it on hand for you, okay Blush?"

She was flustered by his poise and handsomeness, and blurted, "My name is Blaine, not Blush."

"Okay, that's fine. I think Blaine suits you. It's pretty, just like you. You know what, I sensed some feistiness in that response."

She smiled, finally.

"My name is Blaine White. My sister is an upper classman. Flower White. Do you know her?"

"Yes, I do. She's a wonderful young lady. In fact, Flower told me she had a little sister coming here. I play on the football team with her boyfriend, Harry Newman. He's a dear friend. It's a pleasure to finally meet you, Blushing Blaine."

She blushed again. A month later, after the football season ended, Flower called Skylar.

"Can you take my sister out? She just broke up with her boyfriend from back home and is moping around. Her face lights up every time she talks about the football player she met in the bookstore who called her Blushing Blaine. Harry says you're a good guy."

"Your sister, Blushing Blaine, is beautiful. I'd love to take her out."

Two days later, they went on their first date to the campus Rathskeller. Three weeks after that, they were a couple. And they had remained together ever since.

Chapter 48

I Am a Man of God

"How is your wife doing? Have you talked to her?"

"She's overcome with pain and depression," Digby Yates lied to DD2. He hadn't talked to her and continued his lie, "She had a very close relationship with her sister, but I know Flower. She'll come back to me. We'll have her classified as clinically depressed over the loss of her sister. The compassionate Christians and non-Christians alike will understand that, as most of us have experienced the pain of loss. In time, this will pass."

Damon 2 was disturbed by the brazen directness of Yates's thinking. The toughest part of his job as a man of God was managing grief and pain over loss of life. Yates displayed neither. It was a reminder of what he'd long known, but he and DD1 had tried to rationalize and justify it by saying God would intervene and change Yates's heart. Digby's last comments, however, were too much from him.

For DD2, the walls seemed to be coming down around him. Truth and godliness were supposed to be pillars of his daily Christian walk. His son and Yates were epic fails, and he had played some role in their public relevance. Yesterday, he had called his son to account, and now he did the same with the Presidential candidate.

"I've never talked to you in this way, but call it free religious counseling, Senator."

"Huh?" Yates responded.

They had never talked about faith or forgiveness. He wasn't prepared for what came next.

"You need to pray for guidance and forgiveness, and seek God's mercy, Senator. A woman is dead, and you survived a sniper attack. Your chief of staff is dead. I am talking to you as a man of God now, not as an advertiser. I strongly suggest that you have a long talk with God. Seek forgiveness for your part, if you had anything to do with the shooting that took place in New York. That is a petition you must take to God directly."

"Uh, excuse me, DD2," Yates said. The comments by DD2 made him feel defensive.

He'd often bragged to Tommy Tubbs about a super-instinct he had to ward off people who didn't mind their own business and might offer unsolicited advice. Tubbs thought it was arrogance. In this moment he thought DD2 was acting out of place and he needed to level set him.

"Listen, DD2-"

Damon interrupted him, "Don't say another word. You need to listen to me. What I just shared with you is what I am supposed to do as a faith leader. I'll say the same thing as your business agent for this religious network. Talk to God, not me. If you have done wrong by that woman and Tyrone Wheeler, don't double down on your sin. Leave that woman and man alone. Shore up your health, and focus on running for President. That is enough."

"DD2-" Yates said. He tried again to ignore DD2. Being reprimanded in any way never happened to him.

The stern rebuke surprised and embarrassed him. It was a first from any of the Damons. Yates had believed, because his campaign was an advertising partner to SCTV, that DD2 would behave like other sycophants. But DD2 wasn't beholden in the way most were to the sausage king and made his position clear.

"Let me finish," DD2 barked. "My job is to advocate and promote God's teaching, and lead people to his kingdom. We do that around the trappings of this fantastic company, but we will never succumb to the ways of the world. We draw the line there. So, I repeat: You need to pray for God's guidance and forgiveness. I can help you with that. He is a loving God, a forgiving God. You can bring all things to him. Would you like me to pray with you?"

"Uh, um, no. I can pray directly. Thank you, DD2. You're right," Yates said.

He was stunned by DD2's sternness and his words. No one told him what to do. Tommy Tubbs, his longtime loyal chief of staff, but more importantly, a loyal sycophant, was dead. Tubbs would say no to his ego-driven demands, but then relent. It was the pattern. But DD2 didn't work for him. He was as wealthy as Yates, and with his television network, more powerful.

As DD2 spoke, Tubbs's words rang through Digby's head: "Don't ever think that these people, DD1 and DD2, are suckers or loyal servants to you. This is a business deal, nothing more. If they come after you, you're done."

It's why, for the first time ever, Yates shut up and listened. He had no on praying or talking to God, but DD2 had just made it clear that pissing him off could be a huge mistake.

Chapter 49

Decision Made

"**G**overnor, I suppose you know there is a place in hell for the both of us if we do this," Billy One-Shot said.

"Look son, I know this is your chosen profession, but in case you need to know, this is not my first rodeo either," Big Hardy replied.

Hardwick Bivens, Sr. wasn't a triggerman, or a rough 'em up goon. In his mind, he could've been, but lucky breaks in life had catapulted him to the upper crust of society.

In his earlier life as a unionized autoworker and later as an amateur boxer appearing as the "Fighting Counselor," he earned some of the tough guy *bona fides* that the common man and underworld appreciated.

Now, at age 91, his short-tempered brashness remained. Twenty-five years ago, he had Prescott Jefferson poisoned through his covert alliances. The effects of the poison led to Jefferson's forced resignation from the White House. Bivens masterminded the attack in an act of revenge, after the GOP presidential candidate lied to the auto workers union head, Conklin McVeety. Jefferson, during his presidential race against Hardwick Bivens Jr., told the union head that Little Hardy had plans to move the car business and the electronic/tech side of auto manufacturing from Michigan and the Midwest to California. The plans would move tens of thousands of unionized automotive jobs out of Detroit.

Conklin believed Prescott had turned tail on the Democrats. Little Hardy Jr. lost the support of the automotive workers of America, the Michigan electoral vote, and the election.

Big Hardy wanted Prescott dead as revenge, but couldn't get the Guiding Force to approve the assassination of a sitting U.S. President. He had him poisoned anyway, without approval. Prescott recovered but was deemed medically unfit to continue as President, and he resigned from the office.

Two weeks after Yates returned to the campaign, a poisoning again was on Big Hardy's mind, with a twist. He contacted Billy One-Shot on the burner phone. The assassin was still hiding out in Rio.

"How about you earn the money after all, Mr. One Shot?" The Governor asked.

"I thought we agreed that Yates is untouchable," Billy responded. "My sources tell me he has the GPA (government protection agency) securing him now. Nobody will be able to get close to him."

"I know, and that's really too bad. He's deserving of death, but I have a back-up plan that may be just as effective."

"What do you have in mind, Governor?"

"How about those who are supporting him? The ones making his presidential run possible!"

"What are you talking about, Sir? I'm not following you." "Billy, he's getting all of this press from Southern Christian TV."

"Yes, SCTV is a big deal, nowadays. In fact, I've watched it a few times while in the States."

"How about we kill their leader?"

"Huh, what?"

The assassin sighed. In the world of assassins, a contract was supposed to be an unemotional event. Billy often had to calm clients down to fully understand their motivations for ending a person's life. His work with Governor Bivens suddenly required counseling not to get him to understand the finality of a contract, in this case, maybe it was a contract Bivens might want to not have executed.

"Governor, this is a really big deal. Way bigger than killing a scandalous senator. Yates is a known and despised thief from the people. The Damons are beloved."

The Governor had a ready response.

"Billy, the Damon's grandson has been kicked out of the family and their ministry for impregnating a woman just out of her teens. The young woman was working as a stripper at a strip club in Yates. The Damon's, as men of God, have looked the other way on a number of major transgressions by the third generation son/grandson. But his frequenting that strip club, his impregnating that girl who worked there, and the fact that they didn't use their immense power to shut it down loom as huge issues and subjects of embarrassment for their ministry. The untimely death of the patriarch could be viewed as karma visiting them and a reason for SCTV to step away for good from all associations that are not of God, including Yates's campaign."

The governor's plan was now beginning to make sense to Billy One-Shot.

"How do you propose to do this, Governor? I can't put a bullet in his brain. I'd become the target of an international manhunt. Christians all over the world would be hunting me down, and if word got out that you were connected to Damon's murder, they would hunt you down, too, and maybe even your granddaughter."

Bivens had an answer.

"We'll do it the same way I took out Prescott. We'll poison him. Except this time, we kill our target. The old man has to die. If he doesn't, the Damons may just rebound, and the message to step away from Yates may not be effective."

Big Hardy didn't say anything more. Before the call, he assumed that the assassin would take the job, but after hearing Billy's reservations, Big Hardy wondered if killing a religious leader, the most powerful in America, might offend One-Shot. There was much he didn't know about him. Could he be a fan and supporter of Southern Christian Ministries? If so, he'd learn now.

Billy spoke first, "I'm a professional, but if this leader is dirty and embraced Yates, then he had it coming, I guess you could say."

It was an answer with a conviction that given the assassins initial reservation surprised the Governor.

"So, you'll take the job?"

"I will, Governor. This should be easy. I'll make it look like an accident. It will be done next week. I'm out of the country and need to travel discreetly. Where does he live?"

"Jeffersonville, NC. It's the middle of the state. His station and church are the biggest deals in the area. There are no other attractions within several hours."

"I'll map it out, but count on him being dead in a week."

*　　*　　*

Billy landed in Jeffersonville three days after the phone call from Big Hardy. He disguised himself again as Charles Williams. He stayed three nights in the hotel that SCTV had constructed five years earlier. It was four star, and the staffers were not as forward and meddlesome as those he'd encountered at the hotel in Yates.

He spent the first day following DD1 to track his patterns, and did the same the second and third days. DD1's routines were simple. Each morning, he'd stop in town for a cup of coffee and drive leisurely around the entirety of Jeffersonville. It was a five-mile circuit, and he drove below the speed limit. The journey was an event for the patriarch. Along the way, he would gladly stop and pull over to the side of the road to engage in conversation with an old friend or town resident. He drove a wood-paneled station

344

wagon that Billy guessed was forty years old, but the engine purred as if it were brand new.

"That's what money can do," Billy whispered as he trailed DD1's vintage vehicle. By the third day, DD1 hadn't deviated from his travel pattern. It meant that Billy's plan would be easy.

DD1 drove around town with his windows down. He made the mistake of not rolling them up when he stopped to get coffee. On the fourth day, after Damon entered the coffee shop, Billy slowly approached the open car window, leaned in, and applied a deadly untraceable poison to the steering wheel. The remainder he put into a heavy-duty envelope that he sealed and dumped into a nearby trash can. The contents would end up in the Jeffersonville Dump by the end of the day. He then walked into the coffee shop to order his own cup of coffee. He entered as DD1 exited. The church leader smiled warmly at him and said, "Good morning, my good man of God."

Disguised as Charles Williams, Billy nodded, "Good morning to you, kind sir."

Minutes later, DD1 was back in his car. When he touched the steering wheel, the poison began to seep into his bloodstream, starting a countdown to the end of his life. Two miles into his circuit of the town, the venom stopped his heart painlessly and rendered him unconscious. The car crashed at 25 mph into a utility pole.

Ironically, it had been five years earlier when DD1's unrepentant grandson sped out of the parking lot of Pop's Palace and sideswiped the rear end of an SUV driven by a late night shift worker on his way home. That accident caused the driver to lose control of his vehicle and crash into the pole. DD3 fled the scene, of the accident he'd caused. Like many of his local crimes it was not investigated.

Two hours after DD1's demise, Billy One-Shot called Big Hardy to tell him the news.

"Our reservation in Hell is now confirmed, Sir."

The Governor looked at his calendar. It was seven days after the date promised by the assassin. He sat in his backyard garden eating breakfast and raised his face to the warm glow of the southern California morning sun. A smile stretched his lips.

"Fantastic, you got it done!" Big Hardy shouted. "Outstanding. How'd you pull it off?"

"Poisoned him just like you said. It was easy, professional. Exactly how I like to work."

"Tell me more, Mr. One-Shot."

"I slipped into his car while he stopped in town for a cup of coffee this morning. Applied some Zonda to his steering wheel. Ten minutes later, his heart stopped as he drove to the SCTV campus, and he crashed into a utility pole. He's dead, and the drug is untraceable. Toxicology doesn't know to look for it. No one will ever know."

"That's the important part," the Governor said.

"Oh, and one more thing, Governor, the utility pole was live and electrified the body. The authorities won't know that he was already dead. If there is a compassionate element here, it is that Zonda kills you fast. You lose consciousness and are dead one minute after the drug infects the bloodstream. He was dead before the pole fell and electrified the car."

Big Hardy imagined the SCTV leader's final moments. He wondered if Damon 1 knew what was happening and called out to God. And if so, whether God heard him, and what that moment was like.

Billy One-Shot's voice pierced his thoughts.

"Governor, you fell silent. Are you okay?"

"Oh, I'm fine," Big Hardy said. His voice was still amped.

"Good, because you know there is a no return policy. No buyer's remorse in the killing business. Once the job is done. It's done."

Billy then cackled loudly.

The laugh unnerved the Governor and he wondered for a second why Billy laughed, but dismissed the thought as a professional tic unique to being a paid killer. His thoughts shifted to twenty-five years ago when he had Prescott Jefferson sickened with poison, and now today he had a man killed. He was excited by the moment. He'd deal with remorse later, if ever.

"You know, Billy, we conspired here to take down a man who supports an evil force that threatens the peace and sanctity of our great republic. I'm a politician first and foremost, who believes in those protections. I don't know if you can understand it."

Billy paused for a second and answered, "I think I follow you, Governor."

Big Hardy continued, "Politics is like war. You have to bear arms against your enemy at times to make your point. Most people won't understand this. My granddaughter certainly doesn't. Digby Yates is a pox on the character, goodness, and greatness of this fine nation. I didn't know this Damon fellow, but he supported that evil senator with all his resources and power. In war that man, the Damon #1, is akin to a general, and in war you must defeat the generals, the battlefield commanders of your enemy, to win. That's what we've done here. I pray that God forgives me, but I have no remorse. Damon was a conspirator who took sides with our country's most evil foe, and for that I celebrate the death of a warmonger."

Chapter 50

Disaster

"Detrick, this is R.G. Gallery," the Jeffersonville Chief of Police said.

"How are you doing, R.G.? I haven't seen you in a while. How are the wife and family?"

"They are good, Pastor #2," Gallery answered. Pastor #1 and Pastor #2 were his nicknames for the elder Damons. "Sir, this is not a fun call. It's one that I hate making. I am glad I caught you in your office. Are you seated? If not, please sit down, Sir."

Damon knew then something was awry. The warning by Gallery caused the feeling in his legs to escape him. As a church leader and counselor, he'd participated in such calls hundreds of times. Often doctors, and even Gallery, would ask him to be on a call as the consoler when notification of a death or serious injury had to be made. He picked up on Gallery's tell and closed his eyes."

DD2's voice turned cold and his words staccato, "What— is— it, R—G?"

"I'm afraid there's been an accident. Your father's car crashed into a utility pole. Our reports say it wasn't a high speed crash, but live wires fell on the front of his vehicle and electrocuted him. He was pronounced dead at the scene."

Damon 2 felt the blood drain from his face. His arm felt limp. He did the only thing he knew to do at that moment.

The man of God shouted, "Jesus!"

The Chief wasn't an active member of Southern Christian Church. He visited on the high holy days of Christmas and Easter, annually. Other than that, he was there when he profited by hiring outside police departments to supply security for big events, or made official visits that led to payoffs to look the other way when DD3 did something stupid.

DD2's call out to Jesus unnerved Gallery. His personal relationship with God was lacking, and he didn't understand Damon's outburst. He awkwardly moved forward delivering the news.

"I'm very sorry, Detrick but we need you to come downtown and identify the body. It's procedure."

DD2 didn't respond. Gallery watched the second hand on his wall clock. It was a habit he had developed when he delivered news of death over the phone. He counted off five seconds, then ten, and ten seconds more. The Chief knew Damon was shocked and likely had a thousand thoughts running through his head. The shock was the hardest part of delivering notifications of death. There wasn't one single way to snap them out of it. His consoling voice worked the best, most of the time. He slipped into it. It was a low bass where he enunciated each word slowly.

"My friend, I know this is a terrible news. I can come pick you up, but if you need a moment, you don't have to identify the body for a day or two. We all know who your Dad is. For now, I need to know what I can do to help."

Gallery counted off another twenty seconds.

Finally, DD2 muttered, "You said, electrocuted."

"Yes," Gallery answered. "Dr. Duper, the ER head at Jeffersonville Hospital who doubles as the medical examiner, said Pastor #1 likely had a stroke if he crashed into a pole. Bystanders said he wasn't speeding or swerving. The accident occurred in a 35 mile per hour zone right outside the center of town, five miles down the road from your Southern Christian campus. We'll take the body to the hospital, and you can come in when you're ready. Do you want them to determine the cause of death?"

"Yes, please do. I'd like to know."

"Okay, we will. You take care, Detrick. My thoughts are with you, my dear friend."

"Thank you, Chief. I appreciate your kind words."

*   *   *

The accident occurred in the second week of DD3's banishment to Toronto. Detrick 2 called his cell phone. His son answered on the first ring.

"What is it, Dad? We have nothing to talk about. I am banished and told I can't come back to Jeffersonville. You said I have brought a curse on the family. That's what the old man told you, and you didn't stand up for me. I am here in Toronto, where I know no one. You told me to figure out life without your good name, in the wilderness as you call it."

"Son," Damon 2 attempted to interrupt.

"It's fall up here, and cold, Dad. I'm a Southern boy," DD3 whined. It was their first conversation and the prodigal son had rehearsed countless times what he'd say to his dad. He continued with his cries of woe.

"Do you know how humiliating this is? I told you I'm sorry. What can I do to earn my way back into the family? I know I have brought shame to the great Damon dynasty."

DD2 didn't interrupt him. He couldn't make sense out the ramblings anyhow. They went from angry, to sympathetic, to sorry, to angry again, and finally to pleading. DD2 sensed it for what it was: the rantings of a passive-aggressive narcissist, and he lashed out.

"Everything is not always about you, dammit."

The loud rebuke shut DD3 up.

"Get your bags packed. I'm sending the plane to get you. It will be there as soon as it can, probably in eight hours or so. Your grandfather died suddenly this morning. We need to bury him."

The tragic news didn't lead to a relenting of DD3's narcissism.

"Am I back in the family business? If not, I am not coming."

"I don't know, and trust me, Son, on your just-departed grandfather's spirit, you don't want to negotiate with me right now. Continue if you want, and I will not only say no, but I will cut you off entirely. Just do what I say, and shut the hell up. Have I been clear? Do you understand?"

DD3 was bitter. The news of his grandfather's sudden death didn't sadden him; it energized him. His mind swirled. The news meant order would be restored, and he'd be welcome back as the heir-in-waiting. His banishment was over. He determined that it made sense to let the fight go, for now; and so he responded to his father with deference.

"Yes, Dad. You have been clear. You won't have any issues with me."

"Then back your bags and wait for the plane."

"Okay, Dad. I'll pack my bags."

D2 hung up the phone and fell to his knees. He called out to God as his body began to quake.

"God, what is going on here? I need you now more than ever. Please take charge. Order my steps. Make me the servant I need to be. Keep my heart and mind focused on what you want me to do and heal us, God. Give us the strength to make it through these coming days."

Chapter 51

Eyewitness of News

For the past week, Scoop Montgomery had been staying in Harmony, twenty miles away from the Damons' Southern Christian campus. Montgomery was working on the sequel to *God's Town USA.* He was there to get a meeting with DD1 and had five calls into his office. The fifth call was the only one returned.

DD1's secretary, Connie Checks, responded after the fifth call: "Mr. Damon has told me to inform you that he will not sit for an interview with you. He has instructed his son not to speak with you, either. Please don't bother to call again. Mr. Damon will not change his mind."

"But, Ms.-" Scoop said.

"Goodbye," Connie said.

Undeterred, he moved on to Plan B. He had to get the interview with Damon 1 even if it meant a bull-rush ambulance chaser attack. In this case, it meant he would catch Damon 1 in the public square and force him to talk. Public figures hated these attacks by reporters, it carried the threat that he could be misquoted. If the attack worked Damon would agree to an full interview.

The former reporter remembered from his countless sightings during his time at *The Jefferson Standard* that DD1 had a ritual. They both got coffee each morning at Jefferson's Café. The community leader often would hold court there with a number of locals.

Montgomery surprise attack stopped when he witnessed a man, someone he didn't recognize, moving around Damon's car suspiciously. The man reached into DD1s car wearing plastic gloves. Scoop watched him carefully apply a liquid on the steering wheel. He then sealed the liquid's container, placed the container in a thick white envelope, and dumped the envelope in a nearby trash can. Brazenly, the man then walked into Jefferson's Café. He brushed by DD1 as he exited the coffee shop. A few minutes later, after purchasing his own cup of coffee, the man returned to his car and followed DD1 as he began his circuit of Jeffersonville.

Nervously, Montgomery got out of his car and walked to the garbage can where the white envelope sat on top of a pile. He carefully plucked it out, rushed to his car, and took off on the route that DD1 and the mystery man had taken.

"This is not good. It can't be. Mystery man, mystery substance, plastic gloves, thick, sealed, bubble wrapped envelope discarded in a trash can. Nope, it can't be good," Montgomery reasoned.

The road, named SC1, circled the town. A little more than a mile and a half later, traffic ground to a halt. Emergency crews with sirens blaring rushed past him to an accident 100 yards ahead. The accident bore familiar elements: the most compelling was a fallen utility pole. The downed pole was across the street from the now boarded up Pop's Palace . It was also where Damon 3's sports car clipped the SUV of a late night shift worker, causing a pole to collapse and he drove off.

The site was eerily familiar, except today it looked as if death had visited the scene. Live electrical wires bobbed up and down on the vintage wood-paneled station wagon.

"Oh Jesus, that's DD1's car," Montgomery wailed. "This is not good, and I can't go any further. I don't want to be seen, especially if what I think is in this envelope caused the accident."

He looked at the envelope next to him on the front seat.

"I better get out of here. What I witnessed this morning is far worse than a hit and run at a strip club. I may have witnessed the murder of the most powerful religious leader in America."

......To Be Continued....

Coming next is Black Camelot Choices, series book #7

www.ingramcontent.com/pod-product-compliance
Lightning Source LLC
Chambersburg PA
CBHW020349160726
47987CB00022BA/1592